COPPERAS GAP

BY

P.D.MITCHELL

First Published in Great Britain by Jacqui Lessels, Somerset.
April 2019

ISBN 978-0-9955382-4-5

www.pdmitchell.co.uk
e-mail: info@pdmitchell.co.uk

A catalogue copy of this book is available from the British Library

This book is dedicated to my grandfather

Albert Mitchell.

A seafarer and ships' rigger.

1896-1963.

To

Cynthia Sue Stewart

My American friend

For my three daughters,

Louise, Elizabeth & Jessica

Special thanks to my editing publisher

Jacqui Lessels

for her complete support, encouragement and advice

during the writing of this story, without which

this book, *Copperas Gap*, would

never have been published.

Acknowledgements.

With thanks to the following people for their assistance in the proofreading, production or in providing general advice regarding the content of the original manuscript.

Jacqui Lessels, Editor and publisher.

Mrs. S. Reeves

Mr. M. Stringer

Mrs. D. Mitchell.

This book is the first in the trilogy and is the prequel to

The Ghost of the Fishersgate Mariner.

Author website: www.pdmitchell.co.uk

HISTORICAL NOTE

The story told in this book is set before the year of 1971. Before that year the United Kingdom and its dominions used imperial currency units. This comprised of the pound, as it does today, but with coinage values of half-crown, shilling, sixpence, thru-pence, single penny, half-penny and farthing. The pound before 1971 was made up of 240 pennies. Linear measurements before 1971 were set in yards, feet and inches. In context, this book has used the terminology of this old currency and linear measurement.

On the 15th February 1971, the United Kingdom changed from imperial units to metric SI units.

Mawford Arts.

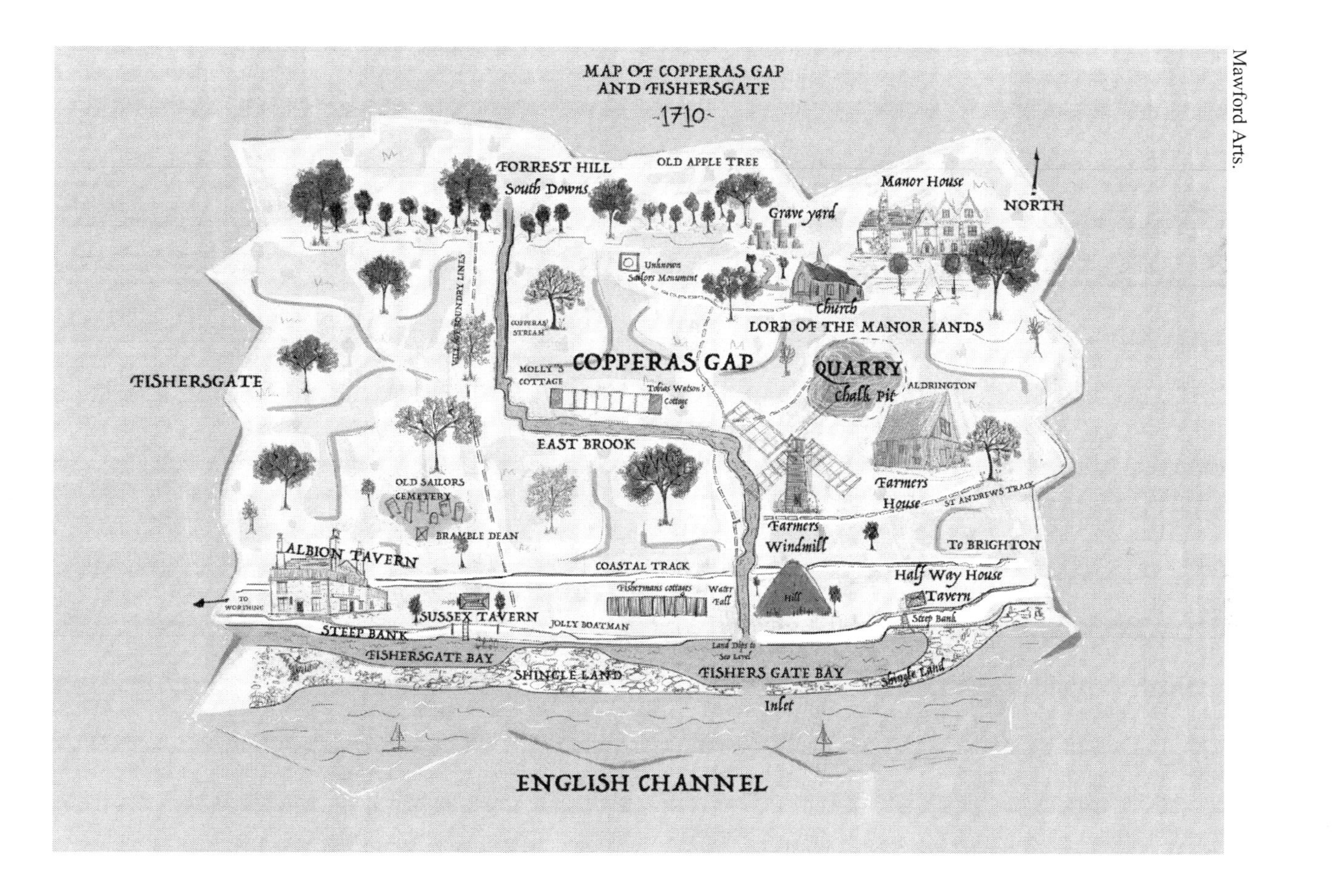

CONTENTS

Chapter 1

First Love, 1713.

"I love you Molly," he said, as he knelt before her, holding her hand in his. They were beneath a mature apple tree, one breezy summer's day in August 1713. The sunlight filtered through the gaps in the foliage and the ripening apples above them, creating moving patterns of light and shade onto her beautiful face. They were alone, except for a few grazing sheep scattered around the meadow. She sat on the ground, her floral dress spread out upon the grass, her back leaning against the rutted tree trunk. She looked deep into the eyes of Tobias Watson.

Tobias moved closer to her. "Molly, will you marry me?"

Molly leant forward and smiled. She kissed Tobias full on the lips. It was a deep lingering kiss with that special intensity of two young lovers locked in a passionate embrace. When it was done and the sensual pulsating pleasure on their lips had faded away, Tobias nibbled her earlobe making her giggle, as it always did.

"Tobias, you ask me that question about marriage every week," said Molly, "you know that I will marry you and we shall raise a family here in Copperas Gap. I would want to have a little girl to start with. I can make pretty dresses for her and tie pink ribbons in her hair. We shall call her Rebecca Alice. Then we shall have a son and I will call him Tobias Henry, after you, and we shall live happily ever after, that is… if you don't leave me to go off to become a sailor on the high seas."

"I will never leave you Molly. Well, not for long. The sea is after all such a special place," said Tobias, "the crashing of the waves on the shoreline and the breeze in the air gives me such a breath-taking feeling. The sound of it draws me towards its sheer magnificence. It is wonderful – just being beside the sea. But I don't want to be beside it. I want to be sailing on the finest ship in the world – travelling across the oceans towards faraway places and experiencing real adventure."

Tobias thought for a moment.

"Sometimes I look out from the shoreline, but I cannot see what is beyond the horizon. Molly, do you ever wonder what is beyond this sleepy village of Copperas Gap?"

"No, I don't," replied Molly, "who cares what is beyond the sea, who cares what adventure may be found in far-off lands. I like it here in this little village that we call home. Our families live here and both of us grew-up here. Tobias, we have everything that we could possibly need – right here in Copperas Gap."

"I have done nothing with my life," replied Tobias.

"But you are almost a skilled shoemaker!" said Molly. "Your father has taught you your trade these past six years. You *have* done something with your life, much more than many other young men in this village. This time next year you will qualify as a shoemaker. You can make enough money for us to rent a cottage from the lord of the manor and we will live our lives together in complete happiness."

Tobias sighed.

"But when I listen to the visiting sailors," he replied, "they tell me wonderful stories about faraway places beyond the seas."

Molly interrupted him. "I don't want to hear any more about this Tobias." She stood up to brush the grass from the back of her dress. Tobias stood up beside her and kissed her once more.

"Molly," he whispered, holding her close in his arms, "I love you more than anything. More than anything in this world."

"Except for the sea," replied a scolding Molly, her bright blue eyes sparkling in the sunlight, "all you do is talk about the sea, sailing ships and those sailors who smell so dreadful. I do believe Tobias Watson that you love the sea much more than you love me."

"That's not true Molly," said Tobias, "just give me some time to explore my destiny and then I will be yours for the rest of our lives. When I have completed my adventures we will live right here in Copperas Gap."

"How long do you want Tobias? Five, ten, twenty years? Why, our lives will be over before we can begin to have a family and then we shall be too old… that is if you do not succumb to hunger, disease or piracy on the high seas and never come back to me," replied Molly.

"Look Molly, I am seventeen years old and you are sixteen. We have been together all our lives. Give me just three months… no… six months… or maybe a year. Yes, give me a year. I shall find my sailor's feet and see what is beyond Copperas Gap. Then, I promise that I shall return home and marry you. Anyway, we cannot marry until you are twenty-one years of age, your mother has said she will not give her permission until then, so there is plenty of time for my adventures in faraway places."

Molly thought for a moment before beginning to speak. "Tobias, my love, it does not matter how much time we have before we marry. What matters is that if you do go on your adventure then we shall be apart. I cannot live my life without you for a year or more?"

"I'll tell you what Molly," interrupted a smiling Tobias – who knew that he was not winning this argument, "let's not talk about the sea anymore, not for today anyway, let's go back to my father's cottage. I will race you down the hill back to Eastbrook."

"You always win these races," exclaimed an amused Molly.

"This time I will give you a head-start," said a playful Tobias, "meet me by the bench seat outside my father's cottage. I'll be there first Molly… at least a minute or two before you."

"No, you won't my lover. Close your eyes Tobias and count to ten," said a cheerful Molly, "I don't want you to see which way I am heading."

"Ok," said Tobias as he closed his eyes and began counting.

"One, two, three, four, five…" Tobias opened his eyes ever so slightly, hoping to see which way she had gone – but she was nowhere to be seen.

He ran down the hill to his father's cottage and was soon standing beside the bench seat. As expected, Molly was not there.

He sat down and waited for a while, but she did not arrive. So, he re-traced his steps back to the old apple tree, but he could not find her. He then went another way – back down the hill to the cottage but could not see Molly at all.

Tobias was beginning to get worried. He re-traced his steps once more and covered both routes from the cottage to the old apple tree – back and forth – several times, shouting out her name but there was no response. Molly was nowhere to be found. He checked inside his cottage where he lived with his parents. Then he checked inside her cottage at the other end of the row of terraced lodges, where she lived with her mother, but he could not find her.

Once more he went back to the meadow and stood beneath the old apple tree where they so often spent time together. Molly was not there.

Suddenly the bright sunlight that surrounded the area turned to darkness. Heavy rain and thunder broke the silence of a summer's day. Forked lightning spread all over the skies, with many powerful million-volt strikes of electricity hitting the earth with tremendous velocity. The ground shook beneath his feet and the apples on the vibrating tree fell all around him, hundreds of them. A howling wind began to take hold. It became increasingly powerful and lifted a rain-drenched Tobias into the air. Tobias grabbed a branch on the tree as the force of nature exerted a wrenching energy on his body, which put a persistent strain upon his grip.

"Hold on Tobias," shouted a voice, "hold on." It was Molly's voice, but he could not see her.

Then, as suddenly as the wind had started – it stopped, and he drifted to the ground, unharmed.

"Molly, Molly, where are you?" called out Tobias. But there was no response.

A deep loud laugh, of what can only be described as a spine-chilling sound, echoed throughout the area. Tobias looked around to try to see where the howling laughter had come from or, more importantly, if he could see Molly.

Then, the menacing laughter echoed around the area once more.

"Who are you? What do you want?" Tobias screamed as he looked around – but he saw no one. The sound of a musical flute could be heard in the distance. It became louder and louder before gradually fading away – until it could be heard no more.

Suddenly the ground beneath him shuddered and a huge crevasse, some ten-yards-long and three feet wide, cracked open in the earth. The apples on the ground rolled into the crevasse, disappearing deep into the planet. Tobias fell down the gap, but not too far, for he had grabbed the root of the old apple tree that was protruding into the crevasse from the side of the broken earth. He hung for a moment, dangling precariously inside the chasm as he tried to gain a foothold in the sodden soil.

His body began shaking. A force beyond his understanding was making him tremble. Suddenly, he lost his grip of the tree root and fell. A long haunting protracted scream of a man in utter distress was emitted from the depths of the earth as he disappeared into the abyss. Then, there was silence.

"Wake up Sir. Wake up," came the request.

A patchy display of unfocused light began to be seen by a wakening man.

"Sir, you asked me to wake you one-hour after first light," said the naval attendant, who was standing over the bunk of a young Captain in the King's Royal Navy.

Almost immediately the Captain was fully awake. His eyes focused on his surroundings within the bedroom. Then, he stood to his feet.

"Yes, thank you sailor. You are dismissed," said the Captain.

"You are sweating, Sir," replied the sailor.

"Yes… I had a bad dream about a girl I once knew in a place where I used to live," replied the Captain as he mopped the sweat from his brow with a handkerchief. "It's hot in this godforsaken place. I cannot wait to get back to sea and have that salty breeze blow through my hair and in my face."

"Yes Sir," said the sailor, "do you want to tell me about this bad dream? I might be able to help you understand it. You see, my Moroccan mother used to be very good at understanding dreams and I believe that she has passed this skill on to me."

"Yes, maybe I should," said the Captain as he bowed his head and looked at the floor. His trusty dog – a long haired Jack Russell – sat quietly in the corner of the room.

The Captain smiled and called, "Good boy, Patch."

The dog produced the sound of a friendly whimper – as if to reply.

The Captain sat on the edge of his bed thinking deeply about the terrible drama that had just been his dream. "I have had this dream a few times before in recent weeks, but no, I shall not discuss it any further today. I have more urgent things to do."

The Captain stood up and sprang into action. "Draw the curtains sailor and then leave this room," he ordered.

"Very well, Captain Watson," came the reply.

The sailor, a personal assistant to the thirty-one-year-old Captain for the past three years, did as he was ordered. He opened the curtains to reveal bright rays of winter sunshine which filled the room with a thousand lumens of natural light. The Captain went into the washroom to sprinkle his face with water. Before long Tobias Watson was in full naval uniform and at his desk in the naval barracks on the Rock of Gibraltar. He began an entry for that day in his diary: Things to do on this day, the 3rd January 1727.

I, Captain Tobias Watson of the King's British fleet shall today begin the task of;

1. *Securing further provisions and more men for my new ship, the Astound.*
2. *Visiting my new ship at the dry dock.*

Pondering for a moment on item two of his itinerary, the Captain went to the window of his barracks and looked down the hill of Gibraltar towards Spain. In the distance he could see a mass of military forces on the Spanish mainland. Further up the hill of Gibraltar he could see the flashes of sunlight from a mirror that was sending heliographic signals over his head.

Unknown to the Captain, the men at that military watch post, James Hodges and Seth Bartlett, had been monitoring the situation of the Spanish forces for the previous hour.

"Looks like the Spanish are playing games again," said Hodges to his mate.

Both men looked downwards from their vantage point high on the hill of the Rock of Gibraltar, watching the Spanish army amass its forces along the border of mainland Spain.

"Well, they have done it before," said Bartlett, a corporal in the British army, the 20th Egerton fusiliers, as he continued to look towards the Spanish army, along the barrel of his musket.

"If we were at war and I were a bit closer I could take some of them out right now – I would blow the bastards to bits. But it's probably just another show of Spanish bravado and I don't want to be the one to start another war. We best be on the safe side though and send a courier message to the Sergeant at arms. The artillery should be prepared – they have the range to hit the Spanish where it hurts."

"You boy," Hodges called to a youngster by the name of John – who was cleaning the brass buttons of a crimson army jacket, "go find the Sergeant and tell him that the Spanish are up to something. Tell him, with respect, he should consider preparing the artillery cannons for battle. Have you got that boy? Tell him also that I tried to send a heliograph signal, but I have received no response from the officers at the command post."

"Yes, Sir," said the boy. The boy put down his cleaning implements and hung the fine military jacket on a nearby tree – before disappearing into the gorse bushes.

"It's probably nothing – but I don't like the look of this," said Bartlett, "the Spanish have been arriving en-masse for the past hour – there must be three-thousand of them."

"How many of us British are here on Gibraltar?" asked Hodges.

"Not sure," said Bartlett, "but it cannot be many more than one thousand British soldiers and eight hundred sailors – and the sailors won't be much good. Well, not in a land battle."

Hodges and Bartlett looked down once more towards the Spanish army – pondering on what might be happening, unsure if these were the final moments before an intended invasion.

Unknown to those two British soldiers keeping guard on the Rock of Gibraltar, communications between the two great countries of Spain and the United Kingdom of Great Britain had been ongoing for days and tension had been building in diplomatic circles.

Indeed, a few days earlier on the 1st January 1727, the Spanish ambassador had sent a letter to the Court of St. James – the Royal Court for the Sovereign of the United Kingdom of Great Britain – explaining why the Spanish Crown believed that British control of Gibraltar was not legal.

This written communication to the British made several demands in the name of his Majesty *King Philip V* of Spain. It was tantamount to a declaration of war. But Spain was not in a good military position to capture Gibraltar by armed force in 1727. Were the Spanish crazy to even attempt it?

Stationed near to Devil's Tounge Battery was Captain Tobias Watson. He had been on the Rock of Gibraltar for the past six-months, waiting for command of his new ship. He was a very experienced seafaring man – for he had joined the Merchant Navy at the young age of eighteen, later joining the Royal Navy and rapidly rising through the ranks. His last ship, *St. Aubyn*, had seen the better part of its service and at the grand age of 55 years was being stripped of its useful assets before being taken to the open sea to be scuttled. There was a tinge of sadness for the passing of this once great ship but new technology in shipbuilding design meant that bigger and faster sailing ships could be built.

The young thirty-one-year-old Captain was preparing his officers and crew to take charge of this new ship the following week. The ship had been named *HMS Astound,* and was being fitted-out in Gibraltar – having been built at Portsmouth three months earlier. The ship was in dry dock number one in the port of Gibraltar at Old Mole. Daily visits were being made to the ship by Captain Watson and his two senior officers. This was one of the first batch of new ships built for this powerful country known as the United Kingdom of Great Britain – a newly formed country of just twenty years. Powerful it was, because England, Wales and Scotland had, at last, become one united country with one parliament. A country that was about to begin its historical journey of becoming the most formidable nation on earth.

Several of King Philip of Spain's senior military advisers had warned the King that the recapture of Gibraltar was, at present, near impossible. The Marquis of Villadarias warned that it would be impossible to take the Rock without Spanish naval support. However, the King was impressed by another of his advisors – the Count de las Torres de Alcorrín, Viceroy of Navarre, who vowed that he could, *in six weeks,* 'deliver Spain from this noxious settlement of British foreigners and heretics'.

King Philip made his decision and the scene was set. The Spanish generals made their plans. The war would begin in earnest in the next few hours. It would be more of a siege of Gibraltar than a war, but nonetheless danger and death would be ever present for the military personnel on both sides of the conflict.

Captain Watson was aboard his ship in the dry dock along with his Lieutenant, Barnabas Roach, and ship's master, Russell Brown. The Captain's trusty dog, Patch, was asleep in his basket under the table. The three men were alone in the Captain's cabin at the stern of this great ship. The door to the cabin was shut but they could hear the banging of tools and the dragging of heavy items across the deck above, as workmen continued with the preparation of making ready this great ship for the sea.

"Gentlemen," called Captain Watson, as they stood beside a large oak table that contained the ship's log and various nautical maps. "In a few days' time we will be taking our ship on to the high sea and it will give us the opportunity to see how she sails."

"It will be a pleasure to sail with you Captain," replied Master Russell Brown. The ship's first Lieutenant, Barnabus Roach, nodded in agreement.

"I have had notification from the Admiral of the British fleet that Spain is about to enter into a war with the United

Kingdom of Great Britain in a dispute over this Rock of Gibraltar," said Captain Watson.

"Wasn't the matter of Gibraltar settled back in 1704?" asked Master Brown.

"It was," replied the Captain, "but it seems that the King of Spain is still not satisfied and has launched this new war to take the Rock of Gibraltar from us."

"But our Navy is far superior to theirs," said Barnabus Roach, "they cannot win."

"Yes, I agree," replied the Captain, "but we British should not rest upon our laurels – the Spanish may have a trick or two up their sleeves."

"Well, what are we to do?" asked Lieutenant Roach.

"Come closer my men, and I will tell you of my orders from the Admiralty."

The Captain moved the ship's log to one side so that the three of them could view the nautical maps laying on the oak table.

Just then, there was a knock on the door.

"Enter," shouted the Captain.

A man holding a two-foot long T-bar auger-bit opened the door.

"Sorry Captain, I have to drill a hole through the bulkhead to insert a wooden peg," said the man.

"Who are you?" asked the Captain.

The man stood to attention, "I am Robert Hotham from Bristol – the ship's carpenter and surgeon. I am assisting with the fitting of essential items aboard this vessel, Sir, in preparation for sail."

"Will you be sailing with us?" inquired the Captain.

"He will," replied the master, Russell Brown. "He is the best ship's carpenter I have come across but he is a better surgeon than carpenter and I hired him when I found that he had become available."

"My last ship was fired upon by the French Navy and sunk. I was one of only three survivors, Sir," said Robert Hotham.

"Must you do this work right now?" asked the Captain.

"I am afraid so Sir, it is part of larger construction works and in order for those to proceed we must drill this hole as soon as we can," replied Robert.

"Will it take long?" growled the Captain.

"About three hours Sir," came the reply.

The Captain resigned himself to the fact that the work must be undertaken. He smiled at Hotham before turning towards his officers and announcing, "Well gentlemen, our war is delayed by a carpenter wanting to drill a hole into the timbers of this fine ship. How can I refuse the request of the finest carpenter and surgeon in the British Navy? We will almost certainly use his carpentry skills in the next few weeks and may indeed require his medical services, so let us bow to his request and resume our discussions back in this cabin in four hours' time."

"Very well Captain," responded Lieutenant Roach. The master of the ship Russell Brown nodded in agreement.

"Thank you, Captain," said Robert Hotham.

"Mr. Brown," called the Captain, as he began to walk through the cabin door that led to a ladder – where he would ascend onto the main deck, "would you be kind enough to secure the navigational charts and the ship's log to a place of safety and security?"

"Very well Captain," replied Brown.

"Then I shall bid you both farewell and I shall see the pair of you in four hours' time – at the afternoon – two bells.

"You stay here Patch," Watson called to his dog, "keep your eye on the ship's carpenter,"

The dog opened its eyes and whimpered, before going back to sleep.

The six-foot two-inch Captain was dressed in the finery of his personal naval uniform, consisting of an embroidered dark blue coat with a golden epaulette on his left shoulder. The coat had a white edged trim and his waistcoat matched accordingly. He wore white breeches, stockings, and leather shoes – which, as a qualified master shoemaker, he had made himself. Each shoe bore a highly polished brass buckle. He wore his natural black hair down to his shoulders and held his tricorn hat in his left hand as he crouched to go through the cabin doorway. His right hand held his battle sword, in place in its scabbard close to his thigh, so as not to hinder his exit from the room as he entered the aperture of the small doorway. Battle swords attached to the waist of an officer had an uncanny knack of getting caught on door frames when their owner was negotiating tight spaces – unless of course it was held firm in a controlled manner. The Captain's officers wore similar uniforms but both Brown and Roach wore wigs because of their individual hair loss, Brown being 42 years old and Roach being 36.

Captain Watson was soon standing upon the dockside, once again admiring the structure of his ship. It would be a few more days before he would take the opportunity to sail her on the high seas on an Admiralty mission that he had yet to impart to his two officers. Brown and Roach were most experienced seafaring men. Both had come from a background of the upper-middle-classes and, like all officers of their day, they had personally chosen their own style of naval uniform within Admiralty guidelines and bought and paid for it themselves. There were no standard issue uniforms provided by the British Navy in those days. Captain Tobias Watson had also purchased his own uniform, as was usual among gentlemen, but there was a big difference between the three men. Whereas Brown and Roach came from privileged backgrounds, Watson did not. He came from the small village of Copperas Gap on the south coast of England and, to date, had achieved great things within the Royal Navy, for Tobias Watson had risen through the ranks to that of a Captain in just eight years. Before joining the Royal Navy, he had been with the merchant Navy, as a boy who could neither read or write. His was an unbelievable achievement based on his natural seafaring skills along with a combination of hard work, sweat and blood as well as an ability to learn quickly. At the age of twenty-three Tobias Watson had been seconded to London's Naval headquarters where he was instructed in the art of gentlemanly ways in presenting himself. His boyish southern Copperas Gap accent was erased and, from then on, he spoke the words of a gentleman. His voice was slightly effeminate, but it was effectual with the decisive efficiency of authority. His very warm personality would ignite his likeability in everyone that he met. He was a man who often advised the Admiralty in matters of war and seafaring techniques.

Today was the first time that Roach and Watson had met. Roach was a man of class distinction, a man that believed that he was born to rule the lower classes and yet, here he was being ruled by a Captain that had originated from a lower class than he. He believed that Tobias Watson was about to take command of a ship that was way above his class-station. He was not sure about Watson – for this story of a lower-class person infiltrating the high ranks of the Navy were just rumours that he had heard. But having now met Watson in person, Roach thought that he seemed quite normal in his mannerisms and demeanour. He spoke well and projected an air of authority as all captains of the fleet should. Maybe the rumours Roach had heard about Captain Watson's background were untrue. Maybe Watson did come from the ruling classes, for he showed not the slightest mannerism which might indicate he was a man born to the lower class. Roach would need to keep an eye on this Captain and, if it transpired that the Captain was of impure stock, he would only have to wait for a mistake to be made. Once an error of judgement had been made, then Roach could legitimately seize control of the ship and report back to the Admiralty as such. It would not be mutiny if the Captain was proven to be unfit to command a King's ship.

Brown, on the other hand, had served with Captain Watson many years before. It was aboard His Majesty's ship *Thunder,* which was then under the command of Captain Stephen Carden, long before Carden was promoted to Admiral of the British fleet. Indeed, behind all of Captain Tobias Watson's success was Admiral Carden who had guided, planned, and nurtured Watson's career.

Later that day Captain Watson met with his two officers.

"Mr. Brown, Mr. Roach," said Captain Watson, "these are our orders from the Admiralty. We are to escort British merchant ships to and from the Rock of Gibraltar. Our merchant ships are tasked with bringing essential supplies to the Rock of Gibraltar. Our common enemy are the Spanish naval forces and our mission is of the utmost importance. We must ensure that supplies get through in order to support our military forces on the Rock."

The Captain proceeded to explain the detail of the operations using maps and drawings.

A few days later the ship was ready to sail. All works had been completed and it was a matter of flooding the dry dock to allow the gigantic ship to float. Once the lock gates were opened the ship would glide into the harbour – pushed from both quays by some five hundred sailors using ropes and pulleys.

Aboard the ship were around 460 crew and of course Patch, the Captain's own dog. The crew included two rifle platoons of the British army – some forty-five fighting soldiers. Among their numbers were regular army men, James Hodges, Seth Bartlett and the boy John – the same three who had been watching the Spanish build-up on main-land Spain a few days earlier.

The giant naval ship *Astound* glided from the dock into the main harbour shortly after the lock-gates were opened. Its magnificent structure, being 150 ft long and 41ft wide with three giant masts, was loaded with firepower of some 68 cannons. Its most deadly cannons were the 24 pounders situated on the lower gun deck.

Captain Watson made a series of orders. "Throw a line to the men aboard the *St. Aubyn*. We will tow her out to sea. Make sail on a southerly course. We have a brisk wind in the air."

A few hours later they were three miles offshore. They unhitched the doomed ship, *St. Aubyn*, and transferred all remaining sailors aboard her ageing structure to the newer *HMS Astound*. "Retreat three hundred yards on a westerly course," ordered the Captain.

"Very well Sir," replied Brown before relaying the order to the lower ranks.

"Prepare cannons, turn *HMS Astound* broadside and await my orders," called Watson.

Fifteen minutes later the mighty ship was in position with the cannons primed.

"Mr. Brown," ordered the Captain, "your orders are to destroy the *St. Aubyn*. Fire at will."

The Captain turned his back on the stricken vessel. It was an upsetting moment for him.

"Destroy the ship *St. Aubyn*," screamed Brown at the top of his voice, "fire at will, begin NOW."

A barrage of cannon fire commenced. Watson composed himself before turning to face the condemned ship.

Twenty minutes later as she began to sink beneath the waves, Watson removed his tricorn hat and held it close to his chest.

"This is the end of a fine ship, but it is the beginning of some wonderful memories of the men who sailed aboard her fine structure. I shall miss you *St. Aubyn*. I shall miss the sailors who are no longer with us." said the Captain before standing to attention and saluting. Captain Watson watched as the *St. Aubyn* disappeared beneath the waves.

During the following weeks Captain Watson and his officers trialled his new ship, *HMS Astound,* against numerous wind forces and sea conditions before he finally concluded that this was the best ship that he ever had the pleasure to command. Patch spent his doggy days wandering freely around the ship, chasing and killing rats – which were plentiful aboard sailing ships of this type. Over the next two years, Captain Tobias Watson and his crew escorted many a British merchant ship to the Rock of Gibraltar and, in that time, his ship *HM*S *Astound* sank seven Spanish ships of aggression. Tobias did not lose a single merchant ship under his supervision and was beginning to make a name for himself among the Navy hierarchy as an excellent Captain and leader of men – his name was mentioned in dispatches more than once at Admiralty House in London. This pleased his mentor, Admiral Stephen Carden, who delighted in telling wonderful stories about his young prodigy at the many after dinner speeches he and his fellow senior officers attended at Portsmouth, England. Tobias Watson was the best young Captain in the entire British Fleet, but future events were about to challenge Captain Watson's skills.

Chapter 2

Into the unknown

Two years later, on a cold winter morning of December 1729, the battle-weary crew of the ship, *Astound,* guided the vessel back into the harbour of Gibraltar. The Spanish War of Succession had ended and the siege of Gibraltar was over. Hostilities had ceased between the two nations a few weeks earlier with the Treaty of Seville being signed on the 9th November 1729. The *Astound* was about to enter the maintenance dock. Once in position, in front of the lock-gates of the maintenance dock, all sails were lowered and stowed away below decks before the giant gates into the dock were slowly opened. The waters in the dry dock levelled to the height of the harbour waters. It was to be a three-month re-fit of the ship – three months of considerable repairs. Though Captain Watson and his men had been very successful in defending against the many attacking Spanish ships in the Mediterranean – the *Astound* had been damaged. Enemy cannon strikes had taken their toll on the ship's superficial structure. It was not enough damage to cause the ship to be unsafe but for aesthetic reasons these repairs had to be done. The ship was looking tatty and tired. And so were most of the crew. What they required was a long rest ashore. Yes, the crew had visited Gibraltar on many occasions during the past two years to replenish the ship's stocks, but they had never stayed more than three days. All the ship's men, including officers, were looking forward to a three-month break while naval engineers re-furbished the ship.

Captain Watson stood on the poop deck along with his officers, Brown and Roach. Two teams of one hundred-and fifty-dock workers formed a line along the length of both quays.

Ropes were winched from the docks to the ship and attached to the port and starboard sides of the bow by the sailors onboard. Each man on the docks took hold of a section of the unravelled rope and waited for further orders.

"Mr. Brown," called the Captain.

"Yes Sir," came the reply.

"Mr. Brown, please relieve the steersman at the main wheel, for you shall now steer the ship into the maintenance dock."

"Very well Sir," replied Brown as he ordered the steersman to release the wheel into his keeping.

The Captain turned to other men on the poop deck, "You men are to leave your posts and wait on the main deck and prepare to disembark."

The cheery men left the poop deck as ordered.

"Pull," ordered Captain Watson to the two teams of men standing on the quays.

Each of the two groups pulled the ropes attached to the bow of the ship. The giant ship slowly glided into the maintenance dock. Other men, on either side of the ship, used timber levers in-between the dock-wall and the ship's hull to ensure that the vessel entered the dock without any further damage being caused to its structure. Once in position the lock gates were closed – leaving the *Astound* floating in its watery containment.

"Remove all ropes tethered to the ship," ordered the Captain, "all men, excepting my officers, are to secure their respective posts, take their belongings and disembark from this ship. Do not leave any of your personal belongings aboard this ship. Accommodation will be found for you on land for the next three months in the Naval barracks. I will see you all, three months from now, at sunrise on the morning of March 10th, 1730, when we shall once more take to the seas and have another go at the Spanish."

There was a huge cheer from the men. Each one of them was looking forward to three months' vacation – with pay.

One of the men shouted, "Three cheers for the Captain, Hip, Hip."

"HOORAY" thundered the booming voices of four hundred men.

A broad smile covered the face of Captain Watson as he looked down on the men and waved to them.

"Hip Hip, HOORAY – Hip Hip, HOORAY," came the second and third cheers.

The men on the ship's deck began their pursuit of getting their belongings from below – while other men below, who had already gotten their personal possessions, swarmed up the ladders to the ship's deck. As the two waves of men met with each other, utter chaos appeared to ensue. Yet it was an orderly sailors' chaos – nothing more than that. And before long the immediate area around the ship was deserted. In the distance hundreds of men could be seen queuing at the doors of the Naval barracks to register for their pay and hammock space or were seen sitting outside the numerous drinking houses that looked out over the docks.

"A successful conclusion," called Roach to Captain Watson.

"Indeed, it has been an orderly finish to the day," replied the Captain, "but there are one or two things for us three officers to do before we ourselves disembark."

"Yes Sir," came the response in unison from Brown and Roach.

"I want you two men to inspect the ship from bottom to top to ensure that everything aboard this ship is safe, that nothing of value is left behind and that no one remains on this vessel," said the Captain, "we have a duty to hand this vessel to the maintenance crew in two hours. They will drain the waters of the dock so that work can begin on the hull of the ship. I have already secured the dock quays with military men to stop any unauthorised persons from coming aboard. Make sure all cooking fires and candles are out and report back to me in my day cabin in one hour. Anyone found aboard this ship shall be ejected and their names reported to me."

"Very well Sir," said Brown. "Come on Roach my old friend," as they both went below deck, "let us complete this one last task for today and as soon as we are done I shall buy you some ale at the Tavern across the way."

"Have you ever bought me ale before?" replied Roach with a wry smile.

Brown grinned at the comment, "Less of your impertinence Mr. Roach."

It sure was a happy day – for the remaining ship's company would soon leave the vessel for some considerable time of leisure on the shores of Gibraltar. The Captain went to his quarters, where he would make a fuss of his dog, Patch. 'It is time for play,' thought Captain Watson, as he took a ball out of his pocket for Patch.

Roach and Brown were now on the lower-deck of the ship.

"So, Mr. Roach," inquired Brown, "you said two years ago that you would keep your eye on our Captain because you believed he was not up to the job – for you feared he was from the lower classes. What do you say about that now Mr. Roach?"

"Well, Mr. Brown," came the reply, "I think I shall have to eat humble words. He is the best Captain I have ever had the privilege of serving and he is very popular with the men. I do not know if he comes from the lower classes but if he does it is of no importance."

"I thought you would say that," replied Brown, "now come… let us go down to the hold and begin checking the ship as the Captain has asked. You start at the stern and I will take the bow. We shall meet in the middle on each level before going up a deck to begin the process again."

"Right Sir," replied Roach.

The two men began their systematic search of the ship. It was not long before Roach came across two soldiers, James Hodges and Seth Bartlett, fast asleep in their respective hammocks. Also asleep on the floor was the boy, John.

"Wake," shouted Roach several times as he stood in between the two hammocks and shook them.

Hodges and Bartlett began to stir. Soon they were both standing beside their respective bunks in the half-light of the gun-deck.

"You two men should be ashore by now, look lively – get your kit and get yourselves off this ship in the next two minutes or you shall be reported to the Captain," bellowed Roach, "and wake that boy up – take him with you."

"Sorry Mr. Roach," replied Bartlett as he gently kicked the sleeping boy, "we were on the late watch," he continued as he scratched his head as if to help wake himself properly.

"I want no excuses," bellowed Roach.

The ship's master, Brown, had heard the commotion.

"What have we here?" he called as he approached the group.

"Two lazy soldiers and their assistant," replied Roach.

The two soldiers stood to a ruffled attention. "Sorry Sir," said one. The boy John had woken. He also stood to attention. "Sorry Sir," said John.

They were soon ejected from the ship.

Roach and Brown reported to the Captain that the ship was secure, bid their farewell and went to the local inn to get their well-earned flagon of ale.

The Captain remained at his desk for a moment, gathering his ship's log and personal papers before putting them into a small wooden chest. He then got-up from his chair and opened the door to his day-cabin before calling for his Moroccan attendant. Leaving the door to his cabin ajar he returned to his desk. His personal attendant, an able seaman, arrived and stood before the Captain.

"It is a sad day for me my friend," said the Captain.

"Sir, it has been an honour to serve under your command these past five years," replied the sailor, "but it is time for me to return to my homeland."

"You have been a good servant of the British navy," said Captain Watson, "you have also been a faithful personal aid to me. I wish you well for the future."

"I shall miss you and the navy Sir," said the sailor with some sadness about him, "but it is time to go... I am fifty-nine years old and though I love being aboard this ship, my legs simply cannot carry me the distance my mind desires. I tire too easily. I am weary. It is time to retire and I have no regrets."

"Yes, yes you have told me all this before. Now what will you do with yourself?" asked the Captain.

"I shall go back to Morocco, the place of my birth," came the reply, "to a dwelling for Islamic learning near to the ruins of the El badi Palace."

"Yes, I remember now – your father was English and your mother Moroccan," said the Captain.

"That is correct Sir," said the sailor, "both of my parents have since passed to the after-world."

Just then, the door to the Captain's cabin moved slightly and made a creaking sound. From behind the open doorway a small golden coloured snub-nosed monkey appeared. Captain Watson laughed out loud while Patch, the Captain's trusty dog, followed every move of the monkey with his eyes, but remained quietly curled-up in his basket.

"And I presume that you are taking your pet Asian monkey with you to Morocco?" asked the Captain.

"Yes Sir," said the sailor, "My primate friend and I have been together for some time now. I cannot leave him behind."

"He is a very fine intelligent monkey," said the Captain.

The monkey wore a scuffed leather collar around his neck that had a short piece of chain attached. He held the excess chain in his left palm and in his right hand he clasped a musical flute that had a pretty pattern of white coloured sparkling beads embedded into its length – maybe they were diamonds. The monkey walked the short distance from the doorway to where the attendant stood – before handing him the flute.

"I must get you a new collar," said the sailor as he touched the monkey's neckline, "your leather collar is worn badly. I know a place in Morocco where I can purchase one."

The monkey's eyes opened wide as he pointed to one of the glass beads on the side of the flute.

"You want a diamond encrusted collar?" asked the sailor.

The monkey nodded.

"I don`t know about that," replied the sailor, "but we shall see what is available at the market stalls in Morocco."

The monkey smiled.

"We have had many pleasant evenings aboard this ship listening to you playing your flute," said the Captain, "play me one more melody before you leave this ship for the last time sailor."

"Very well, Sir," replied the sailor, "I shall play you a tune that you will not have heard before. It emanates from my birth town of Marrakesh which is situated in the foothills of the Atlas Mountains of Morocco. It is a beautiful sound written many years ago by a local musician for the Saadi ruling dynasty. This dynasty ruled the country until the supreme Sultan, Almed Al Mansour, died in 1603. The tune has magical yet hidden meanings."

The sailor sat down on the floor, crossed his legs and began to play a most wonderful tune. It was a *calling* sound. All along, the snub-nosed monkey gazed at his master.

Captain Watson watched on, taking-in every magical musical note. There was a tinge of sadness in his eyes and a wonderment beyond comprehension.

When the sailor had finished playing the tune the Captain clapped his hands together before complimenting him.

"I have heard that tune before sailor," said the Captain, "I have heard that tune in my dreams, when in those dreams I remember my home town of Copperas Gap and a wonderful woman I once knew."

"Molly Moffett?" replied the sailor.

"How did you know her name?" demanded the Captain.

"You speak of her in your sleep captain," said the sailor, "you must dream of her often."

"I do," replied the Captain, "I miss her so much. Her presence in my dreams is always accompanied by that tune of the flute. That same tune you have just played. It is a wonderous tune. Sometimes Molly and I dance to that tune of my dreams."

"Then that is a sign Captain that all will be well for you and Molly in the future," said the sailor. "If you remember, I once told you that my Moroccan mother could interpret dreams and I believed that she has passed that skill onto me."

"Tell me more?" inquired the Captain, "how can you know that all be well for Molly and me?"

"I know no more than I have told you Captain," came the reply, "but believe in me, I truly know that all will be well with you and Molly in the future."

"I wish you were right," said the Captain, "but sadly I cannot share your optimism."

The sailor handed back the musical flute to the golden snub-nosed monkey.

"It is time for me to leave you Captain," replied the sailor. "Thank you once again for all that you have done for me these past few years, but it is time for me to board another ship to begin a final journey to my homeland of Morocco."

"It's a pity that you can tell me nothing more about my dreams. Goodbye my friend," said the Captain as he watched his former attendant and the monkey leave his day-cabin for the very last time.

Three months later the repairs to the ship were complete and the *Astound* was ready to set-sail.

On March 10th 1730, Captain Watson and his crew left Gibraltar for the Chicksaw war in the Americas. This war was a land battle fought by the British Army against the French in Mississippi and Western Tennessee. British Naval action secured supply routes from England. Throughout this war Captain Watson and his crew were mentioned several times in dispatches for heroism beyond the call of duty.

By 1733 the Chicksaw war was over for the Captain and the crew of the *Astound*. Tobias Watson had orders to return to the Rock of Gibraltar. He was to rendezvous with another British ship three miles off the coast of the Rock and wait for further instructions. The journey was uneventful and eight weeks later they were nearing their destination off the coast of Gibraltar.

"A fine day today, Mr. Brown," said Lieutenant Roach, "it's a pity we are below deck on this pleasant day – inspecting the mess area and quarters of the men."

Soldiers Hodges, Bartlett and the boy John were nearby cleaning their uniforms and gun barrels.

Brown did not reply to Roach, for his attention was drawn to a creaking sound emanating from the timber structure of the ship. It became louder and louder. The four men and the boy looked at each other before listening to the unusual sounds. A faint wind began to blow which whistled through the internal structure of the ship. It lasted for a minute or more before a howling gale began. They had not heard anything like this before – aboard this or any other British ship.

"What's happening?" shouted Lieutenant Roach as he held onto a beam for support.

"Not sure," came the reply from Brown.

The gale became louder until they could not hear each other's speech.

Suddenly, the ship lunged forward – the bow falling downwards, leaving the ship at a precarious angle of forty-five degrees. All four men and the boy lost their balance. They rolled downwards towards the front of the ship. Three of them managed to grab onto something, Lieutenant Roach some netting, Bartlett a rope and Hodges a timber upright – but Brown, the oldest of the men, and the youngest – the boy John, were gone. They were thrown the full length of the ship, downwards, towards the bow. Gun batteries were ripped from the ropes that had previously secured them to their fixed positions and their heavy weight caused them to fall forward towards the bow. The ship juddered from port to starboard and then back again, shaking violently before falling, in a downward motion into the depths of an abyss. Suddenly it came to an abrupt and complete standstill before levelling out. The whole episode had lasted about two-minutes.

Then, a deep loud laugh, the laugh of a madman, echoed throughout the area – but this madman was not to be seen.

"Who is that?" shouted Bartlett – no one responded.

Roach, Bartlett and Hodges looked at each other in the stillness – neither of them wanting to release their grip in case the ship moved again.

"I have never, in my entire seafaring career, experienced anything like that," called out Roach to the other two.

"What was it?" replied Hodges.

"Well it can only be a storm of some kind," said Roach, "but no storm I have been through before has been as bad or of such a short duration as that."

"What should we do Sir?" asked Bartlett.

Before Roach could reply, the sound of a musical flute began to play. It started faintly from the bow of the ship and became louder.

"What's happening?" asked a worried Bartlett.

"I am not sure," replied Roach.

The three of them listened to the sound of the flute until it faded away.

Then, without warning, the ship's master, Mr. Brown, came walking past them. But he looked much different to the man they thought they knew. He had an unusual brightness about him. It was a golden glow of happiness. His complexion was fresh and the clothes he wore were spotlessly clean. 'But wait a minute,' thought Roach, 'he is wearing his naval dress uniform – not the working naval uniform he wore some five minutes before.' Brown's arms were outstretched as if he were about to embrace someone. He glided past Roach without saying a word. His mind seemed to be focused on something that only he could see before him. Roach looked in the same direction. He could not see anything – except the inside of the ship's hull.

"Are you okay Mr. Brown?" called out Roach as he let go of the netting that had secured his position during the recent trauma.

Brown did not reply but looked straight ahead as he passed Roach.

"Mr. Brown," Roach called once more.

Brown did not respond. He walked straight into the timber wall at the stern of the ship and disappeared into its structure. He was gone.

There were gasps of disbelief from Roach, Hodges and Bartlett.

"Did you see that?" asked Hodges.

The other two looked on in disbelief.

The three men stood together as they looked towards the plain empty wooden wall where Mr. Brown had been.

"He walked straight into the wall – just like a ghost would," exclaimed Hodges.

Roach stared at the wall for a moment before suddenly coming to his senses.

"Be about you man," he growled.

Roach glared hard at Hodges before he once again looked at the wooden wall, "Brown is not there. Brown is somewhere but he is not there. We must all have had a knock to the head – there are no such thing as ghosts. Come on, let us go forward and find Mr. Brown and the boy, John, and then seek out the Captain who I presume is still in his cabin."

The three of them moved forward to the centre part of the ship to find the step-ladder that would take them up to the Captain's day cabin.

"Oh my God," screamed Bartlett.

"What is it?" called Roach.

"Over there. Look over there under that cannon," as he pointed in a starboard direction.

On the decking was the dead body of the ship's master, Mr. Brown. A loose ship's cannon had crushed him. It was a ghastly sight of blood, guts, broken skin, red soaked bones and matted hair, which was strewn about the immediate area.

"I've seen some horrid sights in my days as a soldier," said Bartlett, as he looked at the crushed remains of Mr. Brown, "but I ain't seen many as bad as that one."

"Come on," shouted a horrified Roach, "he is beyond help now. Let us find Captain Watson, for we must make sure he is safe. We can come back later and deal with Mr. Brown's body."

"So, we did see a ghost walk into the structure of the ship," said Hodges.

"Perhaps," replied a puzzled Mr. Roach as he looked upon his late friend, Mr. Brown, with sorrow and pity.

Suddenly he snapped out of his stare at the grizzly sight of Mr. Brown's mangled body, "Come on – let us find the Captain," he exclaimed.

"What about the boy, John?" said Hodges.

"We will find him later," came the reply.

The three men ascended the ladder to the upper deck where they found an unperturbed Captain Watson sitting in his day cabin making an entry in the ship's log. His trusty dog, Patch, was fast asleep in his basket.

"Captain, I see you are well after our ordeal," said Roach.

"Yes, it was a very unusual experience," replied a calm Captain Watson, "do you know what it was, Roach?"

"No Sir," came the reply, "but the wind was whistling, the voice of an unseen man spoke the words of a madman with a grizzly laugh and a flute began playing."

"A flute playing, you say?" inquired the Captain.

"Yes Sir," said Lieutenant Roach, "we heard a flute playing a gentle sound… it was an enticing sound. Then we heard the deep voice of a madman. It came from no-where and then there was a whistling wind that blew through the underdeck."

"Indeed," said Captain Watson. He pondered on this information while considering his recurring dream of the old apple tree at Copperas Gap. That dream also had a flute, whistling wind and scary voice."

The Captain stood up from his desk.

"Did you hear a girl's voice – Molly is her name?" asked Watson, demanding an immediate reply. The Captain's eyes fixed firmly on Roach's facial expressions.

"No Sir," came the reply from Roach, "should I have heard the voice of a girl? Who is Molly?"

"Never mind," said the Captain.

Captain Watson looked through the cabin's window. He watched the swell of the water that blended into sky, far away on the horizon.

"Might I suggest we go onto the poop deck in order that we may fully view our situation," asked Roach.

"Yes of course, Mr. Roach," replied Captain Watson, "but it is a mystery beyond comprehension. Did you feel the ship vibrate and tip over its usual centre of balance? Did you see any damage on your way to my cabin, Mr. Roach?"

"Yes, Captain, I should report plenty of damage. Cannons and fixtures were ripped from their positions as the ship tipped and rocked. And I am sorry to report that Mr. Brown is dead… crushed and killed by a loose cannon," said Roach.

"He is as flat as a fried egg in a pan," interjected a clearly shocked Hodges as he explained the details of Mr. Brown's fate.

"Hodges, be quiet," ordered Roach, "keep your opinions to yourself man."

"Mr. Brown's death is unfortunate," replied the Captain – as he thought for a moment, "well, let us make haste. You and I, Roach, will go onto the main deck to assess our situation and you two soldiers… what are your names?"

"Bartlett and Hodges," came the reply.

"Yes, Bartlett and Hodges," the Captain continued, "I want you to inspect the hull of this ship from bottom to top in that order and report any leaks or major damage to me on the main deck as soon as you can. After that, would you take Mr. Brown's body into your care and prepare him for burial. AND find that boy, what was his name?"

"John," said Roach.

"Yes, of course," replied the Captain, "find the boy John – he might be trapped somewhere."

"Yes Sir," said both men in unison before they disappeared through the door of the Captain's cabin to attend to his specific orders.

"Mr. Roach," called the Captain, "follow me. Let us attend the poop deck and make what we will of our present situation."

Before long the two men were on the poop deck. In the distance, to the starboard side of the ship, was the outline of land. Behind them, at the stern of the ship, they could see the Rock of Gibraltar on the horizon. They were sailing due west, away from the island. The two men gazed into the rigging high above them to see that the ship was in full sail with a brisk occasional wind blowing from a south-by-east direction. The British white ensign, the flag of the King's Navy, flew from the mast. Yet, there was not an ordinary sailor in sight and no-one at the wheel of the ship, though it was gently turning to take account of wind speed, predisposed direction and tidal forces. It appeared to be steering itself.

"Take the wheel Mr. Roach," said the Captain, "while I assess this perplexing situation. Where is everyone? I have not seen a single sailor aboard this ship since the storm?"

"Very well Sir," replied a puzzled Roach as he took hold of the ship's steering wheel.

"Bring us about Mr. Roach," ordered Captain Watson, "we shall go to the port of Gibraltar.

The Captain raised his telescope and looked towards Gibraltar.

"Sir," called out Roach, "I cannot turn the ship's wheel. Whichever way I try, it will not budge."

"Here… I shall lend you a hand," replied the Captain as he gripped the wheel with both hands, "when I give the word turn the wheel to starboard."

The wheel would not move – no matter how hard the two men tried. They were on a course that seemed to have been pre-set by someone else. Over the next half-hour Watson and Roach tried everything they could to dislodge the wheel from its fixed course – but nothing worked.

"Sir," called out Hodges, who had returned onto the deck, "we have inspected the ship – and though there is a lot of internal damage – the hull of this ship is intact, and water has not breached its structure."

"Well, that's good news," came the reply from Captain Watson, "now, please prepare Mr. Brown's body for a burial at sea."

"Yes Captain," came the reply, "there is one other thing Sir, we found another person aboard this ship. He is in a bad way, unconscious but still alive. Bartlett is tending to him now. I think he will survive."

"Do you recognise him?" said the Captain. "Is it the boy, John?"

"No Sir, it is not John – it's Robert Hotham the ship's surgeon and carpenter."

“Thank you, let us hope he survives,” replied the Captain, “you are dismissed, return to your duties.”

“There is something else Captain,” said Hodges, “there is not a single sailor aboard this ship. They have all gone.”

“Why that’s impossible,” exclaimed Roach, “we are in the middle of the Atlantic Ocean. They couldn’t have been swept overboard. Not all four hundred and sixty of them.”

“I have checked and checked again Mr. Roach and can find no ordinary sailors,” replied Hodges, “the only persons aboard this ship are you Mr. Roach, Captain Watson, Bartlett, Robert Hotham and myself… it’s impossible to understand, Sir, but it is true.”

Captain Watson thought for a moment, “don’t forget that the boy John is here somewhere too. Very well Hodges, thank you for your report. Now return to your duties.”

Hodges disappeared into the hatch that led below decks.

Just at that moment a young voice shouted from above. “Spanish ship preparing to attack, estimate thirty-minutes before contact is made.”

Both men looked upwards towards the crow’s nest at the top of the ship. It was the boy, John, waving his arms and pointing in the direction of the approaching Spanish ship.

“Well done John,” shouted Captain Watson. “Stay where you are boy and keep me informed.”

“Will do, Captain,” shouted John.

Captain Watson turned to Roach. “Well that’s good, the boy is found alive, but we are in a predicament Mr. Roach. An attacking Spanish ship. We have no crew and, even if we did, we have no cannon or shot to fire – for our defences are strewn about the ship.”

“With respect Captain, the only thing we can do is try to outrun them,” replied Roach. “If we can get that wheel turned about we can get to the Rock of Gibraltar. They will not follow us further – once we get near to the Rock.”

“Well, Mr. Roach,” said the Captain, “I agree. Let us evaluate our predicament. The steersman wheel will not turn the tiller. Therefore, it is possible that the ropes to the tiller are jammed. We shall go down to the tiller in the gun room on the middle deck and cut the ropes. Then we can steer the ship directly from there."

"That will not work," boomed a voice.

Both men looked around. Before them stood a strange looking bedraggled man wearing a shopkeeper's lamb-skin apron.

"How did you get aboard?" exclaimed a surprised Lieutenant Roach.

The man ignored Roach's question and continued. "You are set on a pre-defined course for Copperas Gap, England and there is nothing you can do to alter this course."

"Who are you?" shouted Captain Tobias Watson as he drew his sword. "Where did you come from?"

The Captain's dog, Patch, stood up, his ears pricked. He began growling to defend his master.

"Put that toy sword away and get rid of the stupid dog," said the shopkeeper, "you cannot harm me – and you know who I am. Remember Tobias Watson, I once said to you that I would see you in the future. Well, this is the future."

"I do not know you," replied the Captain, "though… wait…" as he studied the shopkeeper's facial features, "I have seen your face before, many years ago."

"Yes, you have," replied the man, "it was in the lodging house of Mrs. Morse."

"Yes, I remember. What do you want?" asked Watson.

"It is not what I want for myself, Tobias Watson. It is your destiny that I want to settle, for it is of the utmost importance," came the reply.

Roach, who had been watching this altercation beckoned the Captain. "Sir, I believe we should arrest this madman and restrain him to the cell below. He is a lunatic."

"You cannot harm me Roach – if you touch me you shall perish. You shall die a slow lingering painful death," replied the shopkeeper. "Now listen, you should both heed my words."

"What words? Well, spit it out man," said Captain Watson, "my patience grows thin. We have enough problems right now aboard this ship and more coming, with that Spanish ship of war approaching."

The shopkeeper held out both his arms before lifting them above his head. As he did so he entered a trance-like state. His body elevated into the air some two feet above the deck.

Roach gasped in disbelief while an unperturbed Watson held his sword firmly in the direction of the shopkeeper.

Then, the Captain's sword turned to wood. He threw the useless implement onto the deck.

"Tobias Watson," wailed the shopkeeper, "you have a destiny to fulfil. This ship is set on a course and it will sail itself to a place where you will seal your fate. I have sent your crew to a parallel world – they are safe. You cannot interfere with this ship or its destination, for your circumstances are now in the hands of the Lord of the Universe. You must use your far-sightedness and providence to the best of your ability to determine your destiny in the coming days – for this incantation cannot be broken. Mr. Brown's spirit is now steering this ship and the spirit of the boy John, in the crow's nest, is helping him.

"You mean the boy is also dead?" asked Roach.

"Can you not see the deathly golden glow about him?" exclaimed the shopkeeper, before his mood changed to reconcile the concept, "but what is death? I shall tell you. It is just another scene in a dramatic play that extends from mortal life to spiritual existence within the regulated theatre of this vast universe, where purgatory and heaven meet under the command of the Lord of the Universe." With that the shopkeeper vanished into thin air.

"Did you see that?" exclaimed Roach, "he just vanished."

"Yes," said the Captain.

Roach looked upwards at the glowing boy, John, who was watching out over the sea, looking towards the approaching Spanish galleon. Then he looked back towards the Captain – who was deep in thought.

"What do you say Captain? I see that you are thinking about matters," said Roach.

"I have seen things that the shopkeeper speaks of before today," said Captain Watson as he recalled past times from his memory, “I have witnessed matters of a spiritual nature in my dreams.”

“You have seen things like that before in your dreams?” came the astonished reply from Roach, “well, Captain, I have never seen or dreamt things like that. What is it about? What is our destiny?”

Captain Tobias Watson looked towards the horizon, once more – in a deep thought.

“We shall see what the future is all about in the fullness of time, Mr. Roach. We shall see…” said the Captain as an inner thought of past times came to fruition in his mind.

“Now Mr. Roach, we have things to do. We must turn this ship about. And we have an unwell ship’s carpenter and surgeon to nurture back to good health.”

“And the spirit of the boy John,” said Roach, “one of us must climb the rigging and talk to that boy to find out what he knows. Do you think it is possible that we could also talk to the late Mr. Brown? That strange shopkeeper seemed to think that Mr. Brown is steering this ship – but I cannot see him. Do you believe the shopkeeper, Captain?”

“Mr. Roach,” said the Captain, “I believe the shopkeeper’s story – though I am assessing the matter minute by minute. I will give my orders, in good time.”

Captain Watson looked out to sea, pondering on their situation.

“Look Captain,” shouted a startled Roach as he pointed towards the wheel of the ship.

The image of Mr. Brown was beginning to appear. He had a firm grip on the ship’s wheel. Patch the dog started to bark at this ghostly image.

Less than a minute later the complete image of Mr. Brown had appeared. Captain Watson looked towards Mr. Brown. He was staring into the distance, steering the ship towards Copperas Gap, England, one thousand three hundred nautical miles due north.

Chapter 3

Copperas Gap - the early years.

Tobias Watson was born at Copperas Gap in 1696 – in a cottage beside a little area called Eastbrook. Copperas Gap and a village known as Fishersgate stood side-by-side on the banks of a minor tidal port called Fishersgate harbour. It was a small natural harbour about a mile in length – connected to the English Channel by a narrow inlet. This narrow inlet leading into the harbour was just wide enough for a single ship to manoeuvre in and out at high tide. At the eastern end of the harbour the waters from the river Adur flowed into Fishersgate bay and about mid-way along its length a watercourse known as Copperas stream flowed down from the hills in the north, via Eastbrook, before terminating into the harbour bay. Fishersgate bay was a place of safety for ships wanting respite from the ravaging seas whenever storms were progressing in the English Channel. It was a place where fishermen landed their catch and traded their wares. It was also where larger ships loaded the inks and dyes that the local people produced from the iron sulphate they extracted from the earth of Copperas Gap. These inks and dyes would be transported to far-away market places in the Americas.

Tobias Watson was the son of a shoemaker named George, who made new shoes to order for the local Lord and gentry. His services were very much in demand. George also repaired damaged shoes. This skill was known as a cobbler. There was a distinct difference between a shoemaker and a cobbler, for shoemakers, as the name dictates, made new shoes with *new* leather whereas a cobbler repaired or adjusted *old* leather shoes and boots. George was an expert at both. It was expected that Tobias would follow in his father's footsteps to learn these highly prized skills so that he could take-over the business when his father became too old to work. Sons often followed their father's trade – it was the only way to maintain consistency of skills through the generations and financial well-being within a family network. Sons would often look after their mother and father when age or illness crept up on them.

By the age of eleven Tobias was helping his father in his workshop and beginning to learn the skills that he would be expected to use for the rest of his life.

On Sunday mornings the Watson family attended St. Nicholas church, which was to the north of the village. The church was situated adjacent to the manor house, where the lord of the manor lived. Nearby was the *old monument.* It was a statue of a man standing on a plinth. The plinth was at least eight feet high. Tobias often stood back from the plinth and looked upwards at the stone statue that stood on top. He did not know who the statue depicted, but he could tell it was some sort of naval commander by the finery of the clothes he wore. There was no name on the brass plate on the plinth – in fact the brass plate was blank, and the facial features of the statue were blurred. The statue was known as the *unknown sailor* to the local people of Copperas Gap.

The coastal road to Copperas Gap from the East, near to where the *Halfway House tavern* stood, was situated high above the harbour – at least ten yards higher than the waters below – and was separated by a steep grassed bank that fell at an acute angle into the shingle harbour beach. Carved into the bank were some ninety-two timber steps that led down to Fishersgate bay, to a small area of the harbour – where several rowing boats were moored. As the road approached the central coastal part of Copperas Gap, if travelling westwards, the road dipped down to almost sea level for a few yards before rising again to a ten-yard height. This was where the *Sussex Arms tavern* was located. On the harbour front, in the lowest part of Copperas Gap and centrally positioned between the two taverns, were nine fisherman's cottages. About a quarter of a mile north of these cottages were several more cottages at the place called Eastbrook. This was where Tobias Watson and his family lived. Copperas stream ran down from the hills in the north – in a southerly direction to Eastbrook where it turned south-eastwards, passing the row of cottages where Tobias lived, before once again taking a southerly direction to the harbour where it terminated. It provided the only source of fresh water to the people of Copperas Gap and the adjoining village of Fishersgate.

Young Tobias was drawn to the sea from an early age. The distant sound of the waves in the English Channel thrashing against the pebbled beach outside of the harbour was music to his ears. The breeze in the air and the fresh but faint smell of salt on the wind was magical. Often, Tobias would go down to the harbour and watch the ships arrive or leave on the high tide. Nothing would move on a low tide. Indeed, the larger ships could not even maintain their grand uprightness without water to support them and they would lay on their side at a forty-five-degree angle when the tide was low. Before low-tide the sailors would stow away all equipment – such as plates, kitchen implements and tools and tie up all large items before reporting to the Captain to tell him that the vessel was *ship-shape* and ready for the low-tide. But, on the high tide, when a vessel was ready to sail, it would display that magnificent sight of glorious sails spread across the rigging, masts and rafts; the ship being thrust forward by natural winds ballooning their canvas expanse to capture natures airstream energy and propel the vessel towards the horizon. Tobias imagined that he was aboard one of those ships. Sailing to a place beyond the skyline. Travelling, he imagined, to a far-away location to engage in adventure and excitement – far-away from the drab boring world of Copperas Gap. Tobias could only imagine where these ships went, for he did not read books – he had never been to school – he could not read or write. The stories he heard from visiting sailors inspired his young mind. They would come ashore and stay at the taverns – either the Sussex Arms tavern or the Halfway House tavern, while their ships were being loaded. They would sit outside the taverns on summer evenings, smoking pungent smelling tobacco pipes and telling wonderful stories about the world that lay beyond the boundaries of Copperas Gap. They would tell those stories to anyone who would listen. And one small person that was indeed listening – was Tobias Watson.

There were several children in Eastbrook. There was Dennis and Suzanne, Richard and Louise, Elizabeth, Leslie, Deirdre, Wendy, Jane… the list was endless, for most families in the village had many children – at least eight per family… oh, and of course, there was Molly Moffatt. Tobias thought that Molly was the special one. She lived at the other end of the terraced row of Eastbrook cottages. The same row of cottages where Tobias and his family lived.

More children populated the fishermen's cottages to the south and there were other children nearby, where the farmer's post-mill and house stood. The children would play together in the summer sun near to their respective adjoining cottages at Eastbrook or go down to Fishersgate bay to use one of the rowing boats belonging to a man named Arlott – the boatbuilder known as the Jolly Boatman. Best of all, for the children, it was free to use a boat – that is, if you did not overstay your welcome or get water in the boat.

"I don't want no water in them, there boats," Arlott would say in a southern Sussex drawl.

The children played nautical games to their hearts content and this further inspired Tobias. He knew that when he was old enough, eighteen perhaps, he would leave Copperas Gap for adventure on the seas.

The next few years passed the children by; while life in the little village of Copperas Gap trundled on. Molly and Tobias grew close and they talked about how their lives would change once they became adults at the age of twenty-one. They still had a while to go – for Molly was sixteen and Tobias seventeen.

Sometimes Tobias and Molly would sit by the shore of Fishersgate bay, holding hands, talking, whispering into each other's ear, or just cuddling-up together while watching the summer sun set against the horizon of the English Channel. Often, Molly and Tobias would go up in the hills and sit under the old apple tree – just to be alone, far away from any other living being. Other times they would dance to the tunes of the village bandsmen. Well, it was not quite a band of the type you would imagine – old John would play the fiddle, George the flute,

Paul the banjo while Richard bashed the drums. When Tobias and Molly danced it was the only time they could get close enough to almost cuddle each other in public view. After the two of them danced together Molly would dance alone, much to the delight of the villagers. She would dance the dance of a ballet dancer to a perfection beyond criticism. Mrs. Fewtrell, the administrational secretary to the local lord of the manor, was her personal dance tutor. That is where Molly had begun her dance training many years before, under the guidance of this elderly lady.

Tobias and Molly had spoken of marriage at some future date, after they had both come of age, though it was clear to Molly that Tobias yearned for adventure upon the seas – adventure that Copperas Gap could not provide. By this time Tobias was indeed a skilled shoemaker and had saved enough money to settle down. He was able to rent a small cottage from the lord of the manor, but he was not ready to do that – not just yet.

The following year, one August morning, Tobias went to look for Molly. He found her beside the stream at Eastbrook – washing her clothes.

He called out in his broad southern English accent "Molly, I have something to tell you."

Molly turned towards Tobias with tears of grief in her eyes. She pulled an item of clothing that she had been washing and hung it over a prop. Tobias held both of her hands in his.

"Molly, I must go to sea. I have to go to sea to find my own destiny," said Tobias.

"I know," replied a tearful Molly.

"How do you know?" asked Tobias.

"I have seen it in your eyes… more than ever before during this past few weeks," said Molly, "I have watched you and I have listened to you, whenever we sat holding hands beside the shoreline or under the old apple tree. You spoke more and more of faraway places that you have never seen. Your heart is out there among the waves. It is not with me anymore Tobias. I just knew that… soon, very soon, you would announce that you would be leaving me."

Tobias took her in his arms and they cuddled for a moment. He smiled as he looked deep into her eyes. Through her tears she smiled too. It was not a smile of joy for she was bitterly upset.

"My heart is with you Molly, it always will be, but I have to do this. I have to get my yearning for adventure out of my system," said Tobias.

Molly began to sob once more. "Who cares about faraway places and adventure?" she screamed.

"Molly listen to me, I love you, you are my best friend in the whole of this world. I promise you Molly that when I return I will marry you and we will take a little cottage at Eastbrook. But first let me find my way in this life; let me have this adventure of my own."

"I don't want you to go," replied Molly, "I know that you love me and I love you so much Tobias. Why, why can't you stay here… stay here with me… stay here with your family. Life isn't so bad in Copperas Gap."

"I have to go," replied Tobias, "for if I do not go I will never see what is beyond the boundaries of Copperas Gap and what the world has to offer. I will always wonder what is beyond the sea. I will only be away for one year."

Molly shed more tears before turning towards her mother's cottage in the distance – to begin running towards the door. Tobias chased her and caught her by the front door of the cottage. He pulled her close to him as she struggled to escape his gentle clutches.

"Molly, please do not let us part like this. I have decided and have made all the necessary arrangements. The ship I am to leave on departs on the high tide," said Tobias. "I am so sorry, this past few weeks I have tried to tell you of my decision. I have tried to tell you many times, but I could not find the courage. It is only now that I find that I *must* tell you, for I will be leaving soon."

Molly suddenly stopped crying. She stood back as Tobias let go of his grip upon her.

"You are leaving today?" she inquired with a startled look.

"Yes," said Tobias.

Molly was lost for words. She threw out a large sigh before slapping Tobias hard across the face with the palm of her hand. “You bastard,” she screamed before disappearing through the front door of her mother’s cottage – slamming the door behind her.

Tobias stood outside the cottage watching, waiting for Molly to come back outside. But she did not.

Time was not on the side of Tobias. He had a ship to board, so he returned to his house to collect his belongings. Afterwards, he went outside, where his father and mother were waiting to bid him farewell; he had at least found the courage to tell them earlier that week of his impending departure. His tearful petite mother hugged his six-foot-tall frame, his long black hair flowing in the sea breeze, his distinguished facial features showing a kind of immature authority.

“Goodbye my boy,” whispered his mother.

“Farewell my son,” said his father.

“I have to do this,” said Tobias, “here father, take this money. It is the better part of my savings. This money should help to keep you and mother in good stead for the time that I am away. I will return in twelve months and I promise you father that I shall take up the family business – that is, if you want me to. And I shall tell you now that on my return I will marry Molly.”

His father nodded as he took the cash. “God speed, my one and only son. Keep yourself safe from all things evil.”

“Look after yourself,” said his mother with a tearful look in her eyes.

“Goodbye to you both,” said Tobias, “God willing, I will see you next year. By that time, I should have earned enough money to pay for your retirement and for me to rent another small cottage nearby.”

He glanced towards Molly’s cottage and saw her in an upstairs window. He beckoned her to come outside but she shook her head from side to side to signal – *No*.

Tears were streaming down her face as she mouthed the word ‘bastard’. Then, she drew the curtains to the outside world and he could not see her anymore. She had gone.

Molly's mother Alice was standing in the front doorway to the cottage. She too looked sad and upset. Tobias glanced at her, as if to ask what he should do. Alice waved him away.

"Just go Tobias," she said, "you have caused enough hurt for today – just go. And it would probably be better, for Molly, that you do not return to her. She deserves a better man than you."

Tobias did not reply.

On that day, at that moment, Tobias could have done something different. He could have changed his mind. He could have stayed with Molly in Copperas Gap. But he did not. He had made up his mind to go.

With a young determined bravado, sureness, and boldness that all young inexperienced men often have within themselves, he turned away and headed towards the harbour to board the ship – *Alliance*. Its destination, Bath County, North Carolina, North America.

On the high tide of the 3rd August 1714, the square-rigged cargo ship slipped out of Fishersgate harbour and into the English Channel. The vessel, a four mast 800 tonne sailing ship based on the carrack design, was one of the last of its type to be built in the 17th century. The ship had been loaded with coal at the northern English port of Hull before making its way to Copperas Gap to collect inks and dyes. A westerly course was set by the Captain and by nightfall the ship had passed the city of Southampton, en-route to the Americas. Tobias Watson, now an ordinary seaman, stood on deck, on this night of a full moon, reflecting on his love for Molly – the girl he had left behind in Copperas Gap. And then he began to think about what exciting adventures lay ahead.

Chapter 4

Alfred

In the immediate days and weeks after Tobias left for the Americas, Molly was so very angry. She never wanted to see Tobias Watson again. But then, of course she wanted to see him because she loved him. She was angry at the way in which he left her – with only a moment's notice – before boarding a merchant ship to sail into the distance to seek adventure.

Then she smiled on knowing that Tobias had been too frightened to tell her that he was leaving – he kept putting it off until, in the end, he simply had to tell her he was going on his adventures. She knew Tobias was just a cuddly, soft, lovable man who worshipped the ground on which she walked. She knew that he loved her more than anything else in this world – except for the excitement of the sea, but she could probably live with that. She remembered those tender moments they so often spent together in the summer sun underneath the old apple tree. But she had made up her mind. The instant he returned to Copperas Gap she would put on her scornful angry look and give him a piece of her mind – before melting into his arms and hoping they would make love. That was the plan. Then she became worried, hoping against all hope that Tobias would not come to any harm and that he would return in eleven months' time so that they could be married, just as Tobias had promised. She would not be twenty-one years old at that time and her mother would have to give her permission for this marriage to take place, but she felt sure that this would be forthcoming.

Molly stood by Copperas stream quietly washing clothes before carefully putting them on several props. Her mother was beside her, grabbing each item of clothing after Molly had washed it, squeezing-out the excess water in a rotary-mangle before hanging it on a washing line to dry in the breeze.

Molly's mother looked on at her subdued daughter.

"Dawdling and dreaming again Molly," said her mother, "thinking about that good-for-nothing, I suppose?"

"If you mean Tobias Watson mother, then yes," said Molly, "he will be back and then I will give him a piece of my mind, and then..."

Molly's mother interrupted, "Don't even speak of marrying that man, he is no good for you Molly. If he's gone off and left you once, he will do it again – you mark my words my girl."

"He just wanted some adventure mother and he told me that when he returns, we will marry and live happily in Copperas Gap," replied Molly.

"They all say that," said her mother. "Your father would be turning in his grave if he heard all this talk."

"Daddy used to go away," replied Molly.

"That's different – he was a soldier in the King's army," said her mother, "he had to go to fight for his King and country. Tobias Watson did not have to leave Copperas Gap for he has a trade as a cobbler. He could have stayed in the village."

"Well, once he gets back, he will stay here forever and we will be married," said Molly.

"Over my dead body. Let's hope he doesn't come back," said her mother with a wry smile.

"Oh, mother," replied Molly, "you can be so wicked sometimes."

Molly's mother put another item of clothing through the mangle before hanging it on the washing line.

"The Lord of the Manor and his family have some very fine clothes," said Molly as she held up a perfectly white wet blouse to inspect its cleanliness before hanging it on a prop.

"This washing provides us with work and keeps a roof over our head," replied her mother, "now come-on, we have a lot to do – I want to return all these clothes to the Lord of the Manor's housekeeper by sun fall."

"Yes mother," said Molly, as she watched her mother put another item of clothing through the mangle, "did you always want to be a mangle woman?"

"A mangle woman is a very honourable profession and so is a washerwoman," replied her mother, "I just wish I could put Tobias Watson through my mangle. I would turn the handle with pride and watch him become trapped in the rollers of my mangle – I would squeeze the life out of him then hang him to dry on the washing line."

"That's so wicked mother. Anyway, one day I won't be a washerwoman anymore... I will be a shoemaker's wife," said Molly. "The wife of Tobias Watson."

Molly's mother tutted.

"Do you remember young Alfred? The Lord of the Manor's fourth son?" asked Molly's mother.

"Of course, I do," replied Molly, "he joined the Army."

"And a very fine Army officer he turned out to be."

"Well he would be an officer, wouldn't he? He is the son of the Lord of the Manor," said Molly, "he would not be an ordinary soldier."

"Alfred always liked you Molly," said her mother, "he is only two years older than you. What a fine husband he would make for you. You would live in the manor house if you married him and maybe you would travel the world with him to exotic places."

"But I don't want to marry him. My love is with Tobias Watson," came Molly's reply.

"At least he can read and write and he speaks like a gentleman... not like Watson, who is an illiterate degenerate," scolded her mother.

"My Tobias is a very clever man," retorted Molly, "one day he will learn all manner of things. He is a very good cobbler and shoemaker. One day he will run his own business and I will help him. We will raise our family here in Copperas Gap."

"And money grows on trees," came the reply. "Well it's all arranged."

"What is?" asked Molly.

"Alfred is coming home on leave and you will visit him next month," said her mother.

"Who said so?" demanded Molly.

"I did, and so did the Lord of the Manor. He always said that you were the prettiest girl in Copperas Gap. Now he wants you to become a part of his family and marry his fourth son."

"We don't marry those sorts mother," said Molly. "Yes, I like Alfred but as a childhood friend. He will always be my friend."

"We do marry those sorts now, not the first-born son and heir, you understand, but the fourth or fifth offspring of the Lord of the Manor," replied her mother, "the gentry need new blood in their pedigree. Molly, you are educated and beautiful. You speak as a lady should and you were trained by the Lord's ballet instructor, Mrs Fewtrell. You are a wonderful dancer and you have been lucky enough to have had an academic education, fit for a princess, all provided by the Lord's household. No other commoner in this village had that opportunity. I, of course, played a hand in your destiny for I know the Lord and his Lady very well. Your father was a soldier in his Lordship's regiment.

"Remember those days Molly, when you were much younger and you frolicked at the Lord's household – you played almost every day with Alfred and attended school with him in his private classes. This training and teaching you received will come to fruition when you marry him. It is the Lord's wish and young Alfred's too that the two of you be married."

"Well, it's the first I have heard of it" retorted Molly, "I have never heard anything sillier than this. Alfred is a nice man, but he is not my type. I don`t really know him anymore, he has been away for such a long time. And anyway, he is... or was..."

Molly stopped. She was about to give away a secret. An old secret about Alfred which she could not be sure was still valid. Maybe Alfred had grown out of this desire for those secret yearnings he held. She turned away from her mother to gather more washing from Copperas Stream. "Yes, he is a nice man. He is too nice. When we were young we used to play with his sister's dolls and push her pram around the grounds of the manor house. Alfred always liked to play that game and many other games too – we played all sorts of games; he was very competitive."

Molly thought for a moment about her childhood days and her visits to the Manor house. It was a wonderful childhood that most other ordinary children had not experienced. She considered herself to have been very lucky to have been educated by the best schoolteachers in the Sussex lands.

"No more talk of this denial towards Alfred," said Molly's mother, "I have spoken openly with the Lord of the Manor in recent days. One day soon I shall hope that Alfred will ask you to be his wife, then you can travel the world with him."

"I want to stay here in Copperas Gap," replied Molly, "and I don't want YOU or the Lord of the Manor to arrange any marriage of mine."

"It's all arranged – well almost. You will marry Alfred. You cannot be a proper lady here in Copperas Gap – too many people know your real background. You will probably go to the new lands that the King's Army has conquered. Maybe the Americas."

"So why am I still a washerwoman?" retorted Molly, "tell me that mother? Tell me why a washerwoman lady who is supposedly about to be married to the fourth son of the Lord of the Manor – as you say I am – is still washing the clothes of the Lord's household?"

"Not for much longer Molly. I have long since dreamt about your future my dear and I just told you why you will be married to Alfred... the Lord of the Manor has ordered it. Anyway, you will need to know about these washer woman things when you are the lady of your own household in some far-off land," said her mother, "but remember your marriage has not been fully agreed yet. It will not be agreed until Alfred asks you to marry him and you say YES,"

"Then I won't agree to see him," retorted Molly, "and I certainly will not say yes to his proposal of marriage."

"Oh yes you will my girl," replied her mother, "you shall be married before that good-for-nothing Tobias Watson returns."

"I will not," replied Molly. "Does Alfred know he is to be married?"

"I would imagine that the Lord of the Manor has told him," came her mother's reply.

Molly's mother opened her arms, beckoning her daughter towards her.

"Molly, you are the best spoken and most educated washerwoman in the whole of Sussex, and you will marry Alfred to become a lady of a household in some far-off land like the Americas. It will be the best life ever. When you are settled in your new home you can call for me."

"Mother, you are intolerable," said Molly with a smile of forgiveness about her mother's simplistic innocence as she moved into her arms. "But I know my own mind mother and one day I shall marry Tobias."

The following month Molly and her mother were summoned to the Manor house. They wore their best frocks and finest shoes. Molly wore a pair of deep brown coloured platform shoes made especially for her by Tobias Watson.

The butler of the house, a man named Murrell, greeted them at the servants' rear entrance doorway. Molly's mother was asked to remain in the servants' quarters while Molly was led to one of the grand household rooms.

In the room was a man about twenty-years old.

"It's so nice to see you again Molly," called Alfred as he held out his hand. He was dressed in the uniform of an officer of the Royal Sussex Calvary, his crimson jacket finely adorned with golden buttons, red ribbons and braid.

Molly went to him and he gently grasped her hand before kissing her on the cheek.

"Six years I think – six years since we last saw each other Alfred," said Molly.

"Yes, and I have thought about you every day," came the reply.

"Don't be silly Alfred, saying that you thought of me every day," said Molly with an impish smile, "you always spoke of being a King's soldier and look at you now – all dressed up as a lieutenant. I bet you never thought of me for one single minute during your army training."

"You still have that way of bringing me down to earth Molly – with your distinctive plain-speaking," said Alfred, "I truly have missed you Molly."

"Why didn't you write if you missed me so much? Not one letter in six years," retorted Molly, "can you not write the King's English?"

"You know I can write Molly – just as well as you can. We were children when I left home to join the army cadets – I was fourteen," said Alfred, "we played childish games up until then."

"And now you are a man Alfred?" smirked Molly.

"Yes, I am twenty-years-old Molly," replied Alfred, "and you Molly, how old are you? No, don`t tell me, let me guess... you are eighteen."

"You should never ask a lady her age, Alfred," said Molly, "we are both grown-up now. Do you remember much about our childhood? Our long summer days playing in the garden of the manor house and those cold winter afternoons sitting in front of the log fire in one of the large rooms in this house."

"I do Molly," replied Alfred, "I remember those wonderful childhood games we played together – just me and you. And here we are now – as you say, all grown-up."

"Did you tell your fellow officers that you used to push your sister's pram around the manor house gardens?"

"You tease me Molly, you always teased me," retorted Alfred with a friendly smile, "and, you pushed the pram too." retorted Alfred.

"Only when you let me," called Molly, "but you always put dolly to bed in the pram."

"I let you play with my tin-soldiers," exclaimed Alfred, "and my toy fort, and my wooden building blocks."

"And your sister's dolls' house," replied Molly. "We had such fun didn't we Alfred."

"Except for when we were in the schoolroom being taught mathematics or English lessons by that monster woman – what was our English teacher's name?" asked Alfred.

"Miss Poole, I believe," said Molly, "and do you remember Mrs Fewtrell? She taught me how to dance. I excelled at ballet... and you did too Alfred. I remember that you were quite light on your feet in ballet classes."

There was a silence for a moment as they both gazed into each other's eyes. Alfred lifted his arm and placed his fingertips on Molly's cheek.

"Molly, you have grown into a beautiful woman," declared Alfred.

Molly thought for a moment.

"We were childhood playmates and friends Alfred, nothing more," came the reply.

Alfred leant his whole body towards Molly. His intentions appeared to be amorous. He aimed his open-mouth towards her crimson lips.

Molly pulled away.

"Is there something wrong?" asked Alfred. "I am not very good at this business of romanticising with a beautiful female – am I Molly?"

"You cannot just come back into my life and try to kiss and caress me," declared Molly, "you never once tried to kiss me before you left to join the army cadets."

"I was only fourteen when we last saw each other Molly," replied Alfred, "kissing girls was not my priority."

Molly thought for a moment. "I suppose we were too young for romance when you were fourteen and I was twelve."

"I'm sorry," said Alfred, "I thought things would be different now we are older..."

"Well, you thought wrongly," interrupted Molly.

"You look even more beautiful when you are angry," said Alfred as he smiled.

"Don't try to flatter me Alfred. Anyway, I am in love with Tobias Watson," snapped Molly.

"Tobias who?" said Alfred as he stood back from Molly. "Tobias, Tobias, I know that name."

"Yes, Tobias Watson, the son of the village shoemaker," replied Molly.

"Ahh yes, I remember Tobias. He used to come to the Manor house with his father to make shoes for my family... You are in love with HIM?"

"Yes, I am," replied Molly.

"Interesting..." said Alfred as he pondered on that thought.

"And where is this Tobias Watson now?" asked Alfred.

"On a merchant ship somewhere in the world I suppose," said Molly.

"You suppose?" questioned Alfred.

"I do," replied Molly, "and he will be back in ten months' time and I shall marry him."

"So, I have ten months to win your heart Molly," queried Alfred.

"Ten months? You are staying in the village for ten months?"

"Well, not quite. I am here for five months before I sail to the Americas to assist in commanding new territorial lands that the King has acquired," said Alfred. "I want you to come with me."

"As your servant?"

"No, Molly. I want you to be much more than that."

"On your father's orders?"

"No, Molly. My father does not rule my life."

"Are you sure Alfred?" said Molly. "Are you sure that your father does not make decisions for you? Well Alfred, what do you want? As if I didn't already know."

They both looked at each other for an awkward moment.

"Alfred, you could have any other woman in the world as your wife."

"I don't want any other woman. I want you... my childhood friend... a woman that I can trust and who understands me and my funny little ways."

"I used to understand all your funny little ways," retorted Molly, "Alfred, I don't really know you anymore... I'm sorry."

Alfred continued to look at Molly before he broke his gaze.

"Molly, I don't expect you to make any decisions just yet. We have five months before us. Let us get to know each other once again. It's a nice day outside, why don't we take a walk within the walled-gardens of the Manor house and talk."

"Promise me you won't talk about romance or anything of that nature," replied Molly, "or try to kiss me."

Alfred smiled. “I promise Molly.”

Alfred held out his hand and Molly took it. Together, they walked arm-in-arm into the garden of the manor house.

During the next six weeks Molly visited the manor house almost every day. The Lord of the Manor ordered that she would be paid a sum of monies not to work as a washerwoman, but to be Alfred’s confidant and mentor. She and Alfred walked in the garden when the weather permitted, and they laughed in each other’s company. Sometimes Molly stayed at the manor house in her own private room and ate dinner with Alfred and his parents, Lord and Lady Hynam. She was even assigned her own maid. Molly found Alfred to be the perfect gentleman. He was amusing, sometimes hilariously funny, generous and handsome... all the things any girl would want in a man of wealth and distinction. But Molly wanted Tobias Watson. She was still annoyed with him for leaving her to travel on his adventures, but she yearned for him to return. Indeed, every morning when she awoke and every evening before she slept, she thought of Tobias and said a prayer to God asking that he would return home to her safely.

And indeed, Molly was not a washer woman anymore. She was a lady of leisure who was a part of the court of the Lord’s household. Alfred was determined to win her heart and take her to the Americas where he was to be posted for the ensuing ten years. They spoke about the Americas often and Alfred even agreed that Molly’s mother could go with them and live in their household. But the one thing they did not speak about was marriage, for Alfred never broached this subject. He would not want to ask for her hand in marriage unless he was certain she would say YES. As far as the Lord and Lady of the manor was concerned the romance between Alfred and Molly was going well. However, Molly discovered that Alfred`s *funny ways* were more prevalent now he was older and contained a dark personal secret – it was a suspicion she had known of long before he left Copperas Gap to join the army cadets – but as a firm friend she would never reveal that secret to any other living soul.

One evening at dinner Molly laughed at something Alfred said before turning to face Lady Hynam. Their eyes met.

"You look so happy and have a warm glow about you tonight Molly," said Lady Hynam.

"Thank you Lady Hynam," replied Molly.

"Come and see me in my boudoir after dinner," said Lady Hynam.

Alfred glanced at Molly, raised his eyebrows and smiled. It was an indication that he knew not why his mother wanted to speak privately.

Later that evening Molly knocked on the door to Lady Hynam's room. A maid opened the door. Lady Hynam was in bed sitting-up.

"Come in Molly," said Lady Hynam before ordering the maid to leave the room.

Molly entered the room.

"Come in my dear and sit yourself down," she continued.

Molly sat down in a wicker chair.

"You know Molly," said Lady Hynam, "you look very well."

"Why thank you my lady," replied Molly.

"And you have put a little bit of weight on these past few weeks," said the Lady of the manor.

"Oh I..." said Molly before Lady Hynam interrupted.

"Do you feel well?" she asked.

"Yes, I do," replied a puzzled Molly.

"Has anything about you changed?"

"Not that I know of," replied Molly.

"Well, if I knew no better, I would say that you are pregnant."

Molly blushed before making a garbled response.

"Are you pregnant?" asked Lady Hynam.

"No," came the reply.

"Are you sure?"

Molly thought about it. "Yes, I am sure," she replied.

However, the facts of the matter were that she was not sure. Things had changed in her wellbeing and she felt differently.

"Well I think you are pregnant my dear," replied Lady Hynam, "believe me Molly I have years of experience in these matters and pride myself on knowing long before one of my female servants declares pregnancy."

"Servants?" asked Molly.

"Oh Molly," replied Lady Hynam, "I do not for one minute liken you to being a servant. What I mean is that I can tell when a young woman is pregnant... call it female intuition if you must. Well, what do you say Molly?"

"If I am pregnant my lady then I am sorry," said Molly.

Lady Hynam rose from her bed and walked towards Molly.

"Stand up Molly I want to hug you and give you comfort," said Lady Hynam, "I knew you and my son Alfred were getting on well together, but I did not realise how well."

"I am sorry," said Molly.

Lady Hynam opened her arms. Molly stood up and went to her.

"This is marvellous news," whispered Lady Hynam, "I have taken the liberty of calling the doctor to confirm this wonderful news. He should be here soon."

"But... if..." said Molly.

"There are no *buts* or *ifs*. There are only whens," said Lady Hynam, "this is wonderful news... we can arrange your marriage to Alfred within the next four weeks. No one need know you are already pregnant with his child. What a good boy my son is – between me and you Molly I never thought he had it in him."

Soon after they spoke the village doctor arrived and examined Molly. He confirmed that she was pregnant.

Molly smiled. But she was dazed – in an almost trance like condition. She knew that Alfred could not possibly be the father for they had never made love. Indeed, since their first meeting Alfred had never made any amorous advances towards her. The child could only belong to Tobias Watson, for he was her only lover and she knew then that she must be at least three months pregnant.

"We must tell the Lord of the Manor straight away. We must tell him that he is to become a grandfather," said a delighted Lady Hynam, "Oh, and of course we must tell Alfred that he is to become a father, then we must get you two married and I shall help you pack for your move to your new home in the Americas."

"Wait," screamed Molly.

"I can tell you are excited Molly," replied Lady Hynam.

"No, wait... I need to think," said Molly.

"Think about what?" asked Lady Hynam, "there is nothing to think about – you must move into the manor house immediately to prepare for your marriage and the forthcoming birth of your baby, my grandchild. You will be pampered by the maids, housekeepers and expert nannies. They will be the best in the land. In a few months Alfred will go to the Americas alone and you will have your baby here in England. Once the child is born, both you and baby will join Alfred in the Americas, maybe sometime next year."

"I have something to tell you Lady Hynam," said a tearful Molly.

"I see tears of happiness about you Molly – speak no more my child," said Lady Hynam gently, "come... let us go through to the gentleman's parlour to find Lord Hynam and my son. I will tell them of the good news."

A few minutes later they were both in the men parlour. Lady Hynam told them of the good news.

"That's wonderful," said Lord Hynam, "well done Alfred,"

Lord Hynam patted Alfred on the back. Alfred said nothing. He seemed to be in a state of shock.

"Don't worry my boy, I know exactly how you feel. I too was in a state of shock when your mother told me she was expecting our first child," said Lord Hynam.

Lady Hynam coughed before pointing to Molly.

"Oh, yes. Well done to you Molly as well," said Lord Hynam, "it takes two I suppose. Alfred, we must celebrate. I have a very rare whisky in the cellar which we should break open to toast your success."

Lord Hynam turned to Lady Hynam and Molly.

"Well ladies, you must leave us now for we are to celebrate into the night. Smoke a cigar or two, you know the sort of thing we men do when we have cause to celebrate. I am sure you ladies have other things to do," said Lord Hynam.

"Come Molly," said Lady Hynam, "let us go to your room and talk. Its early nights to bed for you from now on... that is until the baby is born."

The two women left the room, leaving the men to celebrate.

The following afternoon Molly was in her room when there was a knock at the door. It was Alfred.

"Can I come in," he asked.

"Yes, of course," replied a tearful Molly as she dismissed her maid to another room.

Alfred entered the bedroom and the two of them faced each other beside the white marble fireplace that overpowered the décor in the room.

"The baby," said Alfred.

"Yes, I know, I am sorry Alfred," said Molly.

"Why did you tell my mother of the baby?"

"I didn't intend to. I didn't know myself that I am pregnant though I knew my body was changing – but I thought my mind was playing tricks on my body," said Molly.

"You have not answered my question," said Alfred.

"Your mother already knew. She could tell that I was with child – she called it female intuition," replied Molly.

Alfred turned towards the fireplace and looked at himself in the golden-framed mirror hanging above the mantlepiece before twiddling the end of his waxed moustache.

"I wish my mother was not so damn clever," he said as he clenched his fists, "and what have you told my mother Molly?"

"What do you mean?" replied Molly.

"I take it that you have since told her that the child you bear is not mine," said Alfred.

"I have not said that Alfred," replied Molly, "I tried to tell her but couldn't get the words out in time."

"You mean... she still thinks that the child is mine?"

"Yes, I am so sorry Alfred," said Molly, "I shall make amends and tell her as soon as possible.

Alfred thought for a moment.

"Don't do that Molly," said Alfred, "don't tell her the child is not mine."

"How can I deceive her Alfred? I must tell your parents the truth."

"My darling Molly," whispered Alfred, "promise me you will not tell my mother or any other living soul that this baby is not mine. "Get some rest now Molly and we will talk some more in the morning."

"I cannot promise," replied Molly, "I cannot tell a lie."

"I am not asking you to lie Molly," said Alfred, "let us both take some time to understand this fortunate situation we find ourselves in. Promise me you will not say anything for at least another month... promise me Molly."

Alfred grasped Molly's hand in desperation.

"I know not what you seek Alfred, why do you say this is a fortunate situation?" said Molly, "I do not understand your motive and I will not lie. If I am asked directly if the child is yours, I will tell the truth."

"Please Molly," whispered Alfred, "this is my chance to salvage my life and live as I would want, this is your chance too. We could live our lives in complete happiness."

Molly looked puzzled.

Alfred held Molly's hand before bending down on one knee. "Molly... will you marry me?" asked Alfred. "You know that I have demons and dark secrets – secrets that only you know about. But I know that our marriage could really work in the new land of the Americas. The child will be seen to be mine and yours. We would live happily in each other's company in a big colonial house full of servants and at all other times pursue our own fantasies and interests – doing the things that each of us enjoy."

"I cannot believe what I am hearing," shrieked Molly, "I cannot marry you – I will not marry you – for my true love is with Tobias Watson. I cannot deny my happiness with him."

"Is the child that you bear Tobias Watson's?" asked Alfred.

"Yes," replied Molly.

Alfred thought for a moment.

"Think about our situation Molly, we will live together in relative luxury," replied Alfred as he stood to his feet. "How long is Tobias away for? Never mind... don't tell me... If I have my dates correct, I believe that Tobias Watson will return after your child is born. Do you know the penalty for having a child born out of wedlock?"

"No," replied Molly.

"They take that child away," said Alfred.

"They do not," exclaimed Molly, "they cannot take my child away."

"Listen Molly, my love, my darling Molly, my childhood confidant," murmured Alfred, "I can assure you that they do take away a child born out of wedlock. You will never see your child again. Marry me Molly and your child will be safe. I am sure I can find a job for Watson in our household when he returns – if he returns – and I will not mind if you take him as your lover provided you are discreet. In return you shall understand my needs outside of our marriage, my little *funny ways* and indiscretions and you shall not interfere in this. To the outside world, and to my mother and father, we will be seen to have the perfect happy marriage. I would not lose any of my father's inheritance."

"It would be a sham of a marriage," replied Molly.

"Only we would know that Molly," replied Alfred. "Who knows, we may even have more children and raise a large family – I would like that Molly."

"I will not have a child with you Alfred," retorted Molly.

"We must try sometime my dear – though I admit it will not be easy for me to act against the will of my own mind," said Alfred.

"I know what you are," screamed Molly, "I know of your weakness... I know what your little secrets are. I know why you go into town sometimes and stay overnight. But it does not matter to me. I don't care what you are or what you do. I will never marry you."

"Wait, think about it Molly, I will give you twenty four hours to make up your mind," exclaimed Alfred, "don't leave me

Molly, I am pleading with you – marry me and I will not tell my parents who is the real father of your child."

"And if I don't marry you Alfred?" asked Molly.

"Then I will be forced to tell my parents," said Alfred, "it is something I must do at the earliest opportunity to protect my own reputation. I must be the first to tell them of this family tragedy – I would not want any rumours to fester and destroy their trust in me."

"If I do not marry you Alfred what will happen to me?"

"You will be banished from the court of the Manor house and compelled to go back into employment as a washerwoman while living with your mother in her cottage. When the baby is born, they will seize it and send it for adoption through the church. Your unborn child will fare better under the protection of me and my family's wealth. If you marry me it will be born within the religious confines of wedlock," replied Alfred, "I shall leave you now Molly and I will return tomorrow. I shall hope that your answer is favourable towards me."

Molly began to feel faint – her eyelids flickered before they closed. She fell, collapsing into the arms of Alfred. He gently kissed her forehead before carrying her to the bed. He lay her down on her back to rest – her eyes suddenly opened. Alfred took a glass of water from the dressing cabinet and offered it to her. Molly sat up and sipped the cool water from the glass.

"Are you feeling better my darling?" asked Alfred. "I really do care for you Molly, you must know that."

Molly said nothing. She nodded to acknowledge that she was feeling better but there was a hatred in her eyes. A hatred towards Alfred, that fine young upstanding lieutenant in the King's Sussex Calvary.

"I shall leave you now Molly," whispered Alfred, "I will tell the maid to come into your room and attend to your well-being."

Alfred left the room, before gently closing the door behind him – leaving Molly sobbing on the bed.

The following twenty-four hours was the worst that Molly had experienced at any time in her short life, but by the following afternoon she had made her decision.

That evening Alfred returned to her room and asked Molly if she would marry him and say that the child she bore was his flesh and blood. It was the last chance for her and her unborn child. The alternative was an impossible situation, for she feared for the welfare and safety of her unborn child.

Molly accepted Alfred's proposal of marriage. She had no choice. But there were conditions that she pleaded for.

"The marriage must never be consummated," she demanded.

"I am fairly comfortable with that request," replied Alfred, "of course my dear on occasions we must show some affection to each other in public – a kiss on the hand or a peck on the cheek, maybe a stroll arm-in-arm in the village."

Molly agreed. "And you must agree that Tobias will live in this household on his return from the Americas," she asked.

"I cannot allow that," replied Alfred, "but when we move to our new colonial home in the Americas, Watson can come with us and live with us as a servant of the household. But you must never be seen to favour him any more than other servants. Your private liaisons with him must be discreet and kept secret."

"Very well, I agree," replied Molly.

And so the deal was done. Preparations were made for the forthcoming wedding and everyone in the village looked forward to the event. Molly remained at the manor house for the next month wondering what the future may bring, wondering what Tobias Watson would say on his return from the Americas – she knew he would be devastated. But she had no choice. The safety of her unborn child was paramount in her mind.

Chapter 5

The Americas.

It took a little over eight weeks for the *Alliance* to cross the Atlantic due to some bad weather. Most of the time during the voyage Tobias was tasked with cleaning the decks. It was back-breaking work. Other times he undertook repairs of shoes and boots for his fellow sailors. Sometimes he would be paid in cash, other times he traded goods or clothing for his services. The Captain had given him permission to bring his shoemaking tool chest on board the ship and a few provisions used for the repair and making of shoes and boots. The tool chest was a sturdy oak box some three feet long by two feet high. It contained all the necessary tools that a shoemaker and cobbler would require, such as an awl, hammers, knives, punches and sewing needles – it also doubled-up as a work bench to which a clamp-vice and wooden shoe templates could be affixed. Tobias became a popular boy on this ship. Even the Captain asked him to repair a pair of his shoes.

They arrived in Bath, North Carolina, on Tuesday 2nd October 1714. The ship's goods were unloaded onto the dock – it took nine days to unload. After that, new cargo was loaded aboard the ship in an operation that would take a further week. The ship's hold was to be filled to the brim with local products.

Tobias had learned a lot from the men and merchant officers aboard the *Alliance*. He was a willing pupil. He had that necessary mental skill and persistent desire to achieve well. He strived for perfection in everything he tackled. Most of the work he did aboard the ship involved swabbing the decks and keeping the ship's area clean and clear of obstructions. But he was also given the opportunity to learn about rigging the ship's sails – a most dangerous operation due to the great height sailors had to climb.

The boatswain of the ship was a forty-year-old man named French, a rough rum swilling sort, who supervised the maintenance of the vessel and kept the ship's provisions under his total control. He had taken a liking to Tobias, for he liked hard workers and men with potential seafaring skills. Indeed, Tobias had worked hard and had a natural aptitude for seafaring abilities.

Once the ship was loaded of its new cargo of furs, skins and other animal products it would soon be on its way to various American domestic ports. Over the following months countless cargoes would be distributed between North and South Carolina as well as to Boston, Massachusetts. This tour of duty would take some eight months – ending with their final American destination, Virginia. Here they would load the ship with tobacco products which would be brought back to England. But, for the time being they remained in Bath dockyard while the ship was being loaded of goods.

"Want to do something else other than swab the decks?" called French.

"You bet I do," replied Tobias as he scrubbed the deck with a flat holystone that sanded its surface, "why do we have to throw sand on the decks and clean them so often?"

"Because we do," came the reply, "and anyway, apart from reducing the decomposition of the wooden decks it keeps discipline among you young men."

Tobias laughed as he continued to scrub the deck. French laughed too.

"Here boy, have some rum," called French. He held out a ladle – full to the brim of dark rum.

"No thanks," replied Tobias, "I prefer to keep a clear head."

"Suit yourself boy," said French. "Anyways, credit where credit is due – and you should remember this boy, I don't give much credit or compliment to anyone. But I see something in you. One day, with the right kind of training, you could become one of the best merchant Navy sailors in our fleet."

Tobias stopped what he was doing to look at French, who was sitting on an upturned water butt with his feet on another barrel, supping rum from the ladle. Tobias was unsure if French was paying him a compliment. He had never been paid any kind of compliment aboard the *Alliance* before. French paused for a moment and with a look of honesty about him stared hard at Tobias.

Suddenly, Tobias saw a sincere glint of trustworthiness in French's eyes. "Why thank you Mr. French for your kind compliments," replied Tobias.

"So," continued French, "I want you to put down that there scrubbing stone and go and get yourself cleaned up. Then I want you to get off this ship and go and explore this town of Bath, North Carolina. And be careful of those *Red Indians*." French broke into a laugh before sipping some more rum.

Tobias looked surprised. "Are you sure Mr. French?" he asked. "Where should I go in the town of Bath and why should I watch out for Red Indians – are they dangerous?"

"I am as sure as I am going to be that you should go and enjoy yourself," said French, "and if you continue to ask stupid questions – like *where should I go and are Red Indians dangerous* – then I will throttle you right now." French put down the ladle, broke into a hearty laugh, stood to his feet and mimicked throttling the main mast – not that he could get his hands, or even his arms, around its sheer size.

French continued, "You just get out there and enjoy yourself boy – make the most of your free time and, as I say, mind-out for those Red Indians. They have been causing trouble for a while, ever since 1711 when they attacked Bath town and the surrounding areas. They killed hundreds of white settlers; men, women and children, as well as a few key political figures. This conflict continues between white men and red men, but on a much smaller scale and sometimes, to this day, small groups of die-hard Indians ride into town on their horses and make lightning raids on the people of Bath. But they mainly steal these days – they are nothing more than criminals who have taken a liking to drinking Scottish Whisky – though that does not stop them killing anyone who obstructs them."

"Why are they fighting?" asked Tobias.

"Well, I guess it is because the white settlers took their land," French replied. "The Indians are, after all, the native people of this great land and they were in residence long before the white settlers arrived. It was the white settlers, the colonialists, who started the fighting – for they took the land from the Indians by violent force. They raided the Indian homes, murdered, raped and took Indian prisoners which they sold into slavery. Most slave prisoners from round here were sent to Pennsylvania."

"I don't understand," replied Tobias, "why could they not live side-by-side in peace?"

"I think it became too late for that," replied French. "Their Indian chief, I think it was chief Hancock – not a very Indian sounding name, is it boy? Yes, Chief Hancock, leader of the Tuscarora tribe and his warriors, along with other allied Indian tribes who, in collaboration with each other, fought back against the colonial settlers. Tribes such as the Pamlico, the Coree, Mattamuskeet and Matchepungoe fought side-by-side, but eventually the settlers received colonial army re-enforcements from the south and they beat them on the banks of the river Neuse. More than four hundred Indians were slaughtered and many more captured in that single battle. There were other battles in the years that followed. Chief Hancock was captured and executed in 1712. By 1713 the Tuscarora tribe was defeated at Neherooka when almost a thousand Indian braves were killed. The rest of the tribe, some fifteen-hundred of them, moved north – but a few hard-line stragglers stayed behind."

"How do you know all this?" asked Tobias.

"An educated man needs to know these things," came the reply, "I read books. One day, my boy, I believe that you will want to know about the world around you," said French. "What kind of books do you read Tobias?"

"I don't read anything," came Tobias Watson's dismissive response, "but I do want to know about the world – that's why I am here in the Americas. Mr. French, why are they called Red Indians?"

"It's because of the colour of their skin boy," came the reply, "but we British are the only nation on earth that call them Red Indians, it's so that our government officials can distinguish them from those other Indians."

“What other Indians?” asked Tobias.

“Those ones in Asia who live in a place called India,” replied French, as he sat back on the upturned water-butt before placing his feet on the nearby barrel.

“I see,” said Tobias.

French continued, “I think that the local white Americans call Red Indians, Redskins. Anyways, that’s enough of Red Indians for today, but if you see any riding towards you making noises and wearing war-paint on their faces you get out of the way boy… and do it fast… for they are the savages who are disjointed from the regular Indian tribes. These stragglers live hidden in the hills.”

“But, remember boy not all Red men are enemies,” continued French, “some native tribes have made peace with the white settlers of these lands.”

“It all sounds so very complicated,” replied Tobias.

“Oh, it is my boy, it is,” said French as he supped some more rum from the ladle, “as I was saying boy, there is only one place to go in Bath and all young men find that place, but make sure you find your way back and be on board this ship before dawn in two days’ time – for that is when we sail,” replied French.

“And when you do come back, you won’t be swabbing the decks no more. Tobias, you will be my assistant boatswain and your wage shall increase. And if you are really lucky I will speak to the master of the ship on your behalf and see if I can get him to teach you how to navigate this ship.”

“Why thank you, Mr. French,” said a puzzled but elated Tobias as he collected a clean bucket of water and tipped it over himself before running toward the ladder that would take him below deck for some fresh clothes.

“And one other thing,” called French. “Thank you for making these new shoes for me,” he said as he slowly moved his feet from side to side – pivoting them on their heels, on the top of the barrel that they were resting upon – so as to admire his two new black and shiny acquisitions.

"Your kind thank you is very acceptable to me and I am pleased that you like them," replied Tobias with a grin. "It gave me something to do when I was not scrubbing the decks of this ship. I trust that they will keep your feet in perfect order, for they should last you many years."

"Here," shouted French, "take these twenty shillings as payment for the shoes. You will need it in Bath town."

"Why thank you Mr. French. I was not expecting any payment from you – are you sure?"

"Take it before I change my mind," retorted French.

Tobias disappeared below deck as French muttered under his breath, "If you can stitch a cotton thread into these ship's sails as well as you can stitch together these new shoes of mine, then you my boy will do well aboard this vessel. I intend to teach you everything I know about sails – for it will make my own life easier."

Tobias was soon on his way into the town. It took about ten minutes to walk from the dock to the centre of Bath town, but he was surprised when he got there. There were only about twenty houses scattered around the area and the main high street comprised of just some stables with a blacksmith's yard attached. Beside that was a horse pen with about eight horses enclosed, a saloon bar with a hotel above, a store selling all manner of provisions, an army garrison, and a barber's shop. That was it.

'Why would French say there was only one place to go in Bath,' thought Tobias, 'I see nothing of interest here. Maybe I could do some fishing in the river upstream.'

Tobias needed to find somewhere to purchase a fishing line and a hook. The provisions store looked an obvious place, so he made his way across the street. It was closed. A sign on the door stated, *gone to lunch – in the Saloon bar next door*.

There did not seem to be a Sheriff's office and everyone he passed in the street looked at him in a strange way – a look of mistrust. All bore weapons and their eyes followed his every move. Tobias soon learned that smiling at these people was probably not the best thing to do because most twitched or stood back in surprise – holding their musket, dagger, or sword in defence.

There was a lot of noise coming from the saloon bar. Tobias peered through the window to see what was happening inside. He was surprised to see at least twenty men sitting at various tables with some very pretty women who appeared to be flaunting themselves. A man on a piano played a tune and most of the men were singing along. It looked quite a fun place to young Tobias.

'But wait a minute,' thought Tobias, 'a lot of these men look familiar.'

And indeed, they were, for most of these men were sailors from his own ship – the *Alliance.*

So, as innocent as the day he was born, he ventured inside – through the double swinging saloon-doors.

"Tobias," called out one sailor known as Reg Watts, "come over and join in!"

"Yes Tobias, come in and enjoy yourself. Come and sit yourself down boy," called-out another sailor by the name of Raymond.

"Do you want a drink?" shouted another member of the ship's crew.

Tobias moved towards the inner circle of tables where the men were sitting. One of the pretty ladies came over to him and held his arm. She pulled him towards one of the chairs and sat him down – then sat on his lap, before reaching for a menu card from the table.

"Here, my lovely boy, have a read of this menu and tell me what you want."

Tobias looked at the writing on the board, but it meant nothing to him for he could not read or write.

"Can I get you something to drink while you decide what to eat," her tone changed to a very sexy voice as she brushed her fingers across Tobias's blushing cheek, "or can I take you upstairs and get you something else?" she purred, as she pushed her ample bosom into his face. This brought a loud cheer and deafening jeers from most of the men sitting nearby. Tobias was ever so embarrassed. He had never seen a place like this before or met women that spoke so loud in a sexy way. Neither had he known women who were so forward in their demeanour. He had never met any women who wore bright red lipstick, powdered their faces and showed more bosom in public than they ought to. These women – there were at least eight of them – wore the finest clothes and the smell coming from them was wonderful.

'Why, they must each have a bath every day of the week,' thought Tobias.

The women were draping themselves over the men, moving from man to man, making suggestive remarks, in-between serving food and ale. Now and again one of the ladies would take a sailor up the grand staircase and disappear through one of the many doors that led from the open-plan landing. About fifteen minutes later they would return to join the party. There was even a devilish looking church Rector among the clientele, dressed in his religious black uniform and white clerical collar.

"Have you made up your mind young man?" said the beautiful waitress.

"Umm, I don't think I am hungry or thirsty," said Tobias.

"You must be thirsty, it's a hot day," replied the waitress.

Tobias was too embarrassed to tell the woman he could not read or write but then he had an inspirational thought.

"What do you recommend," asked Tobias.

"That's better," purred the waitress, "well let me see." She looked at the menu and said, "I suggest, young man, that you have beef steak and some ale for one shilling followed by a good time upstairs for a further three shillings."

"What sort of good time?" inquired Tobias with a look of innocence about him.

"This sort of good time," she answered as she rubbed her hand on the inside of his thigh.

The men sitting nearby cheered once more and the Rector stood up on a chair to get a better view. Tobias suddenly realised what kind of a place this was. He pushed the waitress away, jumped up and ran out of the saloon as fast as he could. Jeers erupted from the men in the bar and faded into the distance the further he ran from the establishment. Before long he was back aboard the *Alliance* ship. Mr. French was waiting by the gang-plank.

"Back so soon boy?" he inquired.

"Yes, Mr. French, I didn't much like it there – in Bath town."

"Did you, em… did you find somewhere to go while you were there?" asked French.

Tobias had wised-up by this time. "If you mean, did I find the saloon bar Mr. French then I can tell you that I did. But I did not stay long," replied Tobias.

"You did not stay long?" French replied as he pondered on this response. "Did you go upstairs with one of the young ladies?"

"I did not Mr. French," came the reply.

"Shy was you?" said French with a wry smile.

"Mr. French, I was not shy," said an embarrassed Tobias, "but neither was I in need of their services – for the love of my life remains in England and I do not intend to deceive her. Her name is Molly."

"But she is such a long way away," said French.

"No, she is not," replied Tobias with an angry tone, "she is right here," as he banged his chest with his fist. "Molly is right here in my heart."

"Well, you certainly have some principles about you my boy and a little bit of fighting spirit," said French with a smile, "I like that, boy. Now you best get yourself below deck and get yourself something to eat and drink from the galley… go on."

A hungry Tobias did as he was told and disappeared below decks. After he had eaten he returned to the main deck where he looked into the distance – thinking about Molly and how much he had hurt her before he left England and how much he missed her company. She was his best friend. He thought about those tender moments when they were alone, held each other in their arms and made love in the hay barn. He yearned for the moment when he would return to Copperas Gap to see her again – to make love to her once more. But first, he would apologise to her for making her unhappy on the day he had left Copperas Gap, then he would ask her to marry him and he would hope that she would say – yes. That was his plan. Sailing the sea was all so very exciting but Tobias had come to realise that Molly was so much more important to him than all the seas and oceans of this world. But there was still eight months to pass before he would get back to England.

Chapter 6

Massachusetts.

On the high tide of October 15th, 1714, the *Alliance* left the port of Bath, destination Boston, Massachusetts. It took three weeks to sail to their destination. During this period Mr. French found out that Tobias could not read or write. Another sailor, Reg Watts, who had been in the saloon bar in Bath town, North Carolina had told him.

One afternoon Tobias and French were resting below deck.

"Do you know what these are?" asked French as he held up two white feathers, one in each hand.

"Yes," replied Tobias, "they are the feathers of a swan."

"Correct," proclaimed French, "here… take them." French put the feathers together and held them up in front of Tobias.

Tobias looked at the feathers but was cautious.

"Take them," said French as he beckoned Tobias once more.

Tobias was hesitant. 'Why would French be giving him white feathers? Is this not the sign of a coward,' he thought – 'to be handed white feathers?'

"Take them boy," said French in a more aggressive way.

Tobias took both feathers in his right hand.

"Now give me them back," said French.

"I know not the games you play," said Tobias as he handed back the two feathers.

"The game I play boy is to teach you to write. You have taken these feathers in your right hand which means that you shall write the letters of the alphabet with your right hand," replied French.

"Oh, I see," said a surprised Tobias.

"Do you want to learn to write?" asked French.

"I do," replied Tobias, "I have not had the opportunity to learn before. Few people read or write in my home village of Copperas Gap. I want to learn. I want to better myself."

“Then I shall teach you. I shall teach you to write and read,” said French. “Tobias, you have an excellent memory. I have seen this before in boys that cannot read or write. They have good memories because they cannot refer to the written word to refresh their memory – so they unwittingly train themselves to remember details. You are no different boy, though I must admit your memory excels anything I have ever seen in anyone else. Your talent will help you to learn quickly. You will achieve great things in the future – provided you listen to me and follow my teaching of English.”

“Thank you, Mr. French, I will listen, and I will learn,” replied Tobias.

“So, the first lesson,” said French, as he held up the feathers once more, “these are not feathers of a swan.”

Tobias looked puzzled.

“These are pens, better known as quill-pens. They are used to write words on parchment,” continued French, “they come from the swan, goose or turkey but I only use swan feathers and these two feathers are different to each other, for this one…” French held up one of the feathers, “This one is from the left wing of a swan.” He held up the second feather, “And this one is from the right wing of a swan. You, my boy, are right-handed so it is *this* feather, the right-handed swan feather,” French held up a feather, “it is this one that you need. Do you understand?” said French.

“Well… yes,” replied Tobias.

French put down the left-handed feather and took a knife from his pocket.

“So, whenever you pick-up a feather in the future, you must ensure you use the correct type. Better still, whenever you see a wild swan catch it and grasp it firmly before pulling one, but never more than two feathers from its right wing. That way, you get to select your own pens. But I say this again, do not take too many feathers at any one time. Take no more than two feathers – and never kill a swan, for they are the lifeblood of the written word. You can never have too many quill-pens in your possession, but remember, the swan will die if you take too many feathers. Now, I shall show you how to trim the feather to make a pen-nib – but remember, the feather stem must be specially treated before it can be trimmed. I will teach you how to treat a stem and make it harder wearing on another day. But for now, I shall trim this swan feather that has already been treated and I shall make it into a quill-pen."

French began to trim the right-handed feather to form an implement that could be used to write the letters of the alphabet. Tobias watched him intently.

"Can you see how I am doing this?" asked French, "what am I using to shape the end of the of this feather into a nib, Tobias?"

"Well, it's a knife of course Mr. French," replied Tobias.

"It is not just any old type of knife, it's called a pen-knife," replied French. "It's a small special knife made by the blacksmith for forming pen-nibs on the quill."

French held up the finished product… a quill-pen with a perfectly formed nib.

"There you are boy, it is done. This is your own personal quill-pen – look after it boy. It is arguable that this quill-pen is mightier in power than any sword or dagger – for with it you can destroy your enemies with the written word and those words you write will last forever. Without this pen you have no permanent written voice in this world."

Tobias admired this work of art. A nib with a small slit at its centre.

"Sit down at that table and I will show you what should be done," said French.

Tobias sat at the table and French handed him the quill-pen.

French took a small glass pot and some parchment from a nearby shelf. He put them on the table.

"This is the ink," he said as he removed the lid to the glass pot, "be not clumsy and spill it boy, for you will answer to me. This ink is a very valuable commodity – the dye to produce it is made in a place known as Copperas Gap, the same place you were born Tobias Watson."

"I will not waste any of this commodity," replied Tobias.

“Now dip the pen into the ink and wipe off the excess on the rim of the pot,” said French as he reached up to the shelf to select a book. French opened the book and found the page he was looking for. He placed the book on the table in front of Tobias and pointed to its content.

“In this book Tobias, are the letters of the alphabet. Copy each one of them and write their shape on the parchment, and when you have done that – do it again and then again. And all the while you write those letters learn their name. I shall go through them with you. This is the capital letter A, and this is B.”

French continued to name the letters of the alphabet. Tobias repeated them.

“Keep writing until the ink in the quill-pen runs dry” said French, “then, dip it into the ink pot once more. The stem of the quill-pen is hollow – that is where the quill-pen stores its ink supply. As you write, the capillary action of the ink makes it flow from its storage container onto the nib – then, from the nib onto the parchment to form the letters you choose by the movement and actions of your own hand. Remember boy – after you have finished writing never put your quill-pen away with ink remaining in its storage container, for it will harden and render the quill-pen useless. If you ever do that and destroy a quill-pen while you are aboard this ship, then you shall answer to me.”

“Thank you, Mr. French, I am truly grateful for your advice,” said an enthusiastic Tobias.

Within two-weeks Tobias was able to identify every letter of the alphabet with ease.

Within four weeks Tobias was able to write each letter of the alphabet and instantly identify its name. By that time the ship had arrived in Boston, Massachusetts.

Once they had docked Tobias left the ship and began to explore the area. French, true to his word, had promoted Tobias to boatswain’s mate and, in between the supping of rum, began teaching him all he knew about sailing ships. French had also begun to teach Tobias how to read, using the two books he had aboard the ship.

It was at Boston harbour that Tobias saw a British ship tethered to the quayside. It was a fine looking 60-cannon galleon. He was admiring the masts and rigging when he noticed that one of the high-level ropes was detached. Just then, a man dressed in all the finery of a gentlemen stepped onto the gang-plank that led from the quay onto the ship.

"Excuse me Sir," called Tobias, "I see that you are boarding this fine ship."

"I am," said the man.

"Well, would you be kind enough to tell the Captain that a rope has become detached – up there." Tobias pointed upwards to the offending piece of rope.

"I *am* the Captain," said the man as he turned about and stepped back onto the quay.

They stood side by side. Both looked upwards into the ship's rigging.

"Where?" demanded the Captain.

"There," said Tobias as he pointed again.

"Oh, yes I see it," said the Captain, "well thank you very much for telling me. I shall inform my boatswain and get him to address the problem straight away."

"Good," replied Tobias as he smiled and looked at the Captain.

Then Tobias looked to the ground and spotted that one of the Captain's shoes had a buckle missing.

"Captain, I also notice you have lost a buckle from your shoe."

"No, I have not lost it – I have it in my pocket," said the Captain, "it came off this morning while I was in town."

"Well that's good" said Tobias, "at least it has not been lost. I can fix it for you if you like."

"You can do things like that?" asked the Captain

"Yes, I am almost a time-served cobbler and shoemaker," said Tobias. "as well as being a boatswain's mate on the ship moored next to yours."

"The *Alliance* – is it?" said the Captain.

"That's right Sir – it is the merchant ship *Alliance*."

"Well young man," said the Captain, "how much will you charge to fix my shoe buckle?"

"One shilling Sir."

"How long will it take to fix?"

"I could have it done by tomorrow morning Sir."

"We have an arrangement then," said the Captain as he held out his hand to shake on the deal.

Tobias shook his hand.

"What is your name?" asked the very impressed Captain.

"Tobias," came the reply.

"Well it's nice to meet you Tobias. I am Captain Stephen Carden of His Majesty's Royal Navy and of this ship, *Thunder*," he said.

"Follow me," said the Captain as he stepped on to the gang-plank to begin the short upwards walk to board his ship.

"Captain about to board the ship," shouted a sailor, standing to attention while another blew a whistle. Both saluted as the Captain passed them. The Captain responded with a salute.

"Wait here Tobias," said the Captain before turning to one of his men.

"Jones follow me to my cabin where I will take off this offending shoe and put on my spare pair. Then bring this single shoe to young Tobias here. Go with him to his ship the *Alliance* and see him aboard and make sure he does not get off again until my shoe is fixed. That is all."

"Very well Sir," came the reply.

The Captain turned to Tobias and handed him the buckle.

"Well young man, I shall see you at first light tomorrow when I shall inspect your work. If the repair is suitable I shall settle my account with you. Be sure to bring my shoe back in the morning for I sail on the afternoon tide," said the Captain. "Did you tell me your full name?"

"Tobias Watson," came the reply.

It was not long before Tobias was back aboard *Alliance* effecting the necessary repairs to the Captain's shoe. The following morning, he took the shoe back to Captain Carden who inspected the work.

"Well my boy," said the Captain, "you have done a very fine job on my shoe and I shall pay you your fee of one shilling plus I will give you an extra sixpence for your speedy work."

The Captain opened a small wooden chest situated on his desk. He took some money from within, counted out the correct amount and handed it to Tobias.

"Thank you, Sir," said Tobias as he took the money.

"You know my boy," said the Captain as he admired his shoe, "I noted your observational skills yesterday when you spotted that a ship's rope was not tied properly – a rope that my own men had not seen."

"Thank you, Sir," replied Tobias.

"And I am also struck by your skills with shoe repairs, your skill with the cobbler's needle… for you have made a fine job of attaching my buckle. Your skill with the needle and thread would help maintain our canvas sails aboard this vessel. So I would like to offer you a place on this ship in His Majesty's Royal Navy – that is if your present position in the merchant Navy permits you to take this appointment. We need young men like yourself to build the British Navy into the next generation of fighting forces," said the Captain. "We operate in the Americas protecting merchant shipping – ships like your ship, the *Alliance* – from pirates and we often engage with them in battle, so there will be lots of adventure! Can I tempt you to join us?"

Tobias thought for a moment before replying.

"Thank you, Captain, for your kind offer. I am very tempted, but I cannot join you. You see, in eight months, next July, the *Alliance* will be sailing back to England and I will be on that return voyage, where, upon on my arrival, I will marry my love, Molly."

"There is always some blasted woman involved when it comes to dealing with you young men," retorted Captain Carden as he broke into a smile, "eight months you say – well that is about the same time that my own tour of duty ends – for we also sail back to England next July. Can I still not tempt you to join us?"

"I am honoured Captain," replied Tobias, "but Mr. French, the boatswain of the *Alliance,* is teaching me well and I would not want to let him down by jumping ships at such short notice."

"Very well my boy," replied Captain Carden, "I admire your steadfast loyalty to your ship and crew members. One day I hope to earn your loyalty for myself – should you choose in the future to join me – for my offer of a place upon this ship will always remain open. I am sure that our paths will cross again young man. And if you change your mind you can find me or get a message to me in England at the southern port of Portsmouth."

"Thank you, Sir, Portsmouth is just along the coast from my home village of Copperas Gap," replied Tobias, "and now I must bid you farewell for the *Alliance* also sails on the high tide this afternoon.

Chapter 7

Dead Man's shoes,1715.

That afternoon both ships left the harbour of Boston and headed south, His Majesty's ship *Thunder* heading for the states of Virginia while the merchant ship *Alliance* set sail for a return visit to Bath town, North Carolina.

Over the following seven months the *Alliance* sailed between various ports along the East coast of America picking-up cargoes and delivering them as was necessary. During that time they visited Boston and Bath on at least six separate occasions, as well as many other ports in between.

It was on the first of May 1715 that the *Alliance* entered the harbour of Bath for the last time on this tour of duty, before heading for Virginia to collect a large quantity of tobacco to be taken back to England.

During those past seven months Mr. French had taught young Tobias well; for he had become quite proficient in reading and writing – though there was a lot more to learn. Tobias was devouring one book after another before exchanging his used books for others at the various trading ports they passed through. His first mission at every port, once free-time permitted, was to head into town to see if he could find new books to read. Tobias had also become proficient as a boatswain's mate and the master of the ship, Oliver Green, was indeed teaching him the skills of navigation. French's instinct was correct. He had found a man in Tobias Watson, now nineteen and a half years old, who had a natural seafaring skill with the potential and ability to become a future Captain of the merchant Navy.

After the ship docked in Bath, French told Tobias that he was visiting the saloon bar in town and said he would be back that afternoon.

Later that day Tobias finished the book that he was reading and decided to go to the provisions store in Bath town to see if he could exchange it for another book. Before long Tobias was standing beside a bookshelf in the shop.

Thumbing through the books he found one on ship's navigation and, though Oliver Green had been teaching him about direction-finding and map reading across the globe, he thought he would buy this book as an additional aid to his studies.

Back outside the shop with his new book, Tobias heard a lot of screaming and shouting. He looked along the main street to see four men on horses. Their painted faces and feathers in their hair struck him with horror. They held bows and tomahawks as their armoury. They stored arrows for their bows over the backs of their body, concealed in purpose made pig-skin sacks.

"Indians," Tobias shouted as he dived behind a large wooden barrel.

Settlers came out from all hidden corners of the town as the Indian raiders rallied together high on their horses outside the Saloon bar. The townsfolk began shooting at them.

Just then, Mr. French came out of the saloon to see what the noise was about. On seeing the Indians, he quickly moved back towards the building – but it was too late.

One of the Indians fired his weapon and an arrow took flight towards French. It happened so quickly for within seconds it hit him square on. The arrow penetrated deep into his body just below his heart and he fell backwards to the ground.

One of the white settlers took aim at the Indian and fired his musket. The shot brought him down; he was dead before he hit the ground. The other Indians fled the scene as they continued to whoop and scream in their native language.

Tobias rushed over to French who was on his back outside the door to the saloon, as others began to surround him.

One of the ladies from the saloon bar tore cotton strips from her dress and gave them to a barman tending to Mr. French's wounds. The cotton fabric was pushed hard against the penetration point to stem the flow of blood around the arrow. Tobias crouched down beside the injured man and said, "Mr. French, we will get you inside where we will better tend to your wound."

French was in a bad way. His eyes were beginning to glaze. He looked at Tobias before glancing down at the wound to his chest.

"Give me your hand Tobias," French whispered.

Tobias held French's hand as the ladies and the barman continued to tend to him.

"Tobias," whispered French, "I am done for… this wound is deep. I feel my life ebbing away from my body."

French coughed for a moment. His hand jerked away from Tobias's grasp as he slid towards death.

"Tobias, Tobias, are you still there," French called, "I cannot see you anymore."

"Yes, I am here Mr. French, I am with you. Don't worry we will save your life. Just you hang-on Mr. French."

"Tobias, when I am done, put your hand in my pockets and take every single piece of silver that I own and take it back to England. Take all my possessions from the ship and take everything to my brother. He lives in Portsmouth, England. The Captain of the *Alliance*, Captain Johnson, will give you my brother's details. Tobias, will you do that for me?"

"Yes, of course I will do that for you Mr. French," replied a tearful Tobias as he once more grasped French's hand.

"Don't cry boy, men don't cry." French took a small gasp as the pain from his injury showed on his face. "You're a good boy Tobias and you will do well in this life that extends before you… I… want…you…to," French took several small gasps. His body trembled as death took its hold on his mortal body. Then he was gone. His head fell sideways, his eyes remaining wide open.

A man wearing a top-hat and dressed in black came forward towards this tragic scene. He crouched down beside Tobias and closed French's eyes with the tips of his fingers. Then, he unclasped the hands of French and a clearly distressed Tobias Watson.

"Sit yourself down over there while I deal with the details," said the man, "I will remove all possessions of value from him and, after taking a small fee from his pocket for funeral arrangements, I will let you have the balance to take back to England for this man's brother."

The man looked down to the new shiny shoes that French was wearing, "and I will let you take those shoes with you, for they look brand new."

"They are. I made them for him," whispered a stunned Tobias as he looked at the mortal remains of his deceased friend for the very last time.

Tobias was led away into the saloon bar where he was given a stiff drink that made him feel dizzy. But it did not matter to Tobias for all he was thinking about was the loss of his friend and tutor, Mr. French. A man who had educated him in so many ways and whose spirit was, by now, on its way towards the edge of the universe, to that place called paradise.

Ten minutes later the man in the top hat, an undertaker, brought Mr. French's possessions into the saloon bar and put them on the table where Tobias was sitting. He put the new shoes on the floor.

Another man standing nearby seemed to be very interested in the pair of shoes that belonged to Mr. French.

"Permit me to introduce myself. My name is Charles Ford and I am a travelling comedian and Jester. I reckon those shoes look about my size," he said, "and I don't mind wearing a pair of dead man's shoes. Some people won't wear dead men's shoes, but I will. In fact, they are the best type to wear because the dead man has already worn them in a little and softened the leather."

"They are not for sale," replied an angry Tobias.

"Are you sure?" asked Charles, "I can pay you right now – once we agree the price."

"Yes, I am," said Tobias, "now leave me be."

Charles Ford limped away in a scraggy old pair of shoes at least ten years old and not fit for purpose – claiming that his bunions would never heal until he found himself a better pair of shoes. Howls of laughter from the men in the saloon bar followed him out of the door.

"That's one funny Jester," said Reg Watts to his mate.

“I don’t think he was joking about the shoes,” came the reply.

The funeral of Mr. French was held that same day in a cemetery some one thousand yards behind the saloon bar. By nightfall Tobias was back aboard the *Alliance* with a large bag of Mr. French’s belongings, including the new shiny shoes.

A few days later, on the 8th May 1715, the merchant ship *Alliance* set sail for Virginia where it was loaded with a cargo of tobacco. The following week the ship began the journey across the Atlantic Ocean: destination Copperas Gap, England.

The weather had been good during the journey and they made fair progress. They were just a few days away from their destination of Copperas Gap. Tobias had been promoted to boatswain of the ship for the homeward journey and had command of maintaining the vessel, which comprised of the stores, sails, rigging and anchor. He was easily capable of this command and reported daily to the Captain of the ship.

Mr. French had taught him well. Tobias would always be grateful to his late departed tutor and friend. But his thoughts now turned to Molly. After a long year apart, an excited Tobias was looking forward to seeing the love of his life.

It took a further ten days to reach Copperas Gap. On the afternoon of a sunny day on the 30th July 1715 the giant merchant ship slipped into Fishersgate harbour. Tobias sought permission from the Captain to leave the ship and he ran as fast as he could up the slight incline to Eastbrook to find Molly. As he got near to the cottages, he saw his father tending to the flowers in his garden.

“Father… Father…” called out Tobias.

His father put down the garden implement that he was using and stood up to greet his son.

“My son,” he exclaimed as he opened his arms wide.

Tobias greeted his father with a manly embrace.

“How have you been keeping this past year?” said Tobias.

“Fine,” replied his father, “you look such a strapping and healthy man on your return from the Americas. Where are your things?”

"I left my kit aboard the ship. I will go back later to collect it, for right now I am in a hurry. But first, how is mother? What of her, is she well?" inquired Tobias.

"She is well, she is inside the cottage, go and see her," replied his father.

"I will," said Tobias, "but first I want to see Molly. I will go to her cottage. I have missed her so much. Today, I shall ask her to marry me and we shall set a date."

An excited Tobias began to walk the twenty-yard distance to Molly's cottage.

"Don't go Tobias, she is not there," said his father.

Tobias turned around. "Where is she father? I will go and find her wherever she is in this village."

"Come here my son, I have something to tell you."

He opened his arms once more and Tobias went to him.

"Sit down Tobias and I will sit with you," said his father with a solemn look on his face.

"What is wrong father?" asked a concerned Tobias.

"Sit down my boy," said his father as he directed him to the bench seating outside his cottage – the bench that Tobias and Molly had often sat upon in days gone by watching the waters of Copperas stream flow by.

Tobias sat down.

"Tobias," his father continued as he sat down beside his son, "I have some bad news."

"What is wrong father, tell me," exclaimed Tobias.

"It's Molly," replied his father, "she is dead."

Tobias looked at his father for a moment in disbelief – before realising that what he had said was true. He let out a loud wail, put his head into his hands and began to cry.

"No," screamed Tobias, as the realisation of this personal horror sunk deep into his mind.

"I am so sorry," said his father, "she was a good girl who had grown into a fine young woman."

"How could this happen?" screamed Tobias, as he continued to sob. "When did this happen?"

"She died fourteen weeks ago, here in Copperas Gap," replied his father, "she died shortly after childbirth. There is a child."

"No," screamed Tobias, as he ran down the incline to a little watercourse that they called Eastbrook, which branched from Copperas stream. He sat down beside the brook watching the purified rainwater filtering past him through a narrow purpose-built gap in the gulley; the sparkling water falling through this rivulet from the hills high above. He watched this pure clear liquid of life itself cascade ever downwards making patterns with tiny bubbles, as it passed him by; watching, thinking, wondering. This was too much to bear. Molly is dead, and she had a child. Tobias's father followed him to the brook and sat down beside him.

"How could this happen?" screamed Tobias.

"God moves in mysterious ways," replied his father.

"God… God…" screamed an angry Tobias, "don't tell me about God… there is no God – for a true God would never allow this to happen."

"You will come to understand," said his father. "Right now you are upset, shocked and angry, but in time you will come to understand. Molly is now in paradise – she is up there with the angels."

"And a child," cried Tobias, "tell me who did this to her and I will kill him with my bare hands for my Molly would never have allowed this."

"She did," replied his father.

"No," screamed an angry Tobias.

"And she loved that person more than anything else in this world," said his father.

"What is this life that makes me so unhappy," cried Tobias, "this is not life, this is hell on earth,"

Tobias stood to his feet. "Who is this man that has taken Molly's love from me? I will find him and kill him."

"Wait my son," shouted his father, "it is you that Molly loved more than anything else in this world. Tobias, work it out for yourself… calculate the dates."

A stunned Tobias looked at his father before sitting down once more.

"Me?" he exclaimed as he pointed to his own chest.

"Yes, you Tobias, for she said before she died that the child that she was bearing belonged to you," said his father. "Could that be true my son?"

Tobias sat in a stunned silence for a moment as he thought matters through.

"Yes – it is true my father. I am sorry. Molly and I had spoken of marriage. No... we would have married."

"I had no reason to doubt her word about the child," said his father, "but I wanted to hear it from you."

Tobias thought for a moment. "The child..." he exclaimed, "where is the child? Where is my child?"

"The child is gone," came the reply, "it was a baby girl. She was taken from us. We had no choice."

"You had choices," shouted an agitated Tobias. "What about Molly's mother? Did she not want this child?"

"Listen to me," replied his father, "had you been here you could have married Molly and made the child legitimate. But you were not here – you were away in the Americas."

"We had no choice but to let the child go, for the child was born out of wedlock and had to be sent away, it is the law and the Lord of the Manor enacted upon it. Molly's mother wanted to keep this child and so did your own mother and I too, but the baby was taken by force by the guards of the Lord of the Manor. There was a second baby, but it was very poorly. We believe that it died. The Lord of the Manor's men dealt with it and we were not told where this child is buried."

"Are you telling me that Molly gave birth to twins?" asked Tobias.

"Yes," replied his father, "but information given to us was not clear."

Tobias stood to his feet. "Then I will go and see the Lord of the Manor, this wicked man that snatches children from rightful grand-parents. I will find out where my child is and bring her home."

"Tobias, calm yourself down," said his father, "the Lord of the Manor signed the order that the child should be taken away by the Church. They would have sent this child somewhere far away to be brought up as a Christian by some well-meaning family. The Lord of the Manor will not know where the child has gone. And, such is the secretive ways of the church administration of these matters – they will not know where the child has been sent."

"I cannot believe this situation that I find myself to be in," exclaimed Tobias, "I will find my child…"

His father interjected. "Tobias, let it be. Your child will be better off with another family for they will be a wealthy one. Your child will be brought up in a luxury that you cannot provide. Yes, we would have kept the child had we been allowed but we have been assured that young Rebecca Alice…"

"Wait," said Tobias, "Did Molly name the child Rebecca Alice?"

"Yes, she did. That was her final request. The name Alice is her maternal grandmother's Christian name" said his father, "but that does not mean that her new family will use that name. As I was saying, Rebecca Alice will be well cared for."

"I will find my child and I will bring her home," said an angry Tobias.

His mood suddenly changed. "What of my Molly? I was coming home to marry her. Did she say anything else before she died?"

"I was not there," replied his father, "but her own mother was there just before she died."

"Well, did Molly say anything?" asked Tobias.

"Yes, she did," replied his father. "Her mother told me to tell you that Molly loved you Tobias. She loved you more than anything else in this world."

Tobias began to cry once more before looking up into the sky, "Molly, Molly, I wish you were here with me right now and I am so sorry for the pain I caused you. I wish I had never gone away. I wish I had never left you. I love you Molly. I always will."

"My son," called his father, "let me take you home where you can rest from your journey from the Americas."

"No father," replied Tobias, "I should get my shoemaker's kit and other belongings from the ship as quickly as I can – for due to the large quantity of my possessions it will take me several journeys – and in twelve hours the ship will sail without me."

"Then I will help you," replied his father.

Both men made their way towards to the harbour where the merchant ship *Alliance* was moored.

As they passed the farmer's windmill on their way to the harbour Tobias's father stopped. "Tobias, there is more I must tell you about Molly," he said, "before you find out from others in this village."

"What is it father? It cannot be worse than what you have already told me," replied Tobias.

"Molly was planning to marry the Lord of the Manor's son," said his father.

"WHAT," exclaimed Tobias, as his mood changed to one of anger, "I cannot believe that my Molly would do such a thing – we were in love with each other. She and I agreed that we would marry on my return from the Americas."

"Listen to me Tobias, Molly did love you – she had no choice but to accept this hand in marriage," said his father.

"Which one of the Lord's sons asked her to marry him?" demanded Tobias.

"His fourth son, Alfred," replied his father.

"I know him... I thought he joined the Army," said Tobias.

"He did, but he returned home to Copperas Gap on-leave from the Army soon after you left for the Americas," came the reply.

"Then I will go and see him. I will beat the life out of him," shouted Tobias. "Wait father... you said they were planning to marry – did they marry?"

"They did not, for something happened," said his father, "sit down my son and I shall tell you."

They sat down on a seat outside the farmer's windmill.

"It was around the time that Molly discovered that she was pregnant with your child Tobias. The baby would have been born out of wedlock and taken away from her, so she reluctantly agreed to marry Alfred in order that the child would be born legitimately," explained his father. "That way she could keep the child."

"Lord and Lady Hynam believed that Alfred was the father of the child Molly was bearing. A marriage was hastily arranged. No one in the village knew Molly was pregnant except for her own mother. The whole village was invited to the forthcoming wedding later that month. Molly lived and remained inside the Manor House during this time and no-one outside of the house was permitted to see her."

"My poor Molly," exclaimed Tobias, "what did I do to her? What trouble and anguish must she have been put through because of my own selfish yearning for adventure on the high seas. And why would a man such as Alfred take on another man's child?"

"I don't know, it does seem odd, but let me continue," said his father. "About a week before the wedding Alfred was taken ill and confined to bed. His health deteriorated rapidly and before long he fell into a coma – so the marriage was postponed. He remained in this condition for the next four months while the best doctors in the land attended to him."

"And what of Molly?" asked Tobias.

"She remained in the confines of the Manor house," said his father, "being looked after by the Lord's servants and nursemaids; she had the best treatment available to her Tobias... you should be thankful for that."

"How do you know all this father?" asked Tobias.

"I visited the Manor house often Tobias, to repair shoes for the gentry – you should know that because you used to come with me. You remember one of the footmen called Giles, and another junior butler named Christopher? Well they kept me informed. And twice I got to see and speak with Molly for myself in the Manor house."

"You did?" exclaimed Tobias, "tell me, how was she? Was she well?"

"She was fine and in good spirits because she knew by then that Alfred's condition was terminal and she would not have to marry him," replied his father.

"And what of her child?" asked Tobias.

His father thought for a moment before continuing.

"She knew that the Lord of the Manor had to do something, for word was getting out to the villagers that Molly was eight months pregnant – yet no one was sure if a marriage had taken place in secret between her and Alfred. Molly felt sure that the legitimacy of her child would somehow be dealt with by the Lord of the Manor without her having to marry Alfred – a marriage which was of course impossible by that time because Alfred was not compos mentis."

"What happened father? Tell me more and quickly," asked Tobias.

"It was terrible... it did not have to be said or repeated but it was," replied his father.

"Tell me father," demanded Tobias, "what was repeated?"

His father continued, "One of his Lordship's doctors was overheard by a servant to be telling his Lordship that the disease to which Alfred had succumbed meant that he could not conceive children – and that this condition had been prevalent for at least the previous two years. Alfred could not possibly be the father of Molly's unborn child."

"What happened to Molly?" asked Tobias.

"She was summoned to Lord and Lady Hyman's private quarters to explain her condition. She told them the child was yours Tobias. Meanwhile the whole village got to hear how poor Alfred had been deceived by Molly. He became a local hero. She became the wicked one."

"Oh, my poor Molly," replied Tobias, "it wasn't her fault father."

"I know my son but that is the way of the gentry and indeed the world," said his father. "The weaker people of this world always get the blame for things they do not do."

"What happened next?" asked Tobias.

"Alfred died," was the reply.

"He died?" repeated Tobias.

"Yes, he died," said his father. "After his death the Lord of the Manor decided that Molly should stay within the confines of the Manor house where she had her child, your child Tobias."

A tear began to trickle from Tobias Watson's eyes. His father comforted him for one brief moment.

"You know the rest of the story my son," said his father, "Molly died shortly after childbirth and the child was taken away for adoption. And finally, the people of Copperas Gap were told that you were the father of Molly's baby. A baby girl born outside of wedlock."

Chapter 8

Molly.

Eighteen months had passed since Tobias Watson returned from the Americas. He spent that time adjusting to Molly's death and taking up, once again, his skill of making shoes and selling his wares in the areas around the village of Copperas Gap. Daily, he would visit Molly's grave at the Locks Hill cemetery. Tobias had made an uneasy peace with Molly's mother who had laid the blame for her only daughter's death at his hands. Some of the people of Copperas Gap would not speak to Tobias because of the shame he had brought upon the little village. Others spoke words of hatred – none more so than old Fred the fisherman, who usually started the verbal onslaught.

"Sling your hook Watson," Fred often shouted whenever he saw Tobias, "we don't want wicked murdering people like you in our village."

Ann, Maggie and many others joined in, "Get out of this place, Molly was a good girl and you killed her." It was becoming too much for Tobias. As the months went by he found his cobbler and shoemaking trade difficult, for he had to travel further afield to make a living. Sometimes, he and his only means of transport, a single mule, had to stay overnight at far flung villages across the county of Sussex because the distance was too far to travel home.

Tobias had been to see the Lord of the Manor at East Hill, requesting information about his daughter Rebecca Alice, but to no avail, both the Lord of the Manor and his lady refused to converse with Tobias. The child had indeed been taken by the Lord of the Manor's guardsmen and given to the Church to be removed from the area. Tobias was warned that he should not pursue the matter, for the child would be somewhere safe – being raised by a wealthy family.

But this did not stop Tobias going to see the Vicar at the church. The Vicar could not help – even though Tobias persisted and visited him many times. Each time the Vicar told him to pray and said that when he had prayed enough to redeem his sin he might give him some guidance. One day, Tobias once more visited the church to look for the Vicar. He found a Rector, who he had not seen before, standing by the entrance door to the church. After exchanging pleasantries of the day, Tobias asked, "Have we not met before Rector? – not here at Copperas Gap but perhaps somewhere else?" Tobias studied the facial features of the Rector.

Suddenly Tobias exclaimed, "In the Americas – that is where I have seen you before. You were in the saloon bar in the town of Bath, standing on a chair – if I remember."

"I don't really know," replied the Rector, "though I have been to the Americas several times. I do not recall visiting the town of Bath and certainly not a saloon bar."

"You were in a saloon bar watching those fancy women," said Tobias. Then he thought to himself – 'No… a Rector would not go into a house of prostitution!' Tobias shook his head in disbelief, wondering why he could think such a thing about a religious Rector – before he continued, "Never mind, it is of little importance, I am here because I seek the Vicar and want to know the whereabouts of my daughter, Rebecca Alice?"

"Rebecca Alice – yes I know of the child?" came the reply. "My son, I know everyone in this village and I know your name to be Tobias Watson, the son of a shoemaker."

"While I am indeed the son of a shoemaker, I am also a shoemaker and cobbler in my own right," replied Tobias, "but I have not come here to discuss my parentage or indeed my own trade skills. I have come to see if the Vicar of this church can lend himself to assist in helping me to find my daughter, Rebecca Alice."

"The Vicar is not here right now but let me tell you something. What you should be doing Tobias is praying for forgiveness to your God," said the Rector, "for you have sinned and you should be paying penance for your wicked acts."

The Rector continued. "I have not seen you in this Church this past eighteen-months since you returned from the Americas. You should be coming here every Sunday to attend the church service and to pray to God for forgiveness of your sins."

"Pray to the Almighty!" retorted Tobias. "There is no God, for if there were a God he would not have allowed the death of my Molly."

The Rector smiled. It was a roguish kind of a smile not usual for a man of the cloth. "God did not kill Molly. You killed her Tobias," said the Rector in a calm peaceful voice, before raising his tone very aggressively, "for *you* have admitted that you planted the seed of death within her. You gave her a child."

"I loved Molly with all of my heart," cried a tearful Tobias, "what sort of a wicked person are you to say such a thing."

"I am the appointed delegate here on Earth," replied the Rector, "it is you Tobias who is the wicked person – not me, for you have conceived a child out of wedlock, against the will of your God."

"Lots of women die in childbirth, even those that are married," retorted Tobias. "Where is my child?"

"The child is gone; you will never see that child again. She could not stay in this village because of the stigma of being born out of wedlock. It would not help her as she grows into adulthood. She has been taken to a place where no-one knows of her ordeal or of her natural parent's reputations. She has been adopted by a God-fearing family, who will help to displace the sin attributed to her soul," replied the Rector.

"No child has that kind of sin. Tell me where she is?" demanded Tobias.

"I shall not tell you," replied the Rector, "and, as for the Church itself, in dealing with such matters of this nature, they have made rules that do not permit anyone to know where that child has been sent. Even the Bishop himself does not know where she is – for that is the way of the Church. It prevents people like you from finding her. She has been sent away for her own safety, but let me tell you this Tobias… I know where she is."

"How do you know where my daughter is, and the Bishop does not?" asked Tobias.

"I have special powers," came the reply.

"But she is my child," replied Tobias, "I want to see her."

"She is not your child anymore and the sooner you understand this the better," said the Rector.

Tobias stormed away and headed towards his parent's home in Eastbrook. The Rector followed him and caught up with him by the farm worker's cottages.

"Listen to me Tobias," said the Rector, "for your own sake, you must pray for forgiveness to God. And to be able to live in this village during the rest of your mortal existence in harmony with others you should tell the people of Copperas Gap that you made an error, and that you are NOT the father of this unfortunate child. A denial will take away all stigma shown towards yourself by the villagers. Listen to me Tobias… I can help you."

"I will never say that," said Tobias, "how can you… as a religious man of the cloth suggest such a wicked thing, that I should lie to the people of Copperas Gap!"

"Well, you do not know for sure that you are the father of this child," said the Rector wryly, "there are many young men in this village who could be the father. Molly was a very attractive woman and she flirted with them while you were away in the Americas."

"You lie," screamed Tobias.

Tobias let out a roar of disapproval as he lunged forward to attack the Rector, but suddenly he thought better of this course of action and stopped in his tracks. He composed himself.

"But if I say what you suggest Rector," said an angry Tobias, "that will make Molly out to be a *whore* – if I, as the father of our child, were to retract my declaration. Yes, my own stigma would be gone but her reputation would be in ruins."

"Then you should pray for yourself Tobias, for you will not survive much longer with your reputation tarnished and with this stigma attached to you," replied the Rector. "Molly has passed onto another place and her reputation on this Earth matters no more to ordinary people. If you do not make a retraction, your workload as a cobbler will reduce further and in time you will not earn a living from your trade. You will starve, and you will die all the while you remain with this stigma about you. The choice is yours Tobias. All you need to do is tell a little lie. I am here to help you."

Tobias stood firm, his eyes piercing into the Rector with a hatred he had not experienced before, "But what of Molly's mother? She lives in the village. I could not bring shame on her?" replied Tobias.

"She is only one person in this village – she will not matter. Come back into the Church right now my son and pray to my own almighty God," continued the Rector, "then we can deal with the more practical matters of dispensing with your renunciation of the child. The Lord of the Manor will take the issue forward, accept and sign your evidence contained in a document that he will compose and, once published in Church on Sunday, your stigma will be removed and the people of this village will embrace you once more."

"You are the Devil himself dressed in the fine clothes of a man of the church," replied Tobias, "I will never bring Molly's name into disrepute or bring shame to her mother. I would rather leave this village of Copperas Gap… this land of mine, than renounce my responsibility for my actions. Molly was my only love. And I was her only lover. Molly is still my love now that she has passed. She will continue to be my only love and she will forever be mine until we meet again in paradise."

"You just said there was no God Almighty Tobias, so how is it that you believe that you will meet Molly in paradise," said the Rector in a manner of virtuous sarcasm.

"Rector, I believe that there *is* an all-powerful supreme being," said Tobias. "This supreme being is somewhere in the universe and I know in my heart that there *is* a paradise; a place where one day I shall meet Molly once again. There is certainly not a God like the one that you say you represent."

Tobias marched back to the cottage where he lived with his parents with a rage about him that would take three days to settle.

A few days later Tobias looked out from his bedroom window towards Fishersgate bay and saw his former merchant ship, the giant *Alliance,* berthed in the harbour. These past few months had led him to realise that he could no longer live with the people of Copperas Gap, for daily, the village folk shunned him and some continued to mock him.

It was fortuitous that the *Alliance* was in the port of Fishersgate. As Tobias had worked aboard the *Alliance* before, he knew that the ship's next destination would be the town of Portsmouth. He thought to himself that this was the perfect opportunity to take the late Mr. French's possessions to his brother who lived there. He could then set-up trading as a shoemaker in Portsmouth, for it was a much larger place than Copperas Gap. He would hope that his fortune might fare better in Portsmouth. It would be a new start in a new town where no one knew of his past. Tobias made his way down to the ship and boarded with the permission of the master.

"I bid you good morning Mr. Green," said Tobias to the ship's master.

"Hello Tobias," replied Green, "what brings you aboard? Are you missing the sea and adventure?"

"Well, I do miss the seafaring life just a little. But that is not why I am here. I see that this great merchant ship, the *Alliance,* has returned to Copperas Gap and I know that it is often the case that your next port of call is Portsmouth harbour," said Tobias.

"You are right my friend," replied Green, "Portsmouth is indeed our next port of call."

"Well, I seek passage to Portsmouth in order that I can take the late Mr. French's possessions to his brother, and I will also need to take my own possessions for I intend to set up business as a shoemaker and cobbler in Portsmouth," said Tobias.

"I see no issues with your request," replied Green, "but I will ask the Captain if he will give permission. Wait here and I will ask him."

Green disappeared through a hatch that led below the main deck. Five minutes later he was back.

"Yes, the Captain bids you good morning Tobias and says he will be pleased to have you aboard for the journey to Portsmouth, provided that you assist with the repair of some of the sails en-route," said Green.

"It will be a pleasure," replied Tobias.

"Well, be on board this ship before mid-day tomorrow," said Green, "we sail on the afternoon high tide."

"Very well Mr. Green – and thank you," said Tobias, "I will be back in the morning with my belongings."

Tobias made his way up the hill to the cottage to tell his father and mother that he was leaving the following day. He found them both inside their cottage, sitting in the living room.

"Mother, father," called Tobias, "tomorrow, I will be leaving aboard the merchant ship *Alliance* for Portsmouth. It is for the best."

"I knew this moment would come my son," said his father, "we live in sad times."

"How long will you be away?" asked his mother.

"I do not know for sure," replied Tobias, "I will see how I fare in business as a shoemaker in Portsmouth, but do not fear mother, maybe in time the people of Copperas Gap will forget about me and when they do, I will return to live out my life in this village."

"I am not so sure that they will forget," replied his father, "Portsmouth is a much bigger town than Copperas Gap, they have plenty of room for one more cobbler and shoemaker. But I am very sad that you have to leave us."

"You have been marvellous parents to me," said Tobias, "do not fear, I will send you money by Post Office stagecoach to help you in your twilight years."

"Thank you, my son," replied his mother.

That evening Tobias went to bed in the front bedroom of the cottage, a room that he called his own. It was the same room that he had slept in since childhood. It would be the last time that he would sleep in his bed in this little cottage that his mother and father rented from the Lord of the Manor. He soon drifted off to sleep into his world of dreams.

His dream took him outside of his cottage. He found himself standing before the *old monument* at the North of the village. The stone monument was a six-foot tall figure of a man placed on a large plinth. There was no name on the plinth, and the facial features of the statue were blurred – but he already knew that, for he had walked past this sculpture many times in the past. The statue was known as the unknown sailor to the people of Copperas Gap – for it was attired in a naval uniform.

"Tobias, Tobias," a voice gently called from behind.

Tobias knew that voice, it was a voice that he had yearned to hear this past eighteen months. He turned around and there before him, about twenty feet away, stood Molly.

"Oh Molly, Molly," cried Tobias as he rushed towards her and took her in his arms. "What is this magical place that brings people back to life," as he felt her body with both of his hands. They kissed. It was a long lingering kiss that made them both cry in delightful pleasure. Then Tobias playfully nibbled her ear, as he had always done.

"Stop it," giggled Molly, "you know that tickles me."

Tobias looked at her in a loving way. This truly was Molly.

Molly and Tobias parted slightly, still holding hands, as they looked deep into each other's eyes.

"I am so sorry Molly," said Tobias as he looked at her smiling face while her long blonde hair moved gently in the breeze. The silhouette of her shapely body against the backdrop of the summer's sun showed seductively through the pure-white flowing robe that she was wearing. She was as beautiful as ever. Her soft skin, gentle touch and tender body that he held so close to his own, triggered a quivering of his manly muscle. It was a trembling feeling that they both experienced. It was a yearning to consummate and satisfy an immediate lust that they had so often passionately shared with each other.

"I should have stayed at home with you and not gone to the Americas," whispered a humbling, Tobias.

"You did what you had to do Tobias," replied Molly, "no one on earth can predict the future and we were both so lucky that we spent all our youthful years together. We had so many happy times, loving experiences and tender moments. And we now have a child which we shall both cherish from afar."

"I will find our daughter," exclaimed Tobias.

"Tobias, it is better that you do not find Rebecca Alice just yet," replied Molly.

"Why?" asked Tobias.

"I cannot tell you for I am not permitted to tell you. I cannot tell a human being specific details about the future or some things about the past," replied Molly.

"By who? Who orders you?" questioned Tobias.

"The Lord of the universe has rules that spiritual bodies must abide by," said Molly.

"I don't understand," said Tobias.

"You do not need to understand, my darling," replied Molly.

"Where is our child? Do you know?" pleaded Tobias.

"Yes, I do," replied Molly, "she is safe and well and I watch over her every mortal day. I am her guardian angel."

"What can I do Molly?"

"There is nothing you can do except to remember one thing. You must be in Fishersgate Bay opposite the Halfway House tavern on the 2nd April 1734 at exactly twelve noon," said Molly.

"Why?" asked Tobias, "that's a long time in the future, about eighteen years from now."

"I cannot tell you why my darling, but for your own sake and mine you must be there. Do not forget my lover," said Molly.

"What am I supposed to do when I am there," asked Tobias.

"You will know what to do – for you will see a terrible situation unfold before you," replied Molly.

Tobias thought for a moment before looking at Molly's beautiful face.

"I miss you so much Molly," said Tobias.

"And I miss you too," replied Molly as her body quivered at the delight of being so close to her lover. "Live your life to the full, find your destiny, be honest to yourself and to all others around you. One day, when it is your time to die, you will find me in paradise – I shall be waiting for you Tobias. We will spend the rest of eternity together."

"How can I live my life on Earth without you Molly?" asked Tobias.

"You must, for the sake of my memory, for you will think of me every day when you wake and every day I will be beside you in your thoughts – until that time comes when you shall join me in paradise," said Molly. "In the meantime, I will be known forever to the people of Earth as *The Ghost of Copperas Gap.* Sometimes, Tobias, I will appear before you, but only as an image of a spiritual ghost in your dreams. It will not be often, but it may be necessary. Do not be frightened – but remember, you will not be able to touch me or hold me close like you do now."

“I do not understand,” whispered Tobias, “am I not dreaming right now?”

“You do not need to understand my darling, but you will in time, my lover, when it is your time to die on Earth. There will be things that you will discover just before your death; things that I am not permitted to tell you right now,” said Molly, “but tonight, let us enjoy our moment together – where I can hold your body and you can hold mine in this physical real time territory of your dreams.”

Tobias looked deep into Molly’s eyes once more.

“I love you so much Molly,” said Tobias.

“And I love you too, Tobias,” replied Molly.

Then, hand in hand, they walked down to Eastbrook where the stream from the hills passed by. They sat together on the double bench seat beside Tobias’s parents’ cottage. They had sat here many times before, when Molly was alive, discussing their love for each other and deciding their future together.

For the next half an hour they talked, cuddled and kissed – frantically aware that time was ticking away. Soon they would have to part. Before long, it would be morning and Tobias would wake from his sleep.

Just then a flute began to play in the distance. It became louder and louder. Then, other musical instrumentations began to accompany the flute. Tobias stood up to see where the sounds were coming from but could not see anything.

He turned his attention to Molly once more.

“Tobias,” Molly purred, “whenever there was music on Earth you would ask me to dance. Do you remember?”

“That’s right,” smiled Tobias, “would you like to dance Molly?”

“Of course, I would love to dance with you,” she said.

He held out his hand, which she grasped. They danced together. It was a seductive kind of a dance. They seduced every musical note with stimulating movement. It was a dance that they had never danced before. It was almost like making love in an artistic sensual way. And throughout their tryst they never broke their intense grip, which might have progressed into two tussling bodies – passionately yearning for the fruits of each other – to form one perspiring wrestling form, until the act of love itself had been achieved and lust had been satisfied.

Tobias and Molly knew that before long they would have to leave each other. They held each other close – both with tears of sadness in their eyes. Suddenly, they broke apart and Molly danced alone. Tobias stood motionless, watching her, yearning for her – weeping for her. She danced a beautiful dance of the Copperas Gap ballerina, twirling, leaping, flying in the summer sunlight – her robe flowing in unification with her exacting dance movements. This was no ordinary dance and it lasted for over six-minutes. Finally, she performed a pirouette before coming to a stationary position, holding her arms wide open; the setting sun shining behind her. She faced Tobias with a sad smile on her face – mouthing the words 'Goodbye, my love. I will see you in Paradise, where our love for each other will last for all eternity.'

Tobias rushed towards her to embrace her for the very last time, but as he got near to her she vanished. Tobias waited for a while – in the hope that Molly would re-appear or, at the least, say something more to him, but it was not to be. She had gone.

That was the last thing Tobias Watson remembered, for in the morning he awoke still thinking about this beautiful enchanting yet thought-provoking dream.

Chapter 9

Portsmouth harbour.

The next morning Tobias and his father carried Tobias's personal effects down the hill to Fishersgate harbour where he loaded his belongings onto the sailing ship, the *Alliance*. These possessions included his shoemaker's chest containing the tools of his trade. Later that day Tobias's mother and father stood by the shoreline waving their son goodbye as the giant timber ship weighed anchor and set sail on the high tide – destination Portsmouth. As Tobias waved to them from the main deck he began to think about his dream from the night before. The dream had felt real enough – for when he held Molly in his arms he had felt her unquestionable mortal presence. Molly seemed to be so alive in his dream.

Before that day was done, as the merchant ship *Alliance* headed nearer to its destination of Portsmouth harbour, Tobias concluded that he had experienced something special. He believed that his dream had been put into his own imagination with the help of a spiritual being; a force much more powerful than anything he could comprehend. What other explanation was there? But one thing puzzled him. It was this future meeting that Molly had told him about. She told him that he should attend the Halfway House tavern at Copperas Gap on the 2nd April 1734 at exactly twelve noon – eighteen years in the future. Tobias was mystified.

The following day the mighty ship *Alliance* docked in the harbour of Portsmouth – a naval base since 1194. Tobias bid farewell to the ship's crew and unloaded his personal effects onto the dockside. He sat down on his shoemaker's casket. Dockworkers had begun to unload the cargo of the *Alliance* using ropes and tackles to lift the heavy goods from ship to shore. To his right were a group of fisherwomen gutting the fish that fishermen had brought to the town on the afternoon tide – throwing the entrails into an open half-barrel some five feet away. Seagulls flew overhead – dive bombing the half-barrel in the hope of securing a delicious morsel of fresh fish-innards. Fishermen were repairing their nets. Other men were rolling full sized barrels along the dockside. A fiddler was playing sea shanty songs and two drunken sailors were singing along in their own words – as best they could, each with a different lyric. It was a bustling place.

Tobias watched the world go by, thinking that the first thing he should do was find some accommodation – a bed for the night. However, this would prove difficult because he would have to find somewhere safe to store his shoemaker tools and tool chest while he walked the streets of Portsmouth. He was sure they would be stolen if he left them unattended. Worse, he had Mr. French's personal possessions hidden and these goods were very valuable. Perhaps, in hindsight, he should have left his possessions on board the ship in a place of safety while he looked for accommodation. Lucky for him, at that moment, an official looking man – dressed in a dark blue uniform walked past.

"Good afternoon," called out Tobias.

"Afternoon," said the man, "just arrived, have you?"

"Yes," replied Tobias.

"Looking for somewhere to stay, are you?" inquired the man.

Tobias stood up, "Yes I am. How did you know that?" replied Tobias.

"I see it every day," replied the man, "I am the watchman of the port and I see young men, just like you, arrive with their belongings and sit on the dockside wondering where they should go," said the Watchman.

"Well, seeing you today is my lucky day," exclaimed Tobias.

"There is no luck about me being here today, son," replied the Watchman, "I walk this same path every afternoon on these docks and there is always one or two young sirs like yourself, waiting on the dock, wondering which way to go – out to sea or into the town. Look! there's another one over there." The man pointed to another young man, no more than a boy – sitting on the dock a few yards away. "I shall go and see him in a moment," said the man. "Permit me to introduce myself as superintendent Morse the Chief Watchman of this port."

"Well, my name is Tobias Watson. Is there a place nearby where I can stay for one or two nights until I can find somewhere more permanent?" asked Tobias.

"Yes, there is. It is a place quite reasonably priced just around the corner," replied the Watchman, "I will have one of my men help you to carry your possessions and escort you there. The landlady is a Mrs. Morse, the prettiest landlady in Portsmouth – but I must warn you that she does not take kindly to drunkenness or swearing,"

"She will be happy to know that I do neither," replied Tobias. "I see she has the same surname as you… Morse."

The Chief watchman did not respond to Tobias Watson's observation.

"Good," said the Chief watchman as he beckoned two other uniformed watchmen over. "You men, take this young man to Mrs. Morse's and help him with his belongings."

"Very good Sir," said one of the men as they picked up most of Tobias's belongings.

"Come with us young man – it's not far. It's about one hundred yards up that side-street."

Soon they were at the front door of the boarding lodge and a middle-aged Mrs. Morse bid Tobias good morning before showing him to his room. After he had settled into the room, he thought it best that he should find French's brother to give him the possessions that he had been asked to bring back to England.

The address he had been given was easy to find and soon he was standing outside a small cottage. Tobias knocked on the door and an old woman opened it.

"What do you want?" she asked.

"I seek Mr. Colm French. He is the brother of a Naval boatswain who I had the honour of working for aboard the merchant ship the *Alliance*," said Tobias.

"Stand back for your own safety," said the old woman.

Tobias stood back from the doorway, "Is there a problem?" he asked.

"I fear for your safety," replied the woman, "I have heard of the boatswain Mr. French, I understand that he is a very nice man."

Tobias smiled. "Well, can I see Mr. Colm French?" said Tobias.

"No, you cannot," said the woman, "for he and his wife died of the fever three weeks ago – that is why I am here in this cottage."

"Oh, no… I am so sorry," replied Tobias, "are you his relative?"

"No," replied the woman.

"A friend?" Tobias inquired.

"No," replied the woman, "he had no other known relatives other than his wife and brother, the couple did not have any children either."

"Who are you, if you do not mind me asking?" said Tobias.

"I am here to clear-out this cottage and make it empty, for there is a fever lingering in this household," she said.

"Is that not man's work?" replied Tobias as he moved forward.

"Stand back boy, for if you come closer you will catch the fever," said the woman.

Tobias did as he was told.

"The work that I do is important. It is what old women do when nearing the age of death – I am 83 years of age. Fever could strike me down at any time and the Lord Justice's office pays me well to prepare the deceased persons and their possessions, for removal, before fumigation of the premises takes place. And their fine wage keeps me fed and watered very well indeed. I seems to be immune from the fever and I lives like a Queen on the wages they pay me." The old woman smiled as she took a swig from her gin bottle. "Maybe it's the gin that keeps the fever away from me. Anyway, what do you want? Why have you come here?" she continued.

"I have some treasures and possessions that I am supposed to give to Colm French, they belonged to his brother," said Tobias.

"Well you will have to take them back to him?" said the disgruntled old woman.

"But I cannot for he, too… is dead," replied Tobias.

The old woman's eyes lit up. The thought of treasure appealed to her.

"Is there any money or gold in these possessions?" asked the woman.

Tobias replied, "I cannot tell you that! Are you sure that Mr. French has no other relatives?"

"I am sure," said the old woman, "but if you don't believe me go down to the Lord Lieutenant's office and ask him. Now young man – I have work to do, for I have another cottage to clear before nightfall, so it is better that you leave."

The elderly woman slammed the door shut. Tobias left the area and walked back to his room at Mrs. Morse's guesthouse. He hid Mr. French's possessions deep within his cobbler's chest – while wondering what he should do with them. Perhaps he should go and see the officials at the Lord Lieutenant's office. There was indeed some gold among Mr. French's belongings and about one hundred shillings in cash, but Tobias was not going to divulge that information to anyone except a relative of the deceased or someone in authority. There were too many thieves and tricksters about.

Once back at his room at the lodging house Tobias opened the small security chest containing Mr. French's possessions. It contained a sextant and telescope, plus of course the hundred shillings as well as the gold. He had no idea how much the gold was worth, but it weighed about two ounces. Also among the possessions were Mr. French's new shiny shoes which Tobias had made for him before he died.

'*I cannot let anyone else walk in your shoes Mr. French,*' thought Tobias to himself, '*for I believe that no-one else in this world is worthy of stepping into your eminence and wearing your shoes.*'

Tobias pondered on his thoughts for a moment before taking twenty shillings from his own purse and putting the money with French's possessions.

'I shall buy the shoes back from you Mr. French,' he continued, '*they are too small for me to wear and even if they did fit my feet, I would be unworthy of stepping into your greatness. I will weigh them down and I shall throw them into the deep waters of the Atlantic Ocean to ensure that no other man will ever wear them.'*

Tobias put the shoes onto the floor before securing Mr. French's possessions in the chest.

Then he thought he heard a bell ringing, so he opened the door to his room and listened. The bell rang again – this time much louder.

"Dinner is on the table," a woman's voice shouted – it was Mrs. Morse, the landlady.

Tobias made his way down the flight of stairs from the third floor to the second and headed toward another flight of stairs leading to the dining area on the ground floor. Then, a door opened onto the landing. A young man walked through the door who Tobias recognized in an instant.

"Hello," said Tobias, "I saw you by the dockside earlier today."

"Yes, you did," replied the boy with a southern Welsh accent, "I saw you there too."

"What is your name?" inquired Tobias.

"It's William," came the reply.

"I am Tobias, I am pleased to meet you. Are you staying here?"

"I am," replied William, "but only for one night."

"Are you going somewhere? Aboard one of the ships in the dock perhaps?" asked Tobias.

"No," replied William, "I only have enough money to stay here for one night and then I must sleep on the streets."

Tobias looked the boy up and down. He looked quite clean and had a nice manner about him. He did not appear to be the sort of boy associated with being a street urchin.

"How is it that you come to this misfortune?" inquired Tobias.

"I came over from the Valleys after my mother and father died to find my distant blood relatives," replied William.

"Did you find them?" asked Tobias.

"No, I did not for I have learnt that they died of the fever," came the reply. "It took me two weeks to find out they were dead and by that time I had used up almost all of my money sleeping in various lodgings. Yesterday, I had enough money to go home to Wales by stagecoach – but the coach did not arrive, so I have used the last of my money to stay here. It is so cold outside."

Tobias could see that the boy was clearly distressed at his predicament.

"Yes… I understand that lots of people have died of the fever. What will you do tomorrow?" asked Tobias.

"I don't know," said William, "maybe try to find a job and earn some money so that I can purchase a stagecoach ticket and go home to Wales."

"Is there anyone in Wales who can look after you," asked Tobias.

"No," said William, "all my relatives are dead. I have no-one, but I know the area well and I will feel safer back home, even though my father's farm has been sold and I have nowhere to stay."

"Your father had a farm?" inquired Tobias.

"Yes, he did, it was a stud farm where he trained horses," replied William.

"Would that farm now belong to you, William?" asked Tobias.

"It should be mine, but the horses and stock were taken from me by the Lord of the Manor," came the reply.

"That is unfortunate," said Tobias, "but you must have some redress – even the Lord of the Manor cannot take a farm or its stock from its rightful owner without good reason. Were there many horses?"

"There were around thirty horses at the farm on the day he took the land," said William, "including my own favourite – my personal horse, *Revel.*"

"Do you ride horses?" asked Tobias.

“Yes, I do. I have been riding horses since I was five years old,” replied William.

The dinner bell rang again.

“I said, dinner is served,” called an agitated landlady from the floor below.

“How old are you?” asked Tobias.

“I am sixteen years old,” William replied.

“Come my boy,” smiled Tobias as he patted a very vulnerable William on the shoulder, “let’s eat, and fill our bellies as full as we can, for tomorrow is another day and if we eat well tonight we should both last out until we can find our next meal.”

William smiled. Together they made their way to the dining room where they were ushered to a table where two older men were already seated.

“Evening,” said Tobias. Neither of the men responded.

“Sit down William,” said Tobias to his new friend. They both sat at the table in the warm comfortable surroundings of Mrs. Morse’s dining room, where a fire flickered in the grate at the far end of the stone floored room. Oak beams supported the smooth finished natural coloured ceiling. The walls were not quite so smooth as the plastered ceiling and had lumps and bumps among its coated outer surface, though it was embellished almost entirely in seafaring artefacts such as replica ships, anchors, sailors’ rope knots, pulleys, nets and clay smoking pipes.

Tobias looked around the dining room before taking a brief look at the strange men sitting opposite him at the table

“I said good evening to you two gentlemen,” said Tobias.

“Evening,” one of them growled, the other said nothing. They did not appear to know one another. One of the men, the grumpy one, wore the clothes of a fisherman and had a smell about him that took some minutes to get used to. The other wore a white shirt and grey trousers, covered with what looked like a sheepskin shopkeeper’s apron.

The shopkeeper was to remain silent throughout dinner, but his eyes were to move from side to side, watching, piercing, and thrusting his persona into the personal space of Tobias and

William. It was quite scary. Every now and again Tobias looked at the shopkeeper with puzzled thoughts.

Mrs. Morse appeared from the kitchen.

"What will you gentlemen have to eat?" she said in a southern English accent.

"What do you have?" inquired Tobias.

"We have Fish Pie," she replied.

"And what else?" enquired Tobias.

"Well," replied Mrs. Morse with a smile, "we have Fish Pie and bread."

A huge laugh came from a waiter as he walked towards the table from the kitchen. He was holding a large pot with steam rising from it.

"Mr. Morse the dockside Chief watchman," exclaimed Tobias.

"That is I," replied Mr. Morse, "that is, when I am not in this cottage serving dinners."

"Is this your cottage and business?" enquired Tobias.

"Yes, and that of my lovely wife," he replied, as a large lovable endearing Mrs. Morse raised her head, displaying the seven warts on her face and neck; each wart with a black hair growing from the centre. She giggled like a child underneath the black cloth cap and checked dress that she wore.

Tobias smiled. "Well, Mrs. Morse, given your extensive menu choice I think that I shall have the Fish Pie and bread, and what will you have William?"

"I think I will have the same," said a nervous William.

"An excellent choice," replied Mr. Morse.

The meal was superb. Tobias and William spoke of themselves and got to know each other throughout dinner. Oddly enough, the two men sitting opposite them said nothing. They ate their fish-pie dinner in silence – though the shopkeeper continued to look at them with his beady eyes.

With dinner almost finished Tobias turned to William.

"William, tomorrow I shall look for premises for a new shoemaker's shop that I intend to open here in Portsmouth. You seem like a fine young man and I would not like to see you fending for yourself on these dangerous streets. I believe that you would begin a downward spiral leading to poverty and certain death. I want you to come with me, help me find premises and be an assistant of mine. I cannot promise a wage yet, but I would be able to provide a roof over your head and food on the table. And in return, you would protect and look after my shop and its contents when I am out."

"That is a fine gesture, for I have only just met you, Tobias, but I can see you are a kind man," replied William, "I shall accept your offer."

"Then we are done," replied Tobias, "and now it is time for bed. I shall sleep well tonight for it has been a long day."

"Yes, I think I shall retire as well," said William, not wanting to stay a moment longer near the two odd men that they had shared dinner with. Both Tobias and William stood up from the table.

"Goodnight to you gentlemen," said Tobias.

The fisherman growled while the shopkeeper remained silent.

As Tobias moved away from the table the shopkeeper suddenly blurted out, "I shall see you in the future."

Tobias looked back. "What?" he asked.

"I shall see you in the future," said the shopkeeper.

"I beg your pardon," replied Tobias as he broke into a laugh – William also laughed.

"I shall see you in the future," said the shopkeeper again.

"Can you elaborate?" inquired Tobias.

"I shall see you in the future, Captain Tobias Watson," said the shopkeeper for a final time.

The shopkeeper said no more but stared straight ahead.

Tobias shook his head as if to dismiss the shopkeeper's wild claim. How would he know that they would meet in the future? Unless he was meaning tomorrow morning when they all awoke. And why would the shopkeeper call Tobias a *Captain*? He was a shoemaker not a Captain.

"Come on William," said a laughing Tobias, "let us get out of here before we go mad. This man thinks I am a Captain. What a wild and crazy thing to say to a shoemaker like me."

Both ascended the stairs before saying goodnight and disappearing into their respective rooms. The following morning Tobias did indeed take a walk with young William to get a feel for the town of Portsmouth – to find somewhere where he could set up business as a shoemaker and cobbler. Then he had an idea. He walked down to the docks, because he thought that a shop opposite the quay might be a better location. With the various ships arriving and leaving port he would have a ready-made group of customers who manned those vessels. There would be several hundred new-faces every week, and that meant many clients. As he arrived at the docks he noticed that a few more ships had arrived on the early morning tide. All were tethered to the quayside.

"Well I'll be dammed," shouted a man standing on the deck of one of the ships. "If it isn't young Tobias Watson."

Tobias looked upwards towards the ship to recognise its rigging. 'It's His Majesty's ship, *Thunder,'* he thought. And the man who had shouted was none other than Captain Stephen Carden.

Tobias waved and shouted, "Good morning Captain Carden, how are you?"

"I am fine," came the reply. "Tobias, I have a little job for you. Come aboard and we can talk some more."

Tobias began to climb the gangplank from the dockside to the ship.

"William, you wait here on the docks," shouted Tobias, "I will not be long."

The Captain and two of the crew met Tobias at the head of the gangplank.

"You are looking well Tobias – the last time I saw you was in the *Americas*," said the Captain.

"Yes," replied Tobias, "it seems such a long time ago. Captain Carden, what can I do for you?"

"Well, its these blasted shoes," said the Captain, "I don't know what has happened to them; it could be that the saltwater has shrunk them for they are making my feet sore."

"Unless your feet have grown bigger," replied Tobias.

The Captain looked at Tobias as he thought about the comment.

"Ummm, its possible I suppose," said the Captain. "Anyway Tobias, what brings you to Portsmouth?"

"There are two reasons," replied Tobias. "I am obliged to bring to Portsmouth some personal belongings of a friend who died in the Americas; he was a fellow sailor who hails from this place and I was hoping to find his next of kin. I am also trying to set up business here in Portsmouth as a shoemaker and cobbler."

"Bringing back personal belongings from the Americas, eh Watson," said the Captain "well that's a very fine thing to do. A lot of men would have pocketed the goods. Have you completed your task?"

"I am afraid not Sir," said Tobias, "my friend's relative – his brother – is also dead and there is no one else to deposit these goods with."

"Well, then, they are yours," replied the Captain.

"Is it that simple Sir?" asked Tobias, "I believe that I should not be entitled to take these goods and monies without some authority confirming this?"

The Captain took a step backwards and stared hard at Tobias.

"You know Tobias," he continued, "I saw something in you the very first time that I met you in the Americas – that is aside from your skills as a cobbler or indeed your eye for imperfect ship's rigging. Do you remember when we first met on that dockside in Boston, America?"

"I do Captain," replied Tobias.

"And now I see something more," said Captain Carden, "I see a man of honesty and integrity. Let me tell you what you should do. In common law the goods of your late departed friend could be yours – if he has no other living relatives. I am here in

Portsmouth for the next three weeks, so I will introduce you to my legal friend who will act for you in this matter."

"That is very kind of you Captain," said Tobias. "Now, about your shoes – shall I look at the problem right now."

"I would be delighted," replied the Captain, "come to my cabin where we shall be able to sit."

Tobias followed the Captain below deck to his cabin where he soon identified the problem and said that he would return the following day with his tools to mend the shoes – because he needed to find some premises that day where he could set up trade as a shoemaker and cobbler. But the Captain was not finished with Tobias just yet.

"Tobias," inquired the Captain, "why don't you set-up your shop here, aboard this ship?"

"I cannot do that Sir," replied Tobias, "this is a King's ship. It is a part of the King's Navy."

"Then you shall join the King's Navy," said Captain Carden. "Tobias, you have special skills of seamanship. Forgive me, but I spoke about you to the Merchant Captain of the *Alliance* who you sailed with to the Americas. He highly recommends you. And, I believe that you have a way about you that will take you to great leadership within the King's Navy service. We need young men like you, so I want to offer you a place in this Navy – a place that I shall create for you, given your present skills. I shall appoint you a third Lieutenant – a trainee officer in the finest Navy in the world. You will be paid very well. How about that?"

For a moment a surprised Tobias Watson was lost for words.

"Are you sure Captain?" asked Tobias, "I don't know what to say."

"Then you should just say yes," replied the Captain. "We sail to the Americas in three weeks, patrolling the waters of the Caribbean, protecting British merchant shipping from pirates. There is one pirate causing us problems right now, his name is Blackbeard and I want you aboard this ship *Thunder* to help us catch him and bring him to justice."

"Well I am honoured that you ask," said Tobias, "how can I refuse such an offer."

The Captain interrupted, "Of course we shall need to put in place the legalities of your friend's estate before we leave England. What was his name?"

"Mr. French," came the reply.

"Yes," continued the Captain, "we will see my legal friend before we sail and by the time we return in three years the matter will be settled and you, my boy, I am sure, will be the sole beneficiary of his estate."

"Three years," exclaimed Tobias.

"Yes," replied the Captain, "this tour of duty will be three years, we return in 1719. Is there a problem? Do you have anywhere else to go?"

"Well, no," replied Tobias, "it just came as a surprise. I am astounded."

The Captain turned to look out of the window at the rear of his cabin, as he thought about the word that Tobias had just uttered.

"*Astounded… Astound…* Hmm. Now that's a good name for a ship," he said under his breath.

The Captain turned to face Tobias. "Good, then you must make a decision," replied the Captain.

"Well, my decision is yes," said Tobias with a smile.

"Then it is settled Tobias, welcome aboard," said the Captain, "I shall introduce you to the ship's master and first and second Lieutenants. They will instruct you in the ways of the King's Navy – it is quite different from the merchant Navy. They will arrange for two crew members to collect your belongings and bring them aboard this ship."

"Thank you, Sir," said Tobias, "I will be very pleased to become a member of the King's Navy service.

"Good," said the Captain before murmuring under his breath, "though I wish that my lady wife, Mrs. Carden, was as decisive and accommodating as you. She has not stopped nagging me since I announced this three-year voyage. Mind you she is very busy raising our two young children, we have a boy and a girl – twins they are – and my wife has little time for me, so I am better employed at sea."

"What was that Sir?" asked Tobias.

"Never mind," replied the Captain. "Well, Tobias, you will have to purchase a gentleman's uniform to become a junior officer aboard my ship, but do not worry about the cost for the ship's master will give you a bursary – a loan – to purchase your uniform. You can pay that back when you earn enough wages. Well, what do you say, Tobias?"

"Thank you, Captain," replied Tobias, "I will help the sailors get my belongings aboard,"

"You will not," said the Captain in a firm voice. "You will show them where your belongings are Tobias, but you will not help them by assisting in carrying your own kit. Remember boy, once we have completed the formalities you will be a junior officer of this ship – you do not carry things – you have men under your command to do that for you. Do you understand."

"Well, yes Captain," said Tobias as he tried to stand to attention in an awkward manner before giving a poor naval salute.

"And my other officers will teach you that too – how to properly stand to attention and salute a senior officer," said the Captain as he pointed to Tobias's feeble attempt to salute. "And one last thing Tobias, my attitude towards you will be one of authority from now on. You will not speak to me unless I speak to you first. Your chain of command, superior to you will be the first and second Lieutenant officers and of course the ship's master. You will personally command the men below your rank, all three hundred of them, on the advice of your superiors. Beware of the men below your rank. If they detect a weakness or unsureness about you – then you are done for my boy. Listen to your superiors; follow their instruction to the letter. Do you understand?"

Tobias, who was quite shocked by the Captain's change of tone, replied, "Well… yes Sir, I will."

"Then that is all for now," said the Captain, "you are dismissed, and I shall see you aboard this good ship tomorrow, when you will sign the necessary documents that enable you to join the King's Navy. Goodbye, third Lieutenant Watson."

The Captain turned once more to look out of the window, hands clasped behind his back. It was a sign that all conversation had ended. A nervous Tobias left the cabin. Once the door had closed and Tobias had gone the Captain beamed a broad smile upon his face as he thought. 'Third Lieutenant Watson – a good day's work Captain Carden – if I do say so myself.'

A few moments later there was a knock on the door of the Captain's cabin.

"Enter," shouted the Captain.

The door opened, and Tobias once more presented himself to the Captain.

"I am sorry Sir, I cannot accept your offer of a placement aboard this ship, for yesterday I employed a young boy to assist me with my shoemaking business. If I come aboard with you and join the navy then he will perish," said Tobias.

"Who is this boy?" inquired the Captain.

"His name is William. He is sixteen years of age and he is an orphan from Wales," replied Tobias.

"Well go and get him and bring him to me," ordered the Captain. "As long as he is fit and able bodied I am sure we could find a place for him aboard this ship."

Tobias smiled at the Captain before replying, "Yes Sir, I shall return in a few minutes," before making his way back to the dock where he found William.

"Have you ever sailed aboard a ship as large at that one," asked Tobias as he pointed to *HMS Thunder*.

"No Tobias," replied William, "I have never before been on board a ship of that size."

"Would you want to?" asked Tobias.

"Well, I don't know Tobias, it's a big ship isn't it."

"Look, I shall tell you the facts of the matter," said Tobias. "Yesterday, I offered you employment and I shall honour my word. However, today I have been offered an opportunity to sail the world with some prospects being promised to me. Prospects that would far outweigh setting up a shoemaking business here in

Portsmouth. I want you to come with me on a voyage to the Americas, but you will not work for me you will work for the King's Navy."

"And if I don't come with you Tobias?" asked William.

"Well William, I would honour my commitment to you, I would decline a place aboard this fine ship and stay here in Portsmouth and open a shoemaker's shop," replied Tobias.

"I cannot let you do that," said William, "you have done enough for me already. I cannot allow you to miss an opportunity of a lifetime. I would be pleased to go to sea with you."

"That's great," replied Tobias, "it will be a three-year voyage, is that all right with you?"

"I have no-where else to go," said William, "so yes."

"We shall collect your belongings from the lodgings later today," said Tobias.

"I have no belongings" said William.

"You have no belongings?" asked a surprised Tobias.

"Only what I wear. What few possessions I had were stolen when I left them unattended at the dockside a few days ago," came the reply.

Tobias looked at his new friend with a sadness about him before breaking into a hearty laugh.

"Then, come aboard and meet the Captain of the ship. You will be issued with all the basic belongings required for a sailor's life aboard this fine ship – but, be on your best behaviour when you meet the Captain – for the final decision for you to join this mighty ship is not mine – it is his."

Soon, Tobias was back aboard with William. The Captain agreed to employ William as a cabin boy. He sent him below decks to find one of the ordinary sailors who would show him the place where he would sleep that night, put him to work, provide fresh clothing and show him the ropes over the next few months.

"Well, Tobias," said the Captain, "you are dismissed for the second time today. I shall see you aboard this good ship tomorrow, when you *will* sign the register to join the King's Navy. Goodbye, once again, third Lieutenant Watson."

The Captain turned once more to look out of the window, hands clasped behind his back. It was his signal to Tobias that all conversation had ended. Tobias left the cabin. Once the door had closed and Tobias was gone the Captain, once more, beamed a broad smile upon his face.

Chapter 10

Return to the Americas. 1717.

Word was being sent to the British Authorities in England from their Ambassador in the Americas. It concerned piracy, which was becoming common in the West Indies and along the south-east coast of the Americas.

One such pirate was Edward Teach. This pirate from Bristol, England had begun his naval career several years earlier during the Spanish war of succession, 1701-1714. Authorised by Queen Anne of England, Edward Teach, under the command of a succession of English captains, attacked foreign vessels and plundered them, returning all spoils to the monarch – less a handsome sailor's commission. Later, when the war of succession ended, there was little opportunity for state funded piracy, so this branch of the British Navy was disbanded.

Teach renounced his British citizenship and made his way to New Providence, an uninhabited area where pirates abounded. It was in the New Providence islands (now called the Bahamas) that Edward Teach met Benjamin Hornigold and joined his entourage of pirates. The aggression, boldness, and courage of this bloodthirsty Bristolian was soon spotted by Hornigold – who gave him his own sloop to master. Hornigold's pirates were very successful indeed, though they only pursued soft targets such as lightly armed Spanish ships that carried rum, wine, and cotton, which they later sold via a network of crimelike merchants. But Teach was bolder than Hornigold and wanted to chase bigger prizes. Teach wanted the valuable cargo from the almost invincible ships that carried gold and silver. Hornigold, however, was cautious and delayed pursuing such rewards because this meant taking bigger risks in the deployment of his fleet. Hornigold retired fearing mutiny among his men, who believe that Teach would make a better leader. With Hornigold gone, Edward Teach soon took command of the piracy operations and changed his name – to Blackbeard.

Captain Carden and the ship's crew of the King's ship *Thunder* would encounter Blackbeard during a routine patrol later that same year. But for now, the ship *Thunder* had crossed the stormy seas from Great Britain with a British fleet of some ten ships, under the command of Admiral Hurding, and had arrived at Boston, Massachusetts.

Before they left Portsmouth, Captain Carden, true to his word, had introduced Tobias Watson to his legal friend, a Mr. Soliman of the firm of solicitors Soliman, Soliman and Soliman. Mr. French's possessions, except for his shoes, were deposited into the trust of this noble legal firm while they made legal searches into his background. It would be many years before Tobias would know the outcome regarding the final distribution of Mr. French's estate. But for now, Tobias Watson was sure in the knowledge that Mr. French's valuable possessions were safe and in the care of this practised firm of lawyers.

It had taken eight weeks for *Thunder* to cross the Atlantic.

During that time, one moonlit night, Tobias Watson, working alone, went onto the main deck with Mr. French's shoes. He weighed each shoe with lead-shot before tying the pair together. He stood on the deck looking at the shoes and the waters below, thinking about his late departed friend – the man who had taught him to read and write – a man who had told him so many other important facts about this world in which he lived. Tobias said a prayer for his friend and former mentor before dropping the shoes into the sea waters of the Atlantic Ocean. He would hope that Mr. French would find these shoes in paradise. With a small tear in his eye Tobias Watson bid Mr. French, his hero, a final goodbye.

It was now the end of September 1717, the beginning of the season of Autumn – known as *Fall* in the Americas. The fleet of British ships planned to stay in Boston harbour for four weeks where the ship's stocks would be replenished, and the ship's crew could relax for a while before they began a three-month tour of duty down south, calling at Bath, North Carolina. After that, preparations would be made for the pursuit of these wicked pirates. Admiral Hurding's plan was to enter the area south of St.

Helena, a riskier place known as the buffer zone between Spanish controlled Florida and the British colony in the north. The fleet, with a force of eight fighting galleons planned to sink or destroy all pirate ships they encountered. The British Navy had a cunning plan. The portals in the side of each of the ships, where the cannons stood behind, were to be blocked with balsa wood and painted the colour of the ship. All signs that they were a British Navy ship of war were to be erased. They were to fly the Red Ensign flag to disguise themselves as merchant shipping and sail in convoy from Bath to St. Helena for more provisions, before sailing further south to Jekyll island in South Carolina (now Georgia), via the British Jamestown colonies. These southerly areas were loosely under British dominance, but it was a far riskier area than the relative safety of secure strong British military places to the north like Jamestown and Boston. The British had established grants of colonial land to Native Indians and had made friends with indigenous tribes such as the Yuchi, Muscogee and the Cherokee people.

For now, Tobias was enjoying a break in Boston. It would not be long before his ship containing some three hundred sailors and one hundred soldiers headed for Jamestown, in the Royal county of Virginia; where the Admiral of the Fleet, Admiral Hurding, would order that military manoeuvres would be practiced offshore with the rest of the British fleet under his command. Once the manoeuvres were complete the fleet would separate. Captain Carden's ship, *Thunder,* would sail for Charleston further south while the rest of the British fleet would remain at sea. Admiral Hurding had planned a special mission for Captain Carden and his crew.

William, the boy Tobias Watson had met in Portsmouth and who had secured a place on the ship, *Thunder,* had settled in well. As a cabin boy aboard the ship he had become a popular member of the crew for his enthusiastic hardworking nature. Only one encounter with a less savoury character aboard the ship – a drunken ageing sailor who had taken an interest in William's possessions – had tarnished the voyage. This awful sailor had stolen two, one-shilling coins from him and was quite a bully. It had spoiled the journey. Tobias was there to defend his young friend, for this awful sailor had counter accused William of a similar offence – of stealing tobacco from his bunk, even though it was well known that William did not smoke. Both the sailor and William were put in the cells below deck for two days while the truth of the matter was sought. But in the end, it was proven by Tobias that William had not lied and was innocent of all accusations. William was therefore released, to go about his usual ship's duties. But for the sailor the outcome was quite different. He was hung by the neck until he was almost dead, then thrown overboard where sharks would eat him alive.

It was in the early afternoon when the giant ship *Thunder* entered the harbour to be moored in the dock of Charleston.

"Send this order, Mr. Mechan," called out Captain Carden from the poop deck, "I want thirty soldiers to guard this ship twenty-four hours a day. The soldiers will guard in three watch-shifts. These are difficult and dangerous times. Also, the sailors onboard ship will also stand guard – each ship's watch shall comprise of fifty men situated at various stations around the ship – including the crow's nest, for the three watch-periods."

"Very well Sir," replied the ship's master, Cornelius Mechan, "I will send your orders to the crew."

Mechan relayed the order to third Lieutenant Watson, who had been waiting at his post on the main deck. Watson began implementing the Captain's orders.

"Can't be too careful, Mechan," said the Captain, "this town is full of dangerous people. The fugitive black slaves have formed bands of vigilantes with those renegade Red Indians. Why I do declare and wonder how ordinary white folk in this town sleep in their beds at night."

"I am not sure they sleep easy," came the reply from Mechan, "we are on the edge of the British controlled areas. Any further south and we could come into conflict with the Spanish, on their territory."

"I know all that," interrupted the Captain.

“Might I be permitted to ask why we are here Captain? It seems much more than just stalking pirates; we would be safer out at sea with the rest of our fleet.”

“You think deep and well my friend,” replied the Captain. “Yes we would be safer at sea, but Admiral Hurding has asked us to carry out a special mission.”

“May I ask what it is?” enquired Mechan.

“Yes, you may,” replied the Captain, “but first you should assemble all of my officers in my cabin at six bells.”

“Does that include the juniors, the second and third lieutenants?” inquired Mechan.

“Of course it does,” replied the Captain.

Later that afternoon the officers assembled before Captain Carden in his cabin. They comprised of the ship’s master Cornelius Mechan, the first lieutenant, Mr. Darley, second lieutenant, Mr. Edmund Price and third Lieutenant, Tobias Watson.

“My officers,” said Captain Carden, “I have assembled you here this afternoon because we have a mission of great importance. Our trading partners, the Cherokee Indians, have learned of two Spanish hostages that the Oconee Indian tribe have captured. One, by the name of Ronaldo Delaguila who is a diplomat, an ambassador of Spain. He is a very important man whose knowledge of Spanish political and military matters and their secrets would be of considerable interest to the British government. We need to trade with the Oconee Indians. We must secure this enemy diplomatic man into our care, so that we can transport him to London. This man should not be underestimated for you would not think him to be a powerful Spanish administrator, as he dresses rather scruffy and wears brightly coloured clothing. This is quite out of character for a diplomat, and he smiles quite a lot too.”

“Is it a problem that he smiles?” asked master Mechan, “many men smile.”

“He laughs a lot too,” replied the Captain, “but this is his subterfuge. Be warned, he makes out he knows things that you do not. He is a very clever man. He is always quoting complex mathematical formula that one has never heard of, or he quotes the mis-cited words of famous people. He is a master of mis-information, yet his smile and laughter make you think he is quite frenetic and stupid. He has a way about him that leads you into his clutches and allows you to believe that he is harmless, but he is not."

"But why is our government interested in him?" inquired the master.

"Do not worry yourselves about the politics of our country my good man – leave that to our interrogators in London – our task is to get him back to the United Kingdom of Great Britain alive and unharmed," replied the Captain.

"And the second hostage?" inquired the first Lieutenant.

"She is not to be harmed either – she is a Spanish Princess, a woman said to be of great beauty and demeanour. She is the Princess Serafina of Seville, in the province of Andalusia in southern Spain. She is of no importance to the British – except that she is a Princess in the court of the Kingdom of Spain and probably, once in our custody, would be a useful bargaining tool for our government diplomats," replied the Captain.

"Might I be permitted to speak?" asked Tobias.

"Be quiet," said first Lieutenant Darley.

"Let him speak," said the Captain.

"We are not at war with Spain, why are we taking Spanish hostages?" asked Tobias.

"It is a *cold* war my boy," replied the Captain. "We are not firing shots at the Spanish or sending men into battle for we have an uneasy truce with them. But we do undermine their system of government and authority wherever and whenever possible – and before anyone questions this, the Spanish are doing the same to the British. I have no doubt that one day Spain and the United Kingdom of Great Britain will formally be at war once more. Does that answer your question third Lieutenant Watson?"

"Yes Sir," replied Watson.

"Right, let us continue," said Captain Carden. "The next destination of this most important mission is Jekyll Island, which is further down the coast of the Americas. Once there, volunteers from this room will take a troupe of twenty of our best soldiers and travel some one hundred and fifty miles inland to meet with the chief of the Ocanee Indian tribe. From there you will go with them to a place known as *Little Water* on the shores of Hog Creek bay where you will rendezvous with the Ocanee tribe of Indians and make the trade."

"What are we to trade with?" asked the ship's master, Cornelius Mechan.

"Metal cooking utensils, metal tools, spades, forks, cloth and whisky – that sort of thing Mr. Mechan," came the reply.

"Whisky… I thought it would be that. Do you think it wise Captain that we should give the Indians whisky?" asked Mechan.

"Ours is not to reason why," replied the Captain, "this deal has been arranged at the highest government levels and it is not for us to question. It is a very important deal. Anyway, trading whisky to the Indians is no different to giving whisky to our own men, all men get drunk on the stuff. Now let us discuss the detail. But first, I will need two officer volunteers from this room."

"I will volunteer," blurted out Tobias.

"Good man," said a surprised Captain as all other eyes looked at Tobias.

"Me too Sir," called second Lieutenant Price.

"Well done," whispered Tobias to Price.

"Good man Mr. Price," called the Captain, "the rest of you shall be dismissed. Go about your usual business aboard this ship. Watson and Price, you stay where you are."

The group broke apart and began to leave the room.

"You fool," whispered Darley to Price as he passed him, "you will be dead before the month is finished. It is a dangerous place out there in Indian country – beyond Jekyll Island."

Second Lieutenant Price did not respond but looked at Watson, shrugging his shoulders before giving a look of indifference.

"Mr. Mechan," called out the Captain.

"Yes Sir," replied Mechan as he turned to face the Captain.

"Mechan, would you inform the sergeant at arms that he will be required to escort our second and third Lieutenants into the Americas countryside. Send him to this cabin straight away."

"Yes Sir," replied the ship's master.

Within a few minutes there was a knock on the Captain's door.

"Enter," shouted the Captain.

A soldier with the rank of a sergeant embroidered on his crimson jacket entered the cabin.

"Sergeant Flinders reporting for duty," he called.

"Good man," said the Captain, "now gather round the table with us and we shall discuss your mission. I take it Sergeant Flinders that you know second and third lieutenants Price and Watson."

"Yes" came the reply, "we have spoken on several occasions aboard this ship."

Watson and Price nodded.

"Good," said the Captain, "right then gentlemen, you are to travel to a place known as *Little Water* at Hog Creek bay."

Captain Carden pointed to an area shown on the map.

"It is around here somewhere, though we do not know the exact location. It's about one hundred and fifty miles directly inland from the seaport of Jekyll Island. It will probably take you about one month to get there as the terrain is difficult. You should cover just over seven miles a day in travel distance. I will provide you with a copy of this map. You will need to take three Conestoga wagons with you – each one fully laden with the goods that we are to trade with. The three wagons containing the goods will form part of the trade, so you are to leave them with the Indians. There will be a further two Conestoga wagons that will be going on this journey, which you will bring back to Jekyll Island. One will hold your provisions and tents that you will sleep in at night – the other will contain a mobile military jail box. These Conestoga wagons are the largest type we can secure; each one can carry up to three tons of goods or equipment and are twenty-two-foot-long and five feet wide. Each of those twelve-foot-high framed canvas covered wagons will be pulled by six horses. That is two more horses than is necessary for each of the wagons, but this extra horsepower should ease the burden on the horses over the rough terrain. On your outbound journey, the jail wagon can be used as accommodation for you two Lieutenants or for anyone taken sick. On your return journey you must secure the prisoners in the jail carriage, which will be used to transport those political prisoners. All five wagons are sitting targets for the indigenous renegades and that is why the army is going with you. These wagons and horses have already been prepared by the Governor's men and right at this moment are in Charleston. Soon they will be in transit by cargo ship to Jekyll Island. Sergeant Flinders, you and your men will go with these horses and wagons, aboard the various cargo ships destined for Jekyll Island. There are also another twenty horses that will be ready to be fully saddled for the twenty men under your command. Sergeant Flinders... you shall select your preferred soldiers for this mission first thing tomorrow morning. Take your best men sergeant."

"Yes Sir," came the reply as he stood to attention.

"Oh, and Sergeant Flinders," continued the Captain.

"Yes Sir."

"There will be twelve spare pack horses to take with you."

"Very good Sir," replied Flinders.

"Sergeant Flinders, you shall command this mission and provide the necessary protection in order that the goods we are to trade are delivered to the Indians, and you shall bring back the hostages," said the Captain, "you shall take my second and third lieutenants with you."

"Very well Sir," replied Flinders.

The Captain looked at Watson and Price, "and you two young men shall drive two of the wagons containing the trading items to their destination and assist with the navigation across this rough terrain. You shall also enter negotiations and make the trade with the Indians. Guard these goods with your life for any indigenous renegades who find out that whisky is among your cargo will attack. Over there, in my storage chest," the Captain pointed to an old wooden chest, "is a spare quadrant that you can take with you to plot and record your positions on the maps. Watson, as you are most competent in navigational matters you shall take the lead on plotting and recording the route to the destination. You shall bring back to me a plotted map so that it can be used for future missions to Hog Creek bay at *Little Water*. On this mission however, we have a Muscogee guide who will personally take you there. His name is Sequoya. He will take you to Oconee Chief Attakullakulla at *Little Water*. But I need three more men to drive the remaining wagons. Price…"

"Yes Sir," replied Edmund Price as he stood to attention.

"Mr. Price," called the Captain, "you will select three abled bodied men from the crew of this ship; those who have experience of horses. They shall drive the three remaining wagons to the destination of *Little Water* under your command. You shall all travel to Jekyll Island aboard the cargo ships along with Sergeant Flinders and his men."

"Thank you, Sir," replied Price, "I shall attend to this matter as soon as this meeting is concluded."

"Oh, one last thing," said Captain Carden, "after your mission is completed, I and this great ship, the *Thunder*, will be waiting for you at Jekyll Island. Good luck to you all."

The meeting was dissolved. Both Watson and Price made their way to the main deck.

"Now, where are we going to find three sailors with experience of horsemanship?" asked Mr. Price woefully as the two men walked the main deck.

"I am not sure sailors are best suited to horses," replied a smiling Watson.

"Wait a minute," said Watson as he stopped, to ponder on a thought he had.

"What is it, Watson?" asked Price.

"Young William the cabin boy, I am sure he told me that he and his family kept a farm in Wales and trained horses!" said Watson.

"How old is he?" came the reply.

"Sixteen or seventeen," said Watson, "but no, I suppose that he is too young to be out in the province – to be put in danger."

"We may have little choice," replied Price, "it does depend if we can find older sailors with some experience of horsemanship. Can we not take soldiers instead of sailors for they would be experienced equestrians?"

"Well, the Captain was quite specific," said Watson.

"I'll tell you what Mr. Watson," replied Price, "I will return to the Captain's cabin and clarify the situation."

"Is that wise Mr. Price?" asked Watson.

"I am not questioning the Captain's orders – just clarifying them," said Price.

Price disappeared down the hatch and returned five minutes later.

"He is not in a good mood today," said a deflated Mr. Price.

Tobias Watson smiled at his friend's predicament before asking in a light-hearted manner. "I take it the Captain is not impressed with your request for clarification Mr. Price?"

"Indeed, he is not," came the reply.

"And the outcome?" asked an inquiring Tobias Watson.

"We are to take sailors to drive the horses on the wagons and not soldiers," said Mr. Price.

"Well, then it is settled," said Watson with a smile as he patted his friend on the shoulder, "let us call all-hands on-deck over the next few hours. We have some urgency about us Mr. Price – in finding sailors who can control horses."

"Very well, Mr. Watson," said Price, "call the men to the main deck."

Soon, around two hundred men were on deck and the question was asked about horsemanship. Several men put their hands-up and after some questioning, three of their number were selected for the mission. Their names were Woods, Hamilton and Sykes.

"Well that was easy," said Tobias Watson, "there are many men aboard this ship who have experience of driving horses – many more than one would think."

"I am surprised," replied Price, "well, we have no need for the boy William. It is for the best."

"I agree," replied Watson.

"Right you men. Woods, Hamilton and Sykes," called out Price. "Tomorrow morning at first light you will come with third Lieutenant Watson and I to the town's stables at Charleston where we will lodge. We will spend about a month in Charleston preparing ourselves with horses in readiness for our trip to a place called *Little Water*. Once training is completed those horses and wagons will be loaded onto cargo ships and we shall go with them to Jekyll island. From there we shall undertake our mission."

"May I ask Sir?" inquired Sykes, the tallest and shiftiest sailor among the three, "what is the nature of our mission?"

"You may not," replied Price, "it will become apparent in due course. For now, all you men need to know is that each one of you will steer a wagon and I and third Lieutenant, Mr. Watson, will also each drive a wagon – making a convoy of five wagons in total. We shall be under the protection of the Army who will ride with us. The return mission to a place known as Hog Creek bay, *Little Water* is expected to take about three months."

Tobias continued, "Men, you are to be especially vigilant on this journey and each of you will be armed with a pistol and musket. Keep them close by at all times."

"I don't think I like the sound of this," murmured Woods, as Hamilton nodded in agreement.

"What was that Woods?" called Price.

"Nothing Sir," replied Woods.

"Has anyone among you men any further questions?" asked Watson.

"Will we be going into Indian land?" asked Hamilton.

"Yes, we will," replied Watson, "do you have a problem with that Mr. Hamilton?"

"No Sir," came a faltering reply.

"Then we are done for today," called Price.

The gathering of men faded away from the main deck as they went about their individual business. Watson and Price went below deck. Sykes, Woods and Hamilton remained on deck gathered in this group of three men, discussing their task ahead to *Little Water*. Watching on, not far away from them, at the aft part of the deck was first Lieutenant Darley.

"Sykes… come here man?" Darley called.

Sykes walked down the main deck to Mr. Darley.

"Yes Sir," said Sykes.

"So, you and those other two men are going on this mission," said Darley.

"Yes Sir," said Sykes.

"Well, let me tell you Sykes. Just between me and you. This mission that you embark upon is dangerous, do you understand my meaning?" said Darley.

"I think I do," replied a nervous Sykes.

"Come closer Sykes," ordered Darley.

Sykes moved very close to Darley. Their two bodies no more than ten inches apart as they stood facing one another.

"It is a one-way journey that you embark on," whispered Darley.

"How do you know that?" asked Sykes.

"Oh, believe me Sykes… I know," came the reply.

Darley continued in a firm-mannered low-keyed voice, "Sykes, me and you go back a long way and we have had… shall we say…certain arrangements over the years."

"Yes Sir," replied Sykes.

"And you have done very well out of our, *arrangements*," said Darley.

"Yes Sir," replied Sykes, "what is it that I can do for you this time Mr. Darley?"

"Good… I am glad that you understand my meaning Sykes. Now let us make a new *arrangement*, here and now," said first Lieutenant Darley, "I understand that among a consignment of goods that you are to transport to Little water are several dozen bottles of whisky."

"Whisky?" replied Sykes, "I don't know about that Sir."

"Yes, I can assure you that it is whisky," said Darley, "and I want you to do something for me. I want you to remove eight bottles of Whisky from the stock before the consignment leaves Charleston and put them aside for me. Remember Sykes that this *arrangement*, like all our previous arrangements, is between you and me. No one else must know about it."

"And what's the deal?" asked Sykes.

"You have had your deal Sykes," came the reply.

"Well, begging me pardon Mr. Darley. Have I missed something? I see no deal before me Sir. I guess you will sell the whisky – a very valuable commodity in this part of the world – so I am guessing Sir, that you will give me a percentage of your profit," said Sykes.

"The deal that I have given you is in saving your life Sykes, there will be no exchange of money between us," Darley replied.

"I don't understand," said Sykes.

"The mission you are about to embark on, to *Little Water,* is a death mission," replied Darley. "No one will return alive. The Indians will kill you, scalp you and take the goods that you seek to exchange for a couple of lousy Spanish hostages. You will need to make yourself unavailable for the mission – if you understand my meaning Sykes – that is, once you have delivered the whisky to me."

"How am I going to make myself unavailable for the mission Mr. Darley?" asked Sykes.

"Use your imagination Sykes," came the reply.

Sykes thought for a moment.

"It's a big risk Mr. Darley, getting hold of those bottles of whisky. What would happen if I did not deliver the whisky to you and became ill or something just before the wagons rolled?"

"Then I will shoot you myself as a suspected deserter of his Majesty's Navy… that is… I will shoot you when you run away from me," replied Darley.

"But I won't be running," said Sykes.

"Oh, you will be running Sykes," replied Darley, "with my pistol up your arse, you will be running alright. And who is the Captain going to believe when you are dead on the deck and I tell him that I have done my duty in preventing a coward and deserter from escaping."

"I get your point," said a worried looking Sykes, "how do I get the whisky to you Mr. Darley?"

"I have made some enquiries," said Darley. "The bottles of whisky are in sealed wooden crates marked as kitchen cooking oil. Each crate contains a dozen bottles. There are thirty-six crates being dispatched. So, a mere eight bottles will not be missed; not if you take one bottle from eight of the crates. The difference in the weight of each crate will not be noticeable. You will need a hammer and a crowbar to get the lids off the crates Sykes. And if you like Sykes, take a ninth bottle for yourself."

"That's very magnanimous of you Sir. What you ask of me is a big task," replied an apprehensive Sykes.

"Nonsense man," replied Darley, "you will have at least a month to complete your task before the goods leave by ship for Jekyll."

"I am not so sure," said Sykes as he rubbed his chin, "how will I know where the whisky is stored?"

"Well, I shall tell you now," replied Darley. "There is a storage room at the stables in Charleston. This is where the whisky is stored. No-one but very senior naval officers above the rank of a Captain know it is stored there."

"Well Mr. Darley, with all due respects how do you as a Lieutenant know that the whisky is stored in that building?" inquired Sykes.

"I have my ways," replied Darley, "but that is of no importance to a reprobate such as yourself, Sykes,"

Darley continued, "As I have already said, the whisky is hidden in the storeroom in wooden boxes marked as kitchen cooking oils. The stores are well away from the main-buildings, so it would be easy for a skilled thief to gain entry; and you are a skilled thief Sykes, are you not? A simple hasp on a side door can be removed and replaced without anyone knowing you have been in the room."

"But isn't it guarded by soldiers," replied Sykes.

"No," came the reply from Darley, "there are a few soldiers about the area, but I am sure a man like you Sykes can get in and out without being noticed. So, you *will* – under the cover of darkness, break in to the stores and take the bottles of whisky. You may have to break into the store more than once as you may not be able to carry eight bottles on your own on one journey, but I shall leave the details to you. About a quarter of a mile from the ranch, somewhere in the woods, you will bury the eight bottles."

"But how will you know where I have buried them?" replied a worried Sykes.

"You will be at the ranch for about a month Sykes, so I shall visit you towards the end of your time there and you will tell me where it is hidden," said Darley.

"Well I don't know about this," said Sykes as he rubbed his chin with worry.

"I shall leave you for now Sykes and bid you farewell. Remember, just me and you know about this. Tell no-one," said Darley, as he disappeared down a hatch leading to his quarters below deck.

Chapter 11

Sequoya.

The following day Watson and Price headed into the town of Charleston, where they met with Sergeant Flinders and his twenty men. They were to begin their horsemanship training at a farmstead known as the Black ranch. It was the largest of its kind in this part of the Americas. The area comprised of some five hundred horses spread out over a hundred acres of penned land. To one edge of the land, near the river, were the stables, a large timber building that held a further ninety horses. Next to the stables were several accommodation blocks for the men and women who ran the ranch. The blacksmith's workshop was next, adjacent to two buildings known as the *stores*. In front of the stables was a penned training ground where the livery staff would exercise the horses.

The sixty-two horses that were to be used by Price, Watson, and Flinders on their mission to *Little Water* had been under special military training and grooming for the past six months. The owner of the stables, a man named Barry Stewart, had organised the training. He was there to meet them.

"This is a big order for me," said Stewart, "the King's government wanting the best sixty-two horses from my stocks, plus saddles and grooming kits as well as five Conestoga wagons."

"It cannot be that big an order Mr. Stewart," replied Flinders, as he stood beside the fence looking into the paddock, where some twenty-five of the horses were being paraded by the grooms. "After all, the King's army amounts to several thousand men in the Americas Mr. Stewart. You must have supplied bigger orders than this to the army before now?"

"See those twenty-five horses Sergeant Flinders?" continued Stewart as he pointed towards the paddock, "well those twenty-five horses are my finest. They are the best that I have. The British Army don't normally ask for the finest horses. But they did this time. What is the Army planning? What are you up to Mr. Flinders? We don't want no trouble around here."

"Mr. Stewart, I can assure you that you will get no trouble," replied Flinders. "I shall take these horses from you today and issue them to my men. We will stay nearby in that field over there for the next month while my men familiarise themselves with the horses and receive some training from your people."

"Familiarise, is that what you call it?" said Stewart, "I was told by the army chiefs that your men needed horse training to learn the skills of riding a horse and looking after its wellbeing."

"Yes indeed," replied Flinders, "you are correct, my men may be somewhat lacking in horsemanship because they are infantry soldiers."

"Where are your cavalry men?" inquired Stewart with a wry smile.

"They are not available, Mr. Stewart," replied Flinders, "now, I have twenty men that need to be introduced to twenty of those finest horses. Would you also introduce my men to your grooms? I need one groom for every three horses and those grooms to be assigned exclusively to the Army for the next month. We must saddle the horses today and begin practice. We have one month to turn this rabble of horses into a military fighting force."

"More like a rabble of men than horses I should say," said Stewart under his breath.

"What was that Stewart?" asked Flinders.

"I said, I will do my best," replied Stewart. "I see that you also have Naval men under your command Sergeant."

"Yes," replied Flinders, "they are to be trained on driving the wagons and looking after the pack horses."

"Send your Naval men over to the stable office and my manager will show them the wagons; I'll sort out the grooms for your regular army men – if you would be kind enough to follow me please."

Watson and Price had been standing by the fence and heard this conversation between Flinders and Stewart.

"Mr. Watson," whispered Price as he lent over towards his fellow officer, "are you not glad that we command a single ship's crew and not a rabble of horses that might run off in different directions." Price followed his statement with a hearty laugh.

"An interesting thought Mr. Price," replied Tobias Watson as he smiled, "yes… I think that I would prefer a single ship with all my men contained within its periphery – with full sails and a brisk wind to carry us on our journey."

"What do you know about horses?" inquired Price as they both watched a single horse rear-up amongst a herd of colts, throwing its rider to the ground.

They moved forward to help the unhurt rider. Each man grabbed one arm of the rider before they lifted him to his feet.

"Very little," replied Tobias as he let go of the rider's arm, now that he could see that the slightly dazed man was standing on his own account.

"Where I come from," continued Tobias, "a place called *Copperas Gap* in England – there are very few horses or mules. The Lord of the Manor owns all horses and mules in the village. Indeed, when I was living in Copperas Gap I rented a mule from the Lord of the Manor to go about my business and I can assure you that they are smelly beasts. No, I prefer ships and the sea to these somewhat uncontrollable horses and mules. They seem to have a mind of their own and are rather noisy when they are unhappy, Mr. Price."

"Like you Lieutenant Watson, I too prefer the sails about me aboard a fine sailing ship; where I am in control of my own destination," said Price with a smile, "I do believe that it is not easy for a man to control the destination of a herd of horses, so I think that we shall have some fun and some pain while learning about these huge beasts over the next four weeks."

The two men stood side by side in their fine deep blue naval uniforms – both wearing their tricorn hats with some style – watching the horses and riders on parade.

"Watson, Price, would you come with me?" interrupted Sergeant Flinders.

"Yes, certainly," called Price as he made his way towards him, "what can we do for you Sergeant?"

"Mr. Price," said Flinders, "would you take your men to the stable office, find the manager and take some training from them in looking after the horses and riding aboard the wagons.

"Yes, Sergeant Flinders," came the reply from Price, "we would be delighted," as he turned towards Watson to express a false smile.

Price then turned toward his men who were standing some twenty yards away. "Sykes, Hamilton and Wood, come here men. We have some horse training to undertake."

"Don't need no training. Just give me the wagon and the horses," said Sykes under his breath.

"Don't get funny with the Lieutenant," muttered Woods.

"He can't hear me from here," replied Sykes.

"No, but I bet he can lip-read," interrupted Hamilton with a laugh.

The three men slovenly walked towards their commanding officers.

"Stand up straight man," barked Price. Sykes immediately stood to attention. The other two men did the same.

"Right men, follow me," shouted Price, "let us find those wagons and horses."

Soon, all five men had found the grooms. After various introductions they prepared to receive specialist training in looking after horses in this wild American environment.

"You will be better off without your Tricorn naval hats," said one of the grooms.

"Why would that be?" asked Tobias Watson.

"The temperature in this part of the world gets hot, dry and dusty during the summer months so you would be best suited to wearing a wide brimmed hat that keeps the sun off your head and face," came the reply.

"Our naval tricorn hats do much the same," replied Tobias Watson.

"But the brim of your navy hat is of a design that curls-up at the rim to form a cavity on its three sides. The brim of your hats will be full of dust and grit in no time and they will weigh heavy on your head,"

"A very good point," said Watson, "Where can we get some of these wide-brim hats? What are they called?"

They don't seem to have a name – other than a *wide-brimmed cowboy hat*," replied the groom. "I think they were adapted from the Mexican style of hats in the south west. I shall speak to Mr. Stewart and see if we can supply you with some."

"Thank you," replied Watson, "now let us get to work. Where are these horses and wagons?"

"Follow me Mr. Watson," replied the groom.

The next four weeks passed quickly. Before long all horsemanship training had been completed. Tobias Watson had enjoyed his time at the ranch, sleeping under the stars at night – often beneath a cloudless sky – looking up at the amazing patterns of twinkling celestial bodies that stretched into infinity. To wonder, in bewilderment of the perplexity of this majestic universe and to ponder on the complexity of this phenomenon. This sky above him was indeed a magical place that could only have been created by the miracle of a supreme being. Only the Lord of the Universe could have created it. And then, Watson wondered, where, in the vastness of it all – where in this gigantic cosmos, was his one and only true love, Molly Moffatt? He wondered what she might be doing at that very moment in time. How he missed her. How he loved her so much. How he wanted to hold her in his arms once more. If only he could find a way to be with her right now, he would surely go. But he could not. He would have to wait – for that future moment in time – as Molly had told him on that day at Copperas Gap when she appeared before him in his dream. She told him that when it is his time to die, on Earth, they would be together – for all eternity. How he yearned for that moment. And then, he remembered that day when they enjoyed their last minutes of physical moments together. It was when they danced the dance of true love at Copperas Gap and held each other close.

Tobias much preferred the outdoors to that of the confines of the military tent he had been issued with – but only on a warm night. His daily training wasn't just about horses. Wagon control and maintenance had also been learnt. Repairs to the wheels or the timber frames were necessary, as were repairs to the canvas covers that covered the entire top framework of the carriage – though the stitching of wagon canvas was of little difference to that of a ship's sail.

One dark night as he lay in the field looking at the stars, Tobias heard a rustling noise coming from the storeroom nearby. He looked towards the building but could not see anything as he was too far away. He crept towards the stores to find out what it was. It was fortunate that a full moon provided some light for him to see as he got closer. He saw the outline of a tall man by the door to the stores. It was Sykes.

"Sykes, what are you doing?" called Watson as he moved nearer to him.

Sykes was indeed surprised and hollered back, "Nothing Sir."

"Stand still man," replied Watson as he made his way towards Sykes.

"What are you doing here Sykes?" asked Watson again as he looked around the area. He pulled the hasp on the door of the storeroom to find that it was secure.

"I could not sleep Mr. Watson," replied Sykes, "so I went for a walk."

"You went for a walk, in the dark? A likely story," said Watson.

Watson could see that Sykes was indeed tense, and Sykes was not about to tell him the truth. As the door to the stores was secure there was little else Watson could do. "I have marked your card Sykes," said Watson as he looked at him, "now get back to bed, we have a busy day tomorrow," he ordered.

"Yes Sir," replied Sykes.

Watson watched the silhouette of Sykes walk away from him. He thought to himself that he would need to keep an eye on this man over the next few days.

The next morning first Lieutenant Darley paid a visit to the ranch. He approached Watson and Price as they were tending to some horses.

"How are you getting on with your horsemanship training?" called Darley.

"Very well Sir," replied Price, "and what brings you here Sir?"

"Oh, just interested in seeing the King's finest sailors become skilled horsemen," came a sardonic reply from Darley.

"Well Mr. Darley," interrupted Watson, who had picked up on Darley's sarcasm, "we have been training with these horses and wagons for almost a month now, but we could do with a hand. Can you help us?"

Watson held the reins of one horse and guided it towards Darley.

"I will not touch horses," replied Darley as he stood back, "horses and my good self, do not mix well."

"Can I help you with anything else Mr. Darley?" asked Watson.

"No Mr. Watson," came the reply, "go about your business. I shall take a tour around this establishment and see for myself what our men are doing."

"You may find that the smell of a stable is quite different from that of a ship's deck Mr. Darley," said a smiling Watson as he winked at Price.

Darley walked away towards the training pen where Sykes, Woods and Hamilton were on horseback.

"I don't like that man," whispered Price to Watson, "there is something about him."

"Hmmm..." replied Watson, "but he is our senior officer. We have no choice but to accept his presence."

By this time Darley had reach the fence of the pen and waved to Sykes, who dismounted his horse before walking towards him.

"Now look at that, Mr. Price," said Watson, as he nudged his friend and pointed in the direction of Sykes and Darley.

"What would Darley want with Sykes?" replied Price.

Both men watched for a moment. It was clear that the conversation between Sykes and Darley was more than just a passing congratulations or courteous small talk. But they were too far away to hear anything. Then, Sykes said something to Darley and pointed to the woods in the distance. The resounding expression on Darley's face indicated that he was not happy.

"What's over there in the woods?" said Watson to Price.

"Trees I think," replied Price as he dismissed the question and patted Watson on the back in a friendly gesture. "Come, Mr. Watson we have no time to watch a senior officer make small talk. We have work to do with these horses and I assure you I will keep my eye on Sykes."

"Thank you, Mr. Price," came the reply.

They led their horses back to the stables before washing for dinner.

During the previous month Sergeant Flinders and his men had been assigned their individual horses which each man was to personally look after during the mission. Their training was satisfactory, and soon it would be time to take all horses, wagons, goods and accessories to the docks – ready to be transported to Jekyll Island.

Sykes, Hamilton and Woods were indeed proven to be fine equestrians, though the banter between the three of them was a little edgy at times. But Watson was on to something with Sykes. He did not know what it was. Call it intuition, perception or just an officer's awareness that an honest Naval man often has towards something that appears to be inexplicably wrong. He also thought that there was something suspicious about Darley. Why did Darley turn-up at the stables unannounced and take a great interest in Sykes? Darley took no interest in anyone else, just Sykes. But as Darley was a senior officer to Watson he was not about to question a man above his own rank or indeed tell Mr. Price – for fear of being seen to be mutinous towards a senior officer without some firm evidence. 'But what could Darley and Sykes be up to,' thought Watson? It had to be illegal.

The following day everything had been stowed aboard three cargo ships and they were ready to sail on the following high tide for Jekyll Island.

That morning Sykes appeared beside the ship with Woods and Hamilton. He was limping.

"What is wrong with your leg man?" asked Tobias Watson.

"I fell off a horse yesterday evening and I fear I have broken my leg Mr. Watson," replied Sykes.

"Did either of you men see this happen?" asked Watson of Woods and Hamilton.

"No Sir," came their respective replies.

"Have you seen the doctor, Sykes?" inquired Watson.

"Not yet Sir,"

"Here... let me have a look at your leg. Remove your breeches and lay yourself down on the gangplank," ordered Watson.

"It's okay Sir, no need for that. I shall go and see the doctor right now," replied Sykes.

In a firmer voice Tobias Watson once more boomed his orders at Sykes, "Lay down man."

Sykes, with the help of his two shipmates removed his breeches and lay down on the gangplank while Watson visually inspected a large bruise on his shin. Then he prodded Sykes leg with a stick.

"Does that hurt?" inquired Watson as he poked Sykes leg.

"Ouch, yes Sir, it does. I don't think I am fit enough to go to Jekyll Island."

"Hmmm," muttered Watson as he stood up. "Well, your leg is bruised and if I knew no better, I would have thought that someone has hit your leg with a heavy implement."

Watson took a step backwards to view Sykes in full.

"Stand up man," Watson.

"It's broken Sir," called Sykes.

"Stand up man, "ordered Watson once again.

Woods and Hamilton offered to help Sykes.

"Leave him be," ordered Watson, "let him get up himself."

Sykes rolled over onto his 'good' leg and grabbed the rope that extended up the gangplank. With some huffing and puffing he pulled himself upright and stood to his feet – though it was clear that the weight of his body was resting on his good leg.

"Right," ordered Watson, "very slowly, I want you to transfer your body weight from your good leg to your so-called bad leg. That is an order man."

Sykes made various growling and grunting noises as the attributed pain in his bad leg supposedly got greater as he began to transfer his body weight.

"Stop," shouted Watson.

Sykes transferred his body weight back onto his *good* leg.

"Sykes, you are a malingerer. Your leg is not broken at all and I fear that you have deliberately bruised your leg to relieve yourself from this important mission that we are about to embark on."

"No Sir… I really want to go to Jekyll Island," shouted Sykes.

"Caught you out," whispered Hamilton as he leant over to whisper in Sykes ear, "I told you it wouldn't work. You got me to bash your leg for nothing."

Sykes glared at Hamilton.

"What did you say Hamilton?" asked Watson.

"Nothing much Sir," replied Hamilton, "I asked if Sykes needed assistance to get back to his hammock."

"Oh, he won't need much assistance," said Watson, "push him up the gang plank and get him onto the main deck of this cargo ship. He can lay in the sun until he gets better. Me-thinks that he will soon be up and about once the heat of the day embraces him. Well, get on with it you two men."

Hamilton and Woods helped Sykes get onto the main deck where they assisted him to lay down. They gave him a vessel containing some drinking water.

"Problems, Mr. Watson?" asked Lieutenant Price as he came walking by.

"Not really Mr. Price," replied Watson, "I think we have a malingerer among our ranks."

"Have you solved the problem?" inquired Price.

"Yes Sir, I have solved the problem for the moment, but I have some doubts about this man's intentions. I could leave him behind, but we must not reward skivers and malingerers," replied Watson.

"Quite right," replied Price.

"But as a precaution I think we should take young William with us on our mission. As I have mentioned before, I believe him to be skilled in horsemanship," said Watson.

"Do you think it wise to take a young boy on this dangerous mission?" inquired Price.

"It might be more dangerous without him, if we lose the skills of Sykes," came the reply.

Lieutenant Price thought for a moment.

"Very well Lieutenant Watson," said Price, "go and get young William. He can also help with the cooking. We leave for Jekyll Island within the hour."

"I shall go and get him right now," replied Watson.

Watson returned within the hour with young William.

A few days later they arrived at their destination, but it was not Jekyll Island. They sailed past Jekyll Island and landed further up the river of Fancy Buff Creek, at the docks of Brunswick town – where, over the next five days, all goods and horses were unloaded from the three cargo ships. A scouting party had arrived some two weeks earlier and had cleared an area to make camp. They had also built some horse pens.

"We shall camp here tonight by Brunswick docks and settle ourselves down," called Flinders to Price. "In three days we shall form a wagon train and head for *Little Water* – one-hundred and fifty miles inland."

Sykes, whose leg had made a remarkable recovery, was standing on a grassed area under a tree surveying the area of Brunswick with Hamilton and Woods. They watched the soldiers erect their army issue tents.

"I don't like it here," said Sykes.

"Neither do I," replied Woods, "it's a bit bleak. I hope there are no Indians around here. I don't like Indians, they scalp people. Especially white men." Woods brushed his forefinger across his forehead in an allusion to being scalped, before breaking into a hearty laugh.

"I can't see no Indians, so you are quite safe my friend," Sykes boomed as he laughed in a nervous manner, "anyway, they are frightened of us *white men,* so I guess they have all scarpered."

Suddenly, someone from behind tapped Sykes on the shoulder. Sykes turned around – only to jump backwards before falling to the ground at what he saw.

"An Indian," he exclaimed. Sykes pulled his pistol from his belt and aimed the barrel at the Native American standing before him. It was point-blank range. The Indian had an expressionless look about his face. He stood before Sykes with his arms folded – staring down at the dishevelled sailor.

"Stop," shouted Tobias Watson who had seen what was happening.

"Put your pistol away man and stand up," Watson screamed, "his name is Mr. Sequoya. He is our Indian guide who will take us to Little Water at Hog Creek bay."

Sykes looked at Watson, then back to the Indian.

"I said put your pistol away Sykes," said Watson.

"No Indians around here! Is that what you said Sykes?" exclaimed a laughing Hamilton.

Sykes dropped his outstretched arm and stood to his feet, before putting his pistol away.

"This Indian is our friend; he is from the Muscogee tribe," called Watson.

"Well, he shouldn't go sneaking up on people," retorted Sykes. "I could have killed him with a single shot."

"I have come to scalp you," said Sequoya in broken English as he displayed a deadpan facial expression.

Sykes reached for his pistol once more as a worried looking Woods took a step backwards.

"Put your pistol away," shouted Watson, "can you not see man that the Indian is making fun of you."

"That's all we need," said Hamilton, "an Indian with a sense of humour."

Sequoya smiled at Hamilton's statement. He uncrossed his arms and pulled a hunting knife from a scabbard attached to his belt.

Woods, Hamilton and Sykes took another step backwards as Watson looked on.

"I should teach you men something about this place," said Sequoya, as his wide-open eyes pierced into the retinas of the three sailors with equal velocity. Sequoya then looked towards Watson as if to ask permission.

"Continue," shouted Watson.

Sequoya looked back towards the three men standing before him; each man standing statue-like with fear in their hearts. This imposing Indian brave was wearing a breechcloth that hung from his front and back waistline which was tucked into a leather belt secured around his waist. The belt also supported a pair of full length, fringed, buckskin tunic leggings. Upon his back and chest he wore a matching fringed buckskin fully sleeved shirt that was adorned with small beads, shells, some animal teeth and wooded jewellery. He wore colourful moccasins upon his feet and, attached to a black band around his head, two feathers from a golden eagle. He was an imposing sight to these white men who had not seen such warriors of his calibre before today. The sailor's eyes were fixed on Sequoya's knife as they wondered what this Native Indian was about to do.

Sequoya put the knife back into its scabbard.

"Now that I have your attention, you reckless Englishmen, I should tell you that I could have killed all three of you in an instant. You make the noise of a herd of buffalo and you are not aware of what is around you. Look at the sky… the trees…the bushes… the valleys and the hills of this land. Look around you. If you listen, they will talk to you." Sequoya turned around and, with his back to the three sailors, he held his arms to the sky.

"Look around you," he continued, "look at the tracks in the ground and the squawking or the whistling animals. Look at the soldiers over there. See what they are seeing, hear what they are doing and when you can do all of that, you will see what I see."

"What's he on about? Did he just call us stupid and get away with it." whispered Sykes?

"No," replied Woods, "He said reckless… not stupid."

"Well it's the same thing to my mind," replied Sykes, "I don't have to put up with this Indian – friendly or not."

Hamilton and Woods did not respond further. Their eyes were fixed upon Sequoya.

Sykes took a silent step forward towards Sequoya who was still facing away from him. In an instant the Indian turned around to face Sykes, his legs apart, his knife already drawn – his body positioned in a defensive stance, but the Indian said nothing.

"You will have to be quicker than that," laughed Hamilton.

"That's not funny," replied Sykes.

"Come," beckoned Sequoya to the sailors, "put your pistols to one side and I shall teach you things that you must know in this wild and wonderful country."

"Wait," shouted Tobias Watson, "let me get Lieutenant Price. I assume that you are to teach us the ways of Indian combat to my men. I would wish that Mr. Price and I be a part of this training."

"That is correct," replied the Indian, "yes, I will teach you some of the things you will need to know. Go and get your friend, Mr. Watson."

Soon, Mr. Price and Tobias Watson were standing with the others and facing towards Sequoya.

"I want each one of you to attack me…one at a time. I will turn around and face away from you, so I shall not see you approaching. But remember, I will hear you," said Sequoya, "here, take this small piece of wood. You shall pretend that this is a knife."

"You go first Sykes," called Tobias Watson.

Sequoya handed the piece of wood to Sykes – it was about six inches long and one inch thick – before turning his back on him.

Sykes sneaked up on the Indian but within seconds was dispatched to the ground. He lay flat on his back looking skyward. The wooden weapon Sykes was holding had been removed by the Indian and thrown some ten-foot away.

"He's good," exclaimed Woods.

"Well, Woods, you can go next," called Lieutenant Price as he picked up the wooden 'knife' and threw it to him.

Woods attempted the same approach; he too was thrown to the ground by the Indian. Before long all five men had been beaten by the Indian.

The Indian stood to face all five men.

"Now, I want all five of you to attack me at the same time," called Sequoya, "on my command when I say the word – *begin*."

"Are you sure?" said Sykes, "we will easily beat you, five men against one."

Sequoya raised both of his arms and stood in a defensive position – one leg in front of the other – as he took a moment to look deep into the eyes of each one of the five sailors. Watson, Price, Sykes, Hamilton and Woods stared back at the Indian for what seemed ages, but it could only have been a few seconds.

Suddenly Sequoya yelled his command, "BEGIN."

The five sailors rushed at the Indian but before long each one in turn was pushed to the ground as Sequoya grabbed and wrestled them. It was over in less than a minute.

The Indian folded his arms before he looked down at the five sailors sprawled out on the grass. "Yes, I am sure Sykes," replied Sequoya, "and I have now proven it to you."

Tobias Watson got up from the ground to brush away the grass and twigs from his uniform.

"Well done Mr. Sequoya," said Watson.

The Indian interrupted, "my name is just, Sequoya, I am not a Mister."

"Sequoya," Watson continued with a smile, as he held out his hand to shake the Indians palm, "I am impressed with your combat skills."

Sequoya did not shake hands but kept his arms crossed before saying, "Now, we shall practice this combat some more."

Tobias Watson dropped his arm to his side before replying, "A good idea Sequoya, let us practice this Indian style combat of yours."

William, the cabin-boy, who had been watching these altercations shouted, "Can I have a go?"

"Yes of course you can William," called out Lieutenant Price.

"Now, I shall teach you all of the other things that I think you should know," said Sequoya.

They spent the rest of the day practising the art of wrestling and the different styles of personal combat, including the art of a surprise attack. William joined in too.

Later that day as the sun began to sink low in the sky, Price called a halt to the training before commenting.

"Well, thank you for your instruction in combat skills Sequoya," he said.

"You're welcome," replied the Indian. It was a phrase that seemed to catch-on in later years by the population of America.

Sequoya continued, "It is better that I travel with people who are instructed in combat. Those who can surprise others with the silence of a snake and who can fight as effective as a hungry mountain lion."

"Did you understand what he meant?" whispered Sykes to Woods.

"Nope," said Woods. "This Indian talks in riddles."

"Who cares though," said Hamilton, "I am glad he's on our side."

"I agree," added Woods.

"Well I don't like him," exclaimed Sykes, "this Red Indian is too clever for his own good. He is too big for his boots."

"But he ain't got no boots," ridiculed Hamilton, "he wears moccasins."

Woods and Hamilton laughed once more at Sykes expense.

"Now I have many things to do," exclaimed Sequoya with a smile, "I shall say goodbye for now. Have a nice day, won't you all."

Five slightly ruffled sailors and one cabin-boy looked-on at this powerful one-man army; this amazing Native Indian man known as Sequoya. They watched him as he jumped onto his horse and rode, bare-back, into the dusty American distance.

Chapter 12

Indian Pow wow.

The following morning the wagons were hitched, the goods were loaded, and they began their long journey from Brunswick town to Hog Creek bay, *Little Water.* It was an impressive sight for the few local people looking on. Sergeant Flinders led the men driving the wagon train and beside him was Sequoya the Indian scout. Following behind were ten British soldiers, riding their individual horses: two by two. Behind the soldiers, Tobias Watson drove what was described as a *baggage wagon;* it was a wagon used to store and transport barrels of gunpowder and ammunition for their pistols and muskets. Sitting beside Tobias and enjoying the wonderful experience was young William. Behind them was Hamilton, driving a wagon fully laden with goods. And behind Hamilton's wagon was Sykes, Price and Woods in that order, each driving a wagon containing additional trading goods and the most valuable of all commodities – water. Two water barrels were lashed each side of each wagon – making twelve in total. Enough water for the entire company on this single journey. Following up the rear of this convoy of wagons were ten more of the King's soldiers.

"A nice day William," stated Tobias, as he held the reins of the horses – pulling the wagon they were both riding on.

"Yes Sir," replied the boy.

"No need to call me Sir, William, when it's just you and me and we are not aboard ship," said Tobias. "I have not had much of a chance to speak with you since we left England. How are you getting on in the King's Navy?"

"It's enjoyable but hard work Tobias," came the reply.

"Well, William, it's time for a rest from the trials of seafaring," said Tobias, "here we are travelling across a beautiful country, where the sun shines. We are miles and miles from the coldness of our home towns and enjoying every minute of our experience."

"I would not miss this experience," exclaimed William.

"William, what do you hope to achieve in the Navy?" asked Tobias.

"Oh, I don't know," replied William in his broad Welsh accent, "maybe to make the grade of a Lieutenant Officer, just like you Tobias, and save enough money from my wages to buy a small farm in Wales."

"You need a trade young man," said Tobias, "when are you planning to go back to Wales?"

"Not for a while," came the reply, "I love the adventure of the Navy, but I also miss the valleys of my home country and the people who live there. I will probably give the Navy a good chance, perhaps another ten years – then I would have hoped to have saved enough money to buy my farm."

"Well, in that case there is ample time for me to teach you the ways of the shoemaker and cobbler," replied Tobias. "I'll tell you what William, once we are back aboard the ship, *Thunder,* I will begin teaching you the basics of shoemaking. I still have the tools of my trade in my cabin, but I do not use them much these days as I am too busy aboard ship with my navy duties."

"That's very kind of you Tobias," replied William.

"Well William, I did say before we joined the Navy at Portsmouth that you would be my assistant. When you go back to Wales you will be able to earn yourself a living as a cobbler," laughed Tobias, "I will speak to the Captain to see if he can spare you some extra time so that I can teach you what I know – after all, two cobblers aboard the King's ship are better than one."

William smiled, and thanked Tobias once more. They began to talk about the tools of a cobbler's trade – a boring subject for most people – but to a trained shoemaker and his new apprentice an enlightening experience, no doubt.

The journey to *Little Water* was uneventful and, as ordered by Captain Carden, Tobias Watson kept in close contact with the Indian scout Sequoya who was showing Flinders the wagon train route across the flatlands. It was Tobias Watson's task to take locational measurements with his sextant at various intervals throughout their route and to plot these positions onto a map for future reference. The British believed that there would be further trade deals with the Indian tribe at *Little Water*. Future expeditions would need a certified route map because it was not clear if Indian scouts like Sequoya would always be available to show British trading organisations the best route across this wild country.

The decision to take young William on this expedition had been a good one. For Tobias would often take a spare horse and ride ahead of the wagon train to plot the course on his map, leaving William alone to drive the baggage wagon.

They arrived at Hog Creek, *Little Water* five weeks after they had started their journey. On the banks of the river was a small Indian camp comprising of a few cone shaped tents called teepees. Next to those were animal skins stretched over poles, drying in the afternoon sunshine and women washing clothes in the small river that flowed down to an enormous lake – the shoreline of which was no more than fifty yards away. The lake itself stretched away into its vast distance where a mountainous snow-capped range could be seen about forty miles away – though it was difficult to judge the distance. Other women nearby were basket weaving or tending to children. Horses were tethered to hitch poles. On the lake were canoes – some with two, some with three Indian occupants. All were fishing. About a thousand yards off the shore was a small island no bigger than an acre. The island had several timber and stone huts on its land, with smoke billowing from one of the chimneys.

Chief Attakullakulla of the Oconee tribe was sitting beside his teepee, on a ground mat made from animal hide. He was facing the river. Several of his warriors sat beside him. Smoke from a hand-pipe was pulsating into the air.

"I have come to see you, the great chief Attakullakulla," called Sequoya from his horseback position. Sergeant Flinders was mounted on another horse beside him – followed by a troupe of some ten soldiers, each wearing their standard crimson uniforms, with brass buttons gleaming in the sunlight. Two white leather straps were convoluted across each soldier's jacket, making an X across their chest; one strap holding a bayonet and the other a musket cartridge box. To complete their uniform, they each wore grey trousers, white shirts, black boots and military black caps with their colourful regimental badges affixed.

"I, Chief Attakullakulla greet you once again, my friend Sequoya," came the reply in his native Indian tongue, "put your camp of wagons and men over there on the nearby pastureland and afterwards we shall talk and smoke the pipe of friendship until nightfall."

"What did he say?" whispered Flinders.

"Sergeant Flinders," said Sequoya, "order your men to make camp over there on the pasture. Tonight we rest and tomorrow we shall trade our goods."

"Very well," replied Flinders.

"And when your men are settled, you, I, and the two naval officers, Watson and Price, shall smoke the ceremonial pipe with Chief Attakullakulla to seal our trade covenant," called Sequoya.

Sequoya turned to Chief Attakullakulla, "thank you Chief, we shall set camp to relieve our weariness and we will smoke the ceremonial pipe to our joint covenant before the sun is low in the sky."

"I shall see you later my friend," replied Chief Attakullakulla.

Flinders ordered his men to set up the camp in the nearby pasture.

Sykes, Hamilton and Woods were unhitching the horses after setting the wagons in their final positions on the campsite. They arranged the wagons in a large circle, infilled the gaps with tree branches and rope to pen the horses.

"We're surrounded by Indians," said Sykes.

"Well, aren't you just the brightest person in the toolbox," replied Woods, "what gives you *that* idea?"

"You know what I mean Woods," replied Sykes, "don't get funny with me or I will take my bare hands to you. These Indians will murder us in our beds if we give them a chance."

"Sykes, you have been saying that for the past month," called Hamilton.

"Well it's true," said Sykes, "they are going to take the trading goods and kill us all."

"Why would they do that Sykes?" replied Hamilton as he watched the army pitch their tents.

"Because I've been told," said Sykes.

"Yes, I know," sniggered Woods, "you have said that enough times on this journey. You have said that Lieutenant Darley told you the Indians intend to murder us – but what does he know… huh?"

"If it were dangerous, Lieutenants Watson and Price would not be here," said Hamilton.

"Oh, really," said Sykes, "they are just a couple of boys pretending to be officers and men."

"Well, I trust them *boys* better than Darley; there is something dangerous about that man," said Hamilton.

"Well he's the clever one," replied Sykes.

"Why's that then?" said Woods wryly.

"Coz he ain't here… he's a hundred and fifty miles away – back aboard the safety of the ship, that's why!" declared Sykes. "He ain't stupid."

"Well Sykes, you have had your chances to escape on this wagon train and you never took it," exclaimed Woods.

"That's coz you two would not come with me," retorted Sykes.

"Who's a little baby then, afraid of the dark," jested Woods as he poked him in the chest with his index finger, "a tiny whiney little baby who can't do *nuffing* on his own."

"Shut-it Woods," declared Sykes, "I ain't frightened of nothing or no-one."

"Except Indians!" mocked Hamilton as both he and Woods laughed.

"Look! We are here now at *Little Water*," asserted Woods, "the trade between us and those Indians will probably be made tomorrow. Then we shall be on our way back to the ship before the sunset of the following day."

"And with your scalp in Indian hands, Sykes," said Hamilton as both he and Woods fell about laughing.

"Is there a problem?" came a voice from behind the canvas on one of the wagons.

It was young William. He drew back the canvas covering and stepped over the driver's seat from inside the wagon.

"What have you just heard?" demanded Sykes.

"Pretty much all of it," replied William.

"You had better keep your mouth shut young-un and don't go telling no Lieutenants what's been said."

"Does it matter?" spoke William, "were you really going to escape Mr. Sykes because you are frightened of Indians?"

Woods and Hamilton laughed out loud once more.

"Don't get funny with me boy," pronounced Sykes, "one word from you boy and I will kill you myself."

"That's a bit harsh on the boy Sykes," called Woods, "he is only a boy."

"A boy with a big mouth," came the reply.

"William, you best go and help tend to the horses in the pen," said Woods, before he looked back at Sykes. "You leave the boy alone Sykes."

William looked at Sykes before he scurried towards the sixty or so horses tethered in the centre of the pen, but he was close enough to hear the rest of Sykes conversation.

"Pick on boys – do you Sykes?" said Woods, "what kind of man are you?"

Sykes looked away for a moment. He had a worried look on his face. "I could do with a drink," he said.

"Come on," said Hamilton, "calm yourself down Sykes. Let's get this camp set-up and then we can get some grub and fill our bellies. It's been a long day. There's plenty of water in the wagon barrel if you are thirsty Sykes."

"I don't want that sort of drink you fool," said Sykes, "I mean a proper drink like whisky."

"Well we haven't got any whisky," said Woods.

"We have plenty of whisky in those crates over there in that wagon," came the reply.

"That's not whisky! Its cooking oil; that's what's written on the crates. And, that's a sure-fire way to get yourself hung, stealing the King's cooking oil," replied Woods.

"It's whisky I tell you, and they won't miss a bit of it," said Sykes, "anyway we'll all be dead by morning with our scalps hanging in the trees. At least we shall die with a smile on our faces and a whisky in our bellies."

"The sun's got to you Sykes," said Woods.

Later that afternoon Sequoya, Flinders, Watson and Price went to the Indian camp where Chief Attakullakulla and his warriors were seated.

"Sequoya, it is good to see you once more my friend," said Chief Attakullakulla, "sit down with your associates and introduce them."

The men sat down on the dry animal skins that had been stitched together – which separated their backsides from the dusty, grimy earth.

"I bring you Sergeant Flinders of the British Army and Lieutenants Price and Watson of the King's Navy," said Sequoya in a native Indian language.

"The King and the British, who is he?" inquired Chief Attakullakulla.

"The British. It is they who sit before you, oh wise chief," said Sequoya as he lifted his arms to encompass Watson, Price and Flinders in figurative speech.

All three British men smiled, though they did not know what Sequoya had said.

"Is *British* the name of this tribe?" inquired Chief Attakullakulla.

"That is correct oh wise one," replied Sequoya, "and the King is their chief."

"Where is their King Chief? Why is he not here?" demanded Chief Attakullakulla.

Sequoya held up his hands, both palms facing towards the Chief. This indicated calmness and reckoning among Indians.

"Sergeant Flinders," called Sequoya, "who is your King?"

"King George the 1st," replied Flinders.

“And how many people in your tribe?” asked Sequoya.

Flinders was not sure. “Three million,” called Price.

“What is three million?” asked Sequoya.

“Many thousands of people, more than all the horses and cattle and all the trees and raindrops in this vast land of the Americas,” said Price.

“Well done Mr. Price,” whispered Watson, “I did not know you were a man of knowledge.”

“Wise one, Chief Attakullakulla,” beckoned Sequoya in his native tongue, “the Chief King George of the British tribe is beyond the seas many days and weeks sailing away from here. He has a tribe bigger than all the trees, horses, cattle and raindrops that you have on this land. He must stay with his tribe and look after his people.”

The Indian Chief's eyes opened wide, “Big Chief King George,” he exclaimed in a deep voice – in awe of the information he had received. “I see and understand that Big Chief King George is too busy to come to Pow-wow. Instead, he sends you Flinders. You must be a very important warrior of your King. Now we smoke – we smoke the sacred pipe before we Pow- wow tonight when it is dark, when the fires of our ancestors shall light the sky.”

“What did he say?” said Flinders… “I heard my name spoken.”

“We smoke the sacred pipe. You shall take some smoke Mr. Flinders,” said Sequoya.

“I don't much like smoking tobacco,” replied Flinders.

“It's much more potent than tobacco, Flinders. You must take the sacred smoke otherwise you will insult the Indian chief and his tribe,” said Sequoya, “it is a pungent smoke so, just take a draw on the pipe – hold the smoke in your mouth for a moment and then blow it out. Do not inhale it into your lungs for it will almost certainly make you ill.”

“Very well, if I must,” replied Flinders.

Sequoya continued, “Mr. Watson and Price, you must smoke the pipe too.”

The pipe was passed around each man, starting with Chief Attakullakulla, who took a draw from the pipe which was made of reed, wood and deer horn.

"We trade tomorrow," said Chief Attakullakulla, "our Spanish prisoners are a diplomat and a Princess. They are secured on the island you see before you in the middle of the lake. I will send a boat in the morning to fetch them. What do you bring me in return?"

"The British have brought many implements for cooking. They have brought tools for farming – spades, forks, cloth and grain. They have also brought whisky," said Sequoya.

The Chief smiled. "Whisky, my favourite. We shall have some whisky now," he ordered.

Sequoya turned to Flinders, "Could we bring one crate of Whisky from the wagons for Chief Attakullakulla?" he asked.

"I'll get it," said Tobias Watson as he stood to his feet.

A few minutes later he was standing beside the wagon where the whisky was stored.

"William," called Tobias.

"He is not here, came a slurred reply." It was Sykes who was laying under the wagon.

"Where is he Sykes?" asked Watson.

"Don't know, don't care," came the reply.

Tobias bent down to look at Sykes under the wagon. He was not wearing any clothes – except for a pair of briefs. "You know Sykes… my judgement tells me that you have been drinking."

"That's correct Sir," came the slurred reply from Sykes as he rolled over to look at Watson. Sykes lay on his side with his head held in his hand, "I just had a little taste of the…"

"Where are your clothes man," demanded Watson.

"In the wash," replied Sykes with a hint of sarcasm.

Suddenly Watson confirmed that Sykes had been drinking, for an empty bottle of whisky was laid beside him.

"My God man," shouted Watson, "if that is the King's whisky you have stolen then you shall be executed."

"Does it matter. We'll all be dead soon," came the garbled reply from Sykes.

"Get out from under that wagon," ordered Watson.

"You'll have to come and get me," said a playful Sykes.

Watson stood up. He beckoned two soldiers sitting beside a camp fire about fifty yards away.

"Arrest that man," came the order from Watson.

"Very well Sir," one soldier replied as they both grabbed Sykes by the feet and dragged him from under the wagon.

The soldiers lifted Sykes to his feet – one either side of him. They held him firm in their grip.

"Look at you man," shouted Watson, "you cannot stand on your own two feet. Whose whisky have you been drinking?"

Watson bent down once more and stretched in-between the two wagon wheels to grab the empty bottle. He stood up and looked at the label. It was indeed the King's whisky. It had a blood stain on the whisky label.

"Where did you get this whisky?" demanded Watson, "and where has this blood come from? Are you bleeding man? There is blood on this bottle." Watson looked Sykes up and down. Except for some superficial blood on his hand he could see no cuts or injury on the man's body.

Sykes did not respond. By now he was in a semi-conscious condition, though he kept repeating the words 'I told you Mr. Darley.'

"What's Darley got to do with this?" asked an enraged Watson.

"I told you Mr. Darley," repeated Styles – his head rolling about on his neck – his eyes almost closed.

"You'll get no sense out of him," said one of the soldiers, "he's drunk."

"Wait here," ordered Watson as he clambered onto the wagon.

Tobias Watson pulled back the canvas on the wagon to check on the goods stored inside. The sight that he saw was horrific. It was a sight that would stay with him for the rest of his life. Sykes had indeed stolen a bottle of whisky from one of the crates, for a timber case had been broken open. The lid to the crate, marked cooking oil, was leaning up against the side of the wagon. A crowbar lay beside it. On top of the crates was Woods. He lay on his back, arms outstretched. He was dead. His eyes were open, as was his mouth. His face had the look of horror about it. A dagger was protruding from his body, quite near to his heart. The entire area was a blood-soaked mass of revulsion. Tobias Watson felt physically sick as he looked at this terrible sight. It seemed that not a single crate of whisky – and there were thirty-six of them stacked in a pyramid shape – had escaped being stained by the blood of that unfortunate sailor.

"Quick," shouted Tobias to the soldiers outside of the wagon, "call more soldiers to stand guard and go and get Sergeant Flinders. He is with the Chief Attakullakulla of the Indians.

The soldiers did as they were asked. Their voices were heard calling their companions from the nearby camp.

"Do not let anyone enter this wagon until I give the order," shouted Watson.

Within minutes Sergeant Flinders and Sequoya were outside the canvas door to the wagon. Tobias Watson drew back the curtain.

"This man has been murdered," whispered Tobias Watson.

Sequoya stood on the neatly stacked blood-soaked boxes that formed this pyramid of containers and knelt beside Woods body to inspect the dagger.

"Do you know who owns this dagger?" Sequoya asked.

"No," replied Watson. Flinders also indicated that he did not know its owner.

Sequoya gently closed Woods eyes with his fingertips before saying an Indian prayer to the Gods. He then pulled the dagger from the body and wrapped it in a small piece of animal skin.

"Take this dagger Flinders," as he handed the grizzly package to the Sergeant. "Keep this dagger safe until we decide what to do and do not clean it."

"Very well," replied Flinders, as he took the wrapped dagger.

Sequoya looked to the back of the wagon – towards the pyramid of wooden boxes. He clambered over the top of the pyramid of boxes and was out of sight for a moment.

"There is worse," came the voice of Sequoya from the other side of the stacked boxes, "it is the boy William... he is also dead."

Tobias rushed towards the boxes of whisky and clambered over them to reach the other side. It was another horrific sight. The boys throat had been cut from ear to ear. He lay amongst the congealed blood that had soaked into the wooden crates.

"No," screamed an enraged Tobias, "what wicked person would do such a thing?"

Tobias could look at this gruesome sight no longer. With tears in his eyes and sorrow in his heart he climbed out of the wagon. On seeing Sykes – held upright between the two soldiers – he lunged towards him, fists clenched and began battering his face in a frenzied attack. Other soldiers pulled Tobias Watson away; for if they had not, Tobias Watson would have killed Sykes on the spot.

The following few weeks were a blur for Tobias Watson. The boy William, who he had befriended in Portsmouth and who he had encouraged to join the King's Navy was dead. Tobias blamed himself for William's death, for if he had not brought the boy to the Americas and worse, had he not asked him to go on the wagon trail to *Little Water,* then William would still be alive.

Flinders and Sequoya dealt with the matter of Sykes. The case was clear once Sequoya had found the third sailor, Hamilton. The Indian tracked him down and found him some ten miles from the camp. Hamilton was innocent of any crime excepting that he saw the felony but panicked before stealing a horse, to make his escape.

It seemed that William had taken it upon himself to guard the whisky – after he had seen Sykes take an interest in the wagon containing the alcoholic goods and heard him talk to others that he wanted a proper drink. Sykes entered the wagon to steal a bottle. When William confronted him, Sykes killed him in a brutal manner. Hamilton and Woods heard a noise and got onto the wagon to see what was happening. They were both outraged that the boy had been killed and Woods lunged at Sykes with his own dagger. But Sykes got the better of him and killed him too. Hamilton then ran.

The final proof was the blood-soaked clothes that belonged to Sykes. He had buried them nearby in a drunken attempt to conceal any evidence. Sequoya tracked the clothes and brought them to Flinders.

Two days later, Sykes was hung by the neck until he was pronounced dead. Flinders then had the task of deciding what punishment Hamilton should receive. But, before that decision was made Hamilton decided the outcome for himself. He committed an act of suicide. The man could not live in the knowledge that he, in some small way, was a part of this horrific murder of a seventeen-year-old boy. And for what? A bottle of whisky that Sykes had stolen.

Hamilton stabbed himself in the heart at the first opportunity. No one knew how he got hold of a knife, for he was in the custody of the army, but it was suspected that one of the soldiers guarding him provided this instrument of death.

Hamilton's body was taken to a small area outside of the Indian camp and buried alongside his shipmate Woods, while William was buried in a sacred Indian burial ground. As for Sykes – well, no one knows what happened to his corpse.

There was no dancing that night in the Indian camp and no whisky to be drunk. Chief Attakullakulla ordered a period of mourning and assisted where possible with the arrangements, which helped Flinders and his men.

The trade with the Indians took place a few days later. Soldiers emptied the blood-stained crates, burnt the timber boxes and delivered the cleaned-up bottles of whisky to Chief Attakullakulla along with other goods that they had agreed to trade. This exchange of goods and Spanish diplomats took place on the river bank, near Hog Creek, at a river crossing known as *Knick-knock* way.

The Chief of the Indians kept his side of the bargain and freed the two hostages. They were placed into the care of Sergeant Flinders. The hostages were the Spanish diplomat, the ever-smiling Ronaldo Delaguila and the beautiful Princess Serafina of Seville from the province of Andalusia, Southern Spain. But there was a third hostage. He was Mr. Montez, also Spanish and a diplomatic protection officer.

Tobias did not take much notice of the prisoners at the beginning of the homeward bound journey. Sometimes he smiled at the beautiful Princess when she took evening exercise, after a long day locked in the wagon. Towards the middle of their journey, at the many camps they set up during the homeward trail to Brunswick town, he and the Princess began to speak about ordinary things: for she could speak perfect English. Tobias became attracted to her and it was clear that she liked him too. He and the Princess spoke about William every day. She helped him come to terms with his loss. She used her social skills to help Tobias deal with his personal grief. She was a woman who had a breath-taking beauty that no man could deny. Yet, not even her extraordinary beauty or the astonishing personality of this delightful Princess excited Tobias, for he was grieving the loss of his true friend, William. It was a loss so great. It was as much of a loss as that of his mentor, Mr. French, and almost as great a loss as Molly, his one true love, who lost her life at *Copperas Gap* a few years before. Could Tobias have done more to save William? Could he have done more to save Mr. French? And what of Molly? What could Tobias have done to save Molly? Those were the nagging questions that Tobias kept asking himself. It was those questions which suppressed his usual personality during those long days and weeks on the wagon trip back to Brunswick town.

They drove only two of the five wagons home. Only the baggage wagon and the prisoner wagon. Price rode the prison wagon and Watson the other. The remaining three wagons were given to the Indians.

And during the journey back to the ship at Brunswick harbour Tobias wondered – 'What exactly had been achieved?

Three Spaniard's taken into the care of the King's army for the price of William. It didn't seem worth it to Tobias. There was no comparison.'

Chapter 13

Return to Brunswick town.

Early on the morning of May 29th, 1718, the wagon train arrived back at the docks near Brunswick town. Sequoya, the Indian guide, bid them farewell. But before he left town Tobias Watson went to see him.

"Thank you, Sequoya, for everything that you have done," Watson said, "you have been a real friend to me in my times of trouble and sadness. You are an inspiration to all Englishmen for you have knowledge and skills that my countrymen admire."

"Goodbye my friend," replied Sequoya, "it has been a privilege to ride with you. May the Gods be with you for the rest of your life and for all eternity. Perhaps we shall meet again."

Sequoya mounted his horse before riding into the distance.

The three Spanish prisoners were transferred from the Conestoga wagon onto His Majesty's ship *Thunder*. Tobias Watson thanked the Princess for their many wonderful conversations. He then joined Lieutenant Edmund Price and Sergeant Flinders before reporting to Captain Carden in his cabin aboard the King's ship. The three men stood before the Captain as he sat at his desk reviewing Flinders' daily log of events during the journey to the Indian camp at *Little Water*.

"Sergeant Flinders," said the Captain, "I should thank you and your men for providing protection for the people of this mission. It looks to me that this assignment was a complete success, but I will need to study your report in detail before making my final conclusion."

"With respect Captain, I would not call it a complete success," replied Flinders.

"Well, I would disagree," said Captain Carden, "you have brought the Spanish prisoners back to this ship. Indeed, you have brought an extra prisoner."

"What is his name? Let me see," said the Captain as he began to answer his own question.

The Captain looked at the logbook on his desk.

"It is a Mr. Montez," interjected Tobias Watson.

"Thank you, Watson," replied the Captain, "what do we know about him?"

"Sir," said Watson, "he is a diplomatic protection officer of little importance."

Watson continued, "Might I just say that the mission could never be deemed a success because we lost four of our own King's Navy men."

"We are always losing men, it is the nature of being in the King's Navy – there are plenty more *would-be* sailors waiting to fill the ship's decks," came the reply.

"But Sir – this is different," replied Watson in a firm manner.

"Lieutenant Watson, I don't much care for your tone of voice this morning," said Captain Carden as he stood to his feet, "tell me – please tell me why this mission is different?"

"The boy William was murdered," replied Watson, "and it is my fault."

"It is not his fault," whispered Lieutenant Price.

"What was that Price?" inquired the Captain.

"It was not Lieutenant Watson's fault that young William was murdered," repeated Price.

"Mr. Price," said the Captain, "please explain how this boy was… as you say, murdered."

"He was murdered in one of the Conestoga wagons at the Indian camp in *Little Water* by one despicable sailor whose name was Sykes. Young William was guarding the King's whisky," replied Price.

The Captain thought for a moment before looking at Watson.

"Lieutenant Watson," the Captain asked, "is this the same boy you introduced to me at Portsmouth, a cabin boy who joined this ship at the same time as you did?"

"Yes Sir," replied Watson.

“The boy was your friend?” inquired the Captain.

“Yes Sir,” said Watson, “and it was I that put him on this mission, a mission that led him to his death.”

Captain Carden turned away to look out of the rear windows of his splendid cabin. After some moments thought he turned to Flinders, “Who were the others that were killed?”

Sergeant Flinders told the whole story from beginning to end to a sympathetic Captain Carden. When he had finished his story Carden, once again, turned away towards his cabin window in a moment of reflection.

“It seems to me Mr. Flinders,” said the Captain, before turning to face the three men, “that young William was a hero. I shall see to it that he is considered for a posthumous award from the Admiralty. Does he have a next of kin?”

“No Sir,” said Tobias Watson, “he told me once that he had no known blood relatives who were alive.”

“That’s a pity,” replied the Captain, “so you Tobias, as his friend, will accept any military award – if, and when it arrives. It could take up to three years.”

“I would rather have my friend alive than any award,” replied Watson.

“Lieutenant Watson,” retorted Captain Carden, “it is not your fault that William is dead; I want you to remember that. Now, about this fellow Woods who you say tried to save William. I think he should also receive a posthumous award. It will bring a small pension for his blood relatives.”

“Really Sir?” asked Price.

“Yes Price,” replied the Captain, “Sergeant Flinders, would you meet me here tomorrow at two bells. I need to read and understand your report before I ask you more questions. Tomorrow I will need to speak to you in some detail, before I make my submission to Admiral Hurding.”

“Yes Sir,” replied Flinders.

“You are dismissed,” said the Captain.

Flinders, Price and Watson turned about to leave the room.

“Not you Mr. Watson,” called the Captain.

The Captain waited for a moment while Flinders and Price left the room.

"Pull up a chair and sit yourself down third-Lieutenant Watson," ordered the Captain.

Tobias Watson did as he was told. Both men sat at the Captain's desk, facing each other.

"Mr. Watson," sighed the Captain, "you are a very fine junior officer and I have said many times before that I see something in you that will one day make a fine Captain in the King's Navy."

"Sir, with respect," replied Watson, "flattery is not something I would wish to hear at this moment."

"Listen to me Tobias Watson, it is not your fault that William was killed," said the Captain.

"Oh, but it is my fault Sir, I took him on this mission and now he is dead."

"But did you ask William to guard the cases of whisky on the day he was murdered?"

"No Sir, I did not."

"Then who did?"

"No-one Sir, he decided to guard the whisky himself after he overheard a conversation between Sykes and the two other sailors," replied Watson.

"Had William come to you and told you that the whisky needed to be guarded because of the conversation he had overheard, would you have told this boy to guard it?" asked the Captain.

"No Sir, that type of job requires the strength of a man. Mr. Price and I would have taken it in turns to guard the goods. Remember Sir, the goods were marked as cooking oil. It would have looked odd if we had gotten the soldiers to guard such a worthless commodity. No-one was supposed to know that the cases marked as cooking oil were really whisky."

The Captain stood up. "Mr. Watson, it is my opinion that you were not responsible for the boy's death. Do you understand? I shall make that fact a Navy order if necessary, a military order which you must obey."

A tear began to trickle from the left eye of Tobias Watson; then another from his right eye.

"He was only a boy," came Watson's blubbering reply.

"You are no more than a boy yourself Watson, you cry like a boy," replied the hard-hearted Captain, "how old are you Watson – 23, 24 years old?"

"I am twenty-two," replied a distressed Watson, "and William was my friend. I was his only friend in this world."

The Captain's mood changed. He walked around his desk to Tobias and patted him on the shoulder.

"You, my boy, shall let all those tears out right now," said the Captain. "Sometimes we men must cry, but we must do it in private. Do you understand?"

"Yes Sir," replied a weeping Tobias as he looked up at the Captain.

"I shall leave you now Tobias," said the Captain, "you shall remain in this cabin until I return. Let no-one else into this room and do all your crying in private. Do it now. Let all your sadness and anger out of your body. Hit the wall with your bare fists if it makes you feel better. And when I return in about one-hour I do not want to see a blabbering boy. I want to see a man, an officer in the King's Navy. A man so strong that he can face the world and make important decisions with impunity. That is an order Tobias Watson."

Tobias did not reply. The Captain left the room. Tobias did what he was told. This was a natural human moment; no naval order could change that. It was the first time he had been alone with himself since William's death; where this undiluted wretchedness, worthlessness, despondency, sorrow and sadness that he felt for himself was drained from his body, to be dispatched into the annals of his personal history. He let all that anger and upset out of his mortal frame in one final burst of energy that lasted a full hour. It was a spectacular resounding victory for this tearful individual. It was to be the last time he would grieve for his young friend with tears in his eyes, but it was not to be the last time he would remember William with fondness and positive memories that the late, young hero, deserved.

About two hours later the Captain returned. Lieutenant Watson stood to attention as the Captain entered the room.

"Are you done, Lieutenant Watson," asked the Captain in his usual abrupt manner.

"Yes Sir," came the reply from Watson.

"Good, then we shall continue with the matter of your Navy career when we get back to Boston," replied the Captain. "We sail tomorrow."

"My career?"

"Yes Watson, your career," replied Captain Carden. "You are dismissed Watson."

Lieutenant Watson left the Captain's cabin.

It took several weeks to sail from Brunswick to Boston as other naval duties en-route had to be accomplished. At the end of July 1718 the ship entered Boston harbour where several British ships, the pride of the Atlantic fleet, were moored. The Spanish prisoners were put into the care of the Army in a secure house in Boston town. The *Astound* remained moored at Boston harbour for the next three and a half months, sometimes venturing out to sea to chase and capture pirate ships. Tobias was able to visit Princess Serafina almost every week and their personal friendship flourished during this time.

In mid-November 1718 Tobias Watson was once again summoned to Captain Carden's cabin.

"I have been to see Admiral Hurding this past hour, Watson," said Captain Carden. "His ship is in Boston harbour today. Sit down if you please, I have something to tell you."

Tobias sat down.

"Lieutenant Watson," ordered the Captain, "I am sending you back to England on His Majesty's ship *Grateful.* You sail on the high tide one week from today."

"But I thought my tour of duty was for three years and I have not completed that period of time thus far," said an astonished Watson.

"I have had a change of mind," replied the Captain, "less than an hour ago Admiral Hurding approved my request."

"But I don't want to go back to England Sir," said Watson.

"You *are* going back," said the Captain as he nodded his head several times. "You will escort the three Spanish prisoners to London and deliver them to a government minister at the Tower of London. I shall appoint six soldiers under your command to enable you to do this."

"But why Sir? Why must I go back?" asked Tobias once more.

"Because that is my order," replied the Captain.

"In that case Sir I shall abide by your orders. May I leave now to prepare for my task?" asked Tobias.

"You may not, Lieutenant Watson, I haven't finished with you yet," came the reply from the Captain as he held up a folded piece of parchment with a red wax seal affixing its secret contents in the form of a letter.

"After you have delivered the prisoners to the Tower of London you will make your way to Greenwich where you will register your name with naval command and show them this letter from Admiral Hurding," ordered the Captain.

"What is this letter?" inquired a nervous Tobias.

"This letter is affixed with the personal seal of the Admiral, so we cannot see its content," replied the Captain.

Tobias thought for a moment. This was serious. Lieutenants do not normally get sent to Greenwich without good reason and one of those reasons is a dishonourable discharge from the Navy.

"Captain Carden, I am very sorry that I let my feelings towards the death of my friend William end in tears," said a shocked Tobias Watson, "but I really do want to stay in the Navy. I have overcome my weakness. Please don't let me be discharged at Greenwich. Can you talk to the Admiral and ask him to change his mind?"

"The Admiral will not change his mind and I don't want him to," said the Captain with a stern look, "in fact I suggested the details of your future to him."

"You did?" asked a surprised Watson.

“Yes, I did, and you deserve it Mr. Watson. You are a man of compassion and strength; you are a born leader of men and you have a personal quality that must be nurtured by your mentors,” replied the Captain.

“I have?” said a puzzled Tobias Watson.

Captain Carden’s mood changed.

“Yes Tobias,” he continued in a gentler manner, “and that is why you shall register your name at Naval command headquarters at Greenwich. You will then be taken into the care of the Navy’s training school for senior officers where you will remain for three years to learn the finer details of English gentleman ways and the technical detail of the King’s Navy. If you pass your examinations at the end of your three years Tobias and, after that, pass your mandatory two-year long sea trials, under the command of various captains, it will almost guarantee that you will become a Captain in your own right in the finest Navy in the world. You will be a Captain by the time you reach the age of 28. But if you fail… well… let’s not speak about that because I think I know you well enough: you will not fail.”

Tobias Watson was dumfounded. It took a moment for him to comprehend the situation.

“Well, say something man.” said Captain Carden.

“I am not sure what to say Captain,” replied Tobias, “I should first like to say thank you and that I would be delighted to go to Greenwich college!”

“Well that is enough,” replied Carden, “take this letter from Admiral Hurding and be sure not to lose it, and here, take this also.” The Captain scribbled something on a piece of parchment before dabbing the wet ink with blotting paper and sealing the document with his own mark, “These are your orders to show to the Captain of His Majesty’s ship *Grateful*. I believe that the Captain’s name is Murphy. Yes, that’s it, Captain Richard Murphy. I have arranged for six of the King’s soldiers to take the Spanish prisoners to the *HM Grateful*. All that remains for me to do is to wish you the very best, Tobias, and to say, no doubt, we shall meet again one day in the future.”

"I am very honoured and obliged by your kindness," said Tobias Watson.

"There is nothing kind about my actions Watson," said the Captain, "you have been chosen because I believe that you are one of the very best young men that we have. You volunteered for the *Little Water* expedition without hesitation and you are a fine navigator, but don't let it go to your head young man. Now, go back to England and prepare yourself for learning."

"Yes Sir, I will," replied Watson.

"Now go. Pack up your kit, say your goodbyes to your friends aboard this ship and don't come back… not until you are known as *Captain Watson*," called a smiling Captain Carden.

"Thank you once again Sir," replied an elated Tobias, before leaving the room.

Having packed his kit and instructed one of the men to take it to his new ship *HMS Grateful,* Tobias Watson found his friend, Lieutenant Edmund Price, by the galley taking in some food.

"I shall be leaving this ship today on the Captain's orders," said Tobias.

Price turned to look at his friend, "Leaving?" he inquired.

"Yes, I am being sent back to England," came Tobias's reply.

"Trouble?" probed Price.

"No trouble Mr. Price. I am escorting the prisoners to the Tower of London and handing them over to the warden," said Tobias.

"And then you will be back?" asked Price.

"No Sir," said Tobias as he smiled.

"Well, tell me my friend, where will you go after you assign the prisoners to the warden at the Tower?" said Price.

"Oh… nowhere special, just the Navy training school at Greenwich," replied Tobias.

Lieutenant Price looked at Tobias for a moment – wondering if his friend was pretending. Suddenly, he burst into a laugh with a broad smile across his face.

“Why that’s wonderful news Tobias, congratulations, you must be very pleased with yourself.” Price put down his food and shook the hand of Tobias Watson.

“I am shaking the hand of a future Captain of the King’s Navy,” said Edmund Price, “what an honour that is.

“Well we don’t know yet Edmund – there are a few examinations to pass before I might be considered as a Captain,” replied Watson.

“Promise me, Tobias, that when you become a Captain you will send for me. I would be glad to serve under you,” asked Price.

“Of course, Edmund, I will,” said a cheerful Tobias Watson as he patted his friend several times on the shoulder, “and now I really must say goodbye.”

“Goodbye Tobias,” called Lieutenant Edmund Price, “we will meet again.”

A few minutes later Tobias Watson left His Majesty’s ship *Thunder* and headed along the docks of Boston town towards the ship that would transport him back to England. It was another mighty vessel, His Majesty’s ship, *Grateful,* under the command of Captain Richard Murphy.

Chapter 14

The Pirates and the Spanish.

"Captain Murphy?" inquired Lieutenant Watson on opening the door to the Captain's quarters aboard *HMS Grateful*.

"Yes," said the Captain as he looked up from the book he was reading.

"Sir, I am third Lieutenant Tobias Watson reporting to you and I bring you my written orders from Captain Carden of His Majesty's ship, *Thunder,"* said Watson, as he held out the sealed parchment document with his left hand before saluting Captain Murphy.

"What do you know about electricity?" asked an inquiring Murphy in an almost mad-like manner – his hair sticking-up in all directions as if it were statically charged.

"Nothing Captain, though I have heard of the concept of electricity," replied Watson.

"I am reading about electrostatic generation," replied Murphy, "it's a fascinating subject. I understand it to be the difference between positive and negative currents. But you need conductors and you also need insulators my boy. Did you know that?"

"I did not Sir," replied a puzzled Watson.

"Look over there on the table I have constructed a static generator," said Captain Murphy.

Watson looked towards the contraption on the table, "Very impressive Sir," he replied.

"Who did you say you were?" asked the Captain as he closed the book that he had been reading.

"Third Lieutenant Watson Sir, reporting for duty."

"Yes, welcome aboard Watson, I have been expecting you. How is Captain Carden?" asked Murphy, as he returned a rather sloppy Naval salute that most captains of his day often gave.

"I believe that he is very well," replied Watson.

"Bring your orders to me Lieutenant," said Captain Murphy, as he held out his hand.

Tobias Watson handed over the document to Captain Murphy, who broke the wax seal of the parchment and read its content.

"Hmm," said the Captain as he read the document, "so you are going to Greenwich to train to become a Captain of the fleet, third Lieutenant Watson?"

"Yes Sir," replied Watson, "but first I am to deliver the Spanish prisoners to the Tower of London."

"Yes, I see that is noted on this document, but first let me say congratulations for securing a place at the Navy's most honourable training institution," replied Captain Murphy, "there are not many men who get the opportunity to go to Greenwich. Now to business – we have the Spanish prisoners aboard this ship under lock and key; they came here last night – the army are guarding them below deck.

"Yes Sir," replied Watson.

"My orders," continued the Captain, "are to release the prisoners during daylight hours to move freely around the ship – except for the poop deck. And I am instructed to tell you, Lieutenant Watson, that you are to befriend them. You will look after them and gain as much information as you can, especially from the one known as Ronaldo Delaguila, for he is a Spanish diplomat with secrets."

"What am I supposed to find out from them?" asked Watson.

"Anything you can Watson," came the reply, "get yourself a logbook and record what you overhear or find out. You will record their words daily when you return to your own cabin. But remember, do not attempt to interrogate them or ask too many questions of them – for they may clam-up and tell you nothing. The plan is simple, just talk to them and become their friend, or as friendly as a Spanish and British person can become in these difficult times – they may unwittingly tell you something of importance."

"You mentioned, my own cabin?" asked Tobias.

"Yes, Watson. Unusual as it might be for a third Lieutenant, on this journey you will have your own permanent bed-bunk for security reasons. Lock-up your logbook every day in your cabin and always leave it there – that is until our journey's end in London, when you will bring it to me," replied the Captain. "Is that clear Watson?"

"Yes Sir," came the reply, "did I hear you say we sail to London – not Portsmouth, Captain?"

"That is correct," replied the Captain, "it is deemed safer and far more practical by Admiral Hurding that we should take the prisoners directly to the prison cells at the Tower of London. There is a small landing dock on the North bank of the river Thames, right next to the Tower. Have you been there before Watson?"

"No, I have never been to London, but I have read about it, especially the Tower of London. I believe that William the Conqueror founded the area shortly after the Battle of Hastings which took place on the 14th October 1066. William was crowned King of England in London on Christmas day 1066 and, later, in 1078 King William built the White Tower in the castle grounds. It is a secure prison; the most secure place in England, for it is also a *Donjon,* a place well within the castle's outer walls. I will be pleased to go to this place," replied Watson, "it has a lot of history about it and I would wish to see its structural splendour for myself."

The Captain paused and looked at Watson in disbelief – having listened to him impart such detailed, believable and accurate historical knowledge with some authority. This was expert knowledge that someone twice Watson's age would have difficulty in communicating. The Captain's silent observation and piercing eyes looked Watson up and down. He moved closer to Watson – their faces less than six inches apart. It made Tobias feel uncomfortable and his face blushed. Tobias stood to attention once more in a nervous attempt to alleviate this uncomfortable feeling of the embarrassing closeness – and in doing so extended that six-inch gap between them by a further, yet critical, two inches. The Captain continued with that piercing look as he computed the intentions of Tobias Watson in his own mind. Had Tobias Watson said too much? Had he given the impression of being far cleverer than other men of his own age and way above his own station in life as a third Lieutenant?

'What sort of a man is this?' thought the Captain.

The Captain broke off his stare before he continued.

"Are you sure you know nothing about electricity?" asked the Captain.

"No Sir, I do not," replied Watson.

"Never mind," said the Captain, "once we have delivered the prisoners to the Warden of the Tower and passed on any relevant information to him, such as any useful facts you may have gained from the prisoner's during our seven-week journey aboard this ship, then you will go to Greenwich training school. Is that clear Watson?"

"Yes Sir," replied Tobias Watson. "How far is it from the Tower to Greenwich?"

Tobias already knew the answer to his question but wanted to let the Captain tell him. He did not want to cause himself any further embarrassment.

"We will pass Greenwich on our way from *Mare Germanicum* to the Tower of London," replied the Captain. "Greenwich is on the southern bank of the river Thames and probably about ten nautical miles as the river flows from the Tower of London. Oh, and one last thing third Lieutenant Watson, you will not be asked to assist in the sailing of this ship on our journey from the Americas to London. You may speak freely with my officers about our methodology of sailing aboard this ship or to pass the time of day with them but remember your period aboard this ship is to be dedicated to those Spanish prisoners. Do you understand?"

"Yes, Captain Murphy," replied Watson, before pausing…

"Come on Watson, if you have something else to say then you must say it?" said the Captain.

"Forgive me Sir," said an uneasy Watson, "it's interesting, Sir, that you use the Latin phrase *Mare Germanicum* instead of simply saying the southern part of the Northern sea or simply, the

German sea, when you refer to sailing into the estuary of the Thames river."

The Captain laughed as he stood back from Watson, allowing that extra personal space between them. "I test every one of my new Lieutenants with a difficult nautical question and when I can, I use the one about *Mare Germanicum.* Mr. Watson, I am impressed with your knowledge; and with you being such a young age. Never, in my experience, has a third lieutenant got that question right. Come to think of it, I don't think any of my first Lieutenants have got that question right. Most have asked where *Mare Germanicum* is located. It is no wonder that Admiral Hurding is sending you to the British Navy training school at Greenwich."

"Thank you, Sir," said an apprehensive Watson.

The Captain thought for a moment. "How old are you Watson?" he asked.

"I am twenty-two years old, almost twenty-three Captain and I read books. I read lots of books, books on all sorts of subjects. I read two or three books a week when I can get hold of them – they are a valuable commodity. I read these books on top of my usual naval duties and that is how I learn these things that I know," came Watson's jumbled nervous reply.

The Captain smiled, "Now I think I understand you Tobias Watson. Be careful aboard this ship my friend – do not make yourself out to be a man of knowledge that is way above your superior officer's capabilities for you will make enemies among them. Save your knowledge for when you become a Captain in the King's fleet – and never give up reading books. Well done Lieutenant Watson."

"Sir, thank you for your advice," replied Watson

"Books, books and more books Watson. You have come to the right place for a book," said Captain Murphy as he threw his arms in the air with delight, "I too am an avid book reader, though these days I prefer electrical technical book or shorter quizzical books about the ancient Roman civilization."

The Captain pondered before continuing, "I retire from the Navy soon. This voyage to England will be my last as a Captain.

I am 65 years old and I shall miss the Navy – for I have led a wonderful life. Anyway, that is not the point I make. What I should say is that I have over two-hundred books on all manner of subjects in my study aboard this ship and I would be pleased if you will take the opportunity to read some of them on your journey to London.

"That's very kind of you Captain," replied Watson, "I will take you up on this offer of borrowing a book or two from you, once I am settled aboard this ship."

"You are dismissed Watson, go and find my first Lieutenant, Jock Colville, who will direct you to your cabin."

"Very good Sir and thank you," replied Watson as he saluted the Captain – before leaving Murphy's quarters to go on-deck.

On the 26th November 1718, on the early morning tide, the ship slipped out of Boston Harbour with a brisk wind filling its sails. The British white ensign flew with authority from the mizzen mast. The mighty ship travelled at a constant five-knots and, by late afternoon, was just over fifty-five miles from shore. Tobias Watson had settled into his cabin and went on deck to take in the sea air.

It was such a marvellous feeling being at sea. Standing starboard side of the ship, below the fore mast, Watson held on to a rope that extended from the skid beams on the deck, right to the top of the mast. He felt the rope flex and slack with the movement of the ship. Tobias looked towards the stern and upwards to marvel at the sight of the sails in full flow. They never ceased to amaze him, billowing in the wind – affixed to the many yards and booms situated around the ships structure. Eighteen thousand yards of hemp-rope threaded through five-hundred pulley blocks – so finely adjusted by expert sailors to provide the perfect pitch – depending on wind velocity. Treble-sheaved jeer blocks, lower yard jeer tackles, main topgallant yard and the yard arm; all parts of the ship that Tobias Watson could recall from memory. This ship was a three-mast vessel and, as usual, Tobias looked upwards to mentally list the names of the masts and the booms; names such as the mizzen boom, crossjack yard, foremast and flying jib boom. It was a game he played with himself. A game to pass the time when he was usually alone on watch. He looked at the poop deck where two officers were standing, booming orders to the two hundred sailors on deck who adjusted the fine balance of the sails and weighted ballast in the hold to suit the ever-changing weather conditions. It was a marvellous feeling. It was a marvellous sight.

The ship still had its surreptitious status, for it had been in the south seas chasing and catching pirates. There was no sign of cannon portals in the sides of the ship, for they had been blanked with soft wood. The cannons were hidden behind this camouflage of wood – which had been carefully painted on the ship's external elevation, with colours to match the rest of the ship – to make *HMS Grateful* look like a merchant ship. The only give-away on this day was the white ensign flag which flew high above them, for they only used the red ensign of merchantmen while chasing pirates.

Just then a voice called from behind Tobias Watson.

"Mr. Watson I do believe."

Tobias Watson turned around to face the Bow of the ship. It was first Lieutenant Darley from *HMS Thunder*.

"Mr. Darley," said an astonished Watson as he broke into a naval salute, "I am surprised to see you aboard this ship."

Darley returned the compliment of a salute, "So am I Watson," came the reply.

"Well, are you going to tell me what brings you aboard this ship?" inquired third Lieutenant Watson.

"Bit of bad luck old chap," replied Darley, "two of the officers aboard this ship were taken ill last evening and have had to stay in Boston town while they recover."

"And you have taken one of these places?" said Watson.

"Yes Mr. Watson," replied Darley, "I only knew early this morning that I would be changing ships. Just about got most of my kit together and onto this ship before she sailed – that's how tight it was. It's a bit of a nuisance though as I have had to leave some of my belongings behind. Still it is not so bad, I get to go back to England earlier than I should and see my wife and children in London. That will come as a surprise to them. No doubt I shall be back in the Americas in the next year or so."

"You hail from London?" asked Watson.

"Yes, I do, it is quite fortunate that this ship is bound for London. It's very unusual for a ship of this type to go directly to London," said Darley.

"I am sure it will be a pleasant journey Lieutenant Darley," replied Watson, "and a restful one, for I too go to London, to start my studies at Greenwich college."

"You are a lucky man," said Darley, "I have been trying to get into Greenwich naval training school for a while now. What did you have to do for the Captain to get into the training school?"

"Why nothing Mr. Darley," came the reply.

"Come come, man you must have done something of a favour for him. They don't often send young men such as you, men with poor regional Sussex accents as broad as yours to Greenwich," replied Darley in a most hurtful manner.

But Tobias had learnt not to rise to the bait of men such as Darley and merely smiled – much to the apparent annoyance of the first Lieutenant.

"I also hear that you are to oversee three Spanish prisoners while aboard this ship," asked Darley.

"You hear well – for that is correct," replied Watson.

"Hmm... well if you need some help let me know," said Darley.

"I shall need no help from you Mr. Darley," said Watson with a smile, "it is an easy task for a man like me."

Darley sneered. "I have no time to continue this pointless conversation and must make haste. I am due on the poop deck," he said, as he brushed past Watson deliberately pushing him aside.

Watson smiled as he watched Darley climb the steps to the poop deck. Tobias Watson had no time for Darley. He didn't trust him, but as a first Lieutenant Darley out-ranked Watson. There was nothing Watson could do or say, though he knew he would need to watch him. Tobias had not forgotten that Darley was an associate of the late sailor, Sykes, the man who had stolen the King's Whisky. And he was still puzzled by the fact that Darley had visited Sykes at the ranch in Charleston in the Americas, for he believed that he had been up to no good.

Two days later the three prisoners were released from their cells below decks and escorted onto the main deck by two soldiers. Watson was there to greet them.

"Good morning," he called, "do any of you gentlemen speak English?"

"Las condiciones son terribles en las celdas, exijo estatus diplomático," shouted one of the men known as Montez. "Y yo podría hacer con una bebida." He looked a little perturbed, almost violent. And he kept pointing his finger at Tobias. The guards pushed him away.

Then the woman prisoner was brought forward. She stepped towards Mr. Montez. She appeared to scold him. "Sr. Montez. Por favor desistan, no tenemos elección, estamos prisioneros," she said.

Tobias once again noted her exceptional beauty. She was five-feet-tall, petite, with bronze facial features and deep-brown coloured eyes. Her auburn shoulder length hair flowed in the breeze. She wore a turquoise and gold full length dress which showed off her ample, seductive figure. She was, of course, the adorable and beautiful Princess Serafina of Seville, from the province of Andalusia.

The other man Ronaldo Delaguila also spoke in Spanish – only he had a smile on his face throughout the conversation, "Tu, Ingles, nunca nos vas a vencer! Se cuál es tu juego y exijo inmunidad diplomática." Tobias did not understand what either of the two men or the princess had said but it was noticeable to him that this diplomat Ronaldo Delaguila was a man *with flair*. Tall, thin, wearing yellow trousers and a green shirt, this diplomat was truly flamboyant. He wore a wide-brimmed raffia hat dressed with two ostrich feathers, and he smoked a cigarette with some style.

The Princess Serafina spoke in a perfect soft English voice, with a hint of a Spanish accent.

"Hello, Tobias," she purred.

"It is so nice to see you again Princess," said Tobias. "If you are the only one among you who can speak English then you shall translate for me."

"We all speak English," said Ronaldo Delaguila, "we are diplomats – except for him," as he pointed to Mr. Montez, "he is a diplomatic protection officer. He is supposed to protect me and the Princess. What is it that you want from us?"

"My name is Lieutenant Tobias Watson. You three are to be taken to England," replied Watson, "and it is my job to escort you."

"I have diplomatic status as a Spanish Ambassador. She has diplomatic status as a Princess," said Delaguila, "I demand that we are released into the care of the Spanish government."

"Not while there is a war on I believe," said Watson, "as you know, it is the war of the *Quadruple Alliance* between Spain and the British Allies."

"It does not matter that we are at war with you, we have diplomatic immunity – all three of us do." demanded Delaguila.

"That is correct, Tobias Watson," called the Princess, "and we have special rights while we are your prisoners."

"And what are your rights?" asked Tobias.

"First, we should not be in the cell of a common prisoner. We should be in a suite of rooms and secondly, I, as a woman, should not have to share a room with these two gentlemen," said the Princess as she pointed to Delaguila and Mr. Montez.

Tobias thought for a moment. "I agree madam – you should have your own room though you will agree with me that we have limited space aboard this ship. I will speak to the Captain and see if the arrangements can be changed. As for your request of diplomatic immunity I cannot comment – for you will see by my uniform that I am a third Lieutenant. My task is to make your journey to England as comfortable and as pleasant as is possible, that is all."

"But you can speak to the Captain about our diplomatic status?" said the Princess.

"I cannot madam," replied Watson, "even those matters are above his command. Our orders are to deliver you into the care of our superiors in London, England and that is that. Do not ask me again."

"Very well," said Delaguila, "how many days sailing is there before we reach London?"

"About forty days," came the reply, "if the weather is kind to us."

Mr. Montez began growling under this breath, just like a Jack Russell dog.

"Are you well?" asked Watson as he looked at Mr. Montez.

"Take no notice of him," said a smiling Delaguila, "he growls when he is unhappy – he growls when he needs a drink – we have got used to him. Have you some rum to keep him quiet?"

"Not right now, I will see what I can do later. You seem a very happy man Mr. Delaguila," said Tobias, "you have not stopped smiling since I first met you."

"He smiles a lot," said the Princess.

"I smile because I know things that you do not, Lieutenant Watson," said Delaguila.

"And what is it that I know not?" asked Watson.

"Well, I cannot tell you that, because then you will know what I know, and I shall have no secret," said Delaguila.

"You only have one secret then?" asked Tobias.

"I have many secrets," came the reply, "one of which is the secret formula of resistance."

"Resistance?" asked Tobias, "you mean the resistance that the waters of the sea impose on the bow of a ship travelling upon and partly below its surface?"

Ronaldo Delaguila was surprised by Watson knowledge, "something like that," replied Delaguila with a smile.

Tobias Watson smiled too. "You are a very confusing man Mr. Delaguila – you too Mr. Montez. What should I make of you all? What is this misperception that I have before me? I have a man who growls when he is unhappy, another who smiles most of the time and who says he has secrets that he will not impart.

Then, and among all of this – a Princess. What am I to do with you all?"

Tobias turned to the two army guards who had been listening to this conversation. They were leaning against the perimeter of the ship dressed in their fine crimson red uniforms – holding their muskets to hand.

"What am I to do with them, guards?"

Both guards smiled but said nothing.

Tobias Watson looked towards the stern of the ship. He could see Lieutenant Darley high on the poop deck – standing with his hands clasped behind his back – watching him and the prisoners on the main deck.

Tobias raised his hand and made a perfect naval salute. Darley returned the compliment.

Tobias looked back towards his prisoners before noticing, once more, the exceptional beauty of the Princess.

"You are very beautiful madam," said Tobias.

Tobias never meant to say that. It was not in his usual character to give such a compliment to any woman – not since the loss of his one true love, Molly Moffatt. But nonetheless he had said it. And he soon regretted it, for he found himself mildly embarrassed.

"That is very kind of you," replied the Princess with a smile.

Mr. Montez growled some more and Delaguila laughed out loud.

Watson changed the subject and his tone of voice.

"Right, let me set some ground rules. The Captain has said that you three prisoners can use the main deck during daylight hours, but at night you must return to your room. You are not allowed on to the poop deck, aft of the ship, or beyond the forecastle towards the bow. You must not speak to any of the crew – except the guards or officers. The guards will watch over you twenty-four hours a day. If bad weather takes hold, or we come under attack or you are ordered by a guard to remove yourself from the deck you will go below to your room immediately and without question. You are not allowed anywhere else on this ship. You will eat and sleep in your room. Every day, at two bells on the ship's second watch, we will meet here on deck. Do you understand?"

"Yes," replied Delaguila, "but why do we need to speak every day?"

"I want to know if your well-being is in order and we shall speak each day to talk about your fears or concerns," replied Watson.

"My only fear," replied Delaguila, "is that I am prisoner aboard a British ship."

Watson ignored this comment.

"Will you talk to the Captain about a separate room for me?" asked the Princess.

"Yes, I will madam," replied Watson.

"And you will talk to the Captain about my diplomatic status," inquired a smiling Delaguila.

"I will not," replied Watson, "I have already told you that your diplomatic status counts for nothing aboard this ship. Now, if there is nothing else, then we are finished for today."

Watson left the area to climb the steps to the poop deck. He turned to look downwards onto the main deck and saw that the three Spanish prisoners were engaging in conversation.

"She is very beautiful," came a voice from behind, "I might just pay her a visit one evening."

Watson knew that voice. He turned to face Darley.

"With respect Sir. You will not be permitted to see the female prisoner alone," said Tobias Watson.

"You take matters too seriously Watson," laughed Darley, "can you not see that I am jesting with you."

Tobias looked Darley in the eye. He knew that his superior officer was not jesting.

"Yes Sir," replied Watson.

"Ship ahoy off the starboard side," shouted one of the boys in the crow's-nest.

"Darley looked in the direction and raised his telescope. It's a ship flying the flag of pirates and its heading this way. Call the Captain onto the poop deck."

"One more ship on the horizon," came another call from the boy in the crow's-nest.

Darley raised his telescope once more.

The Captain soon arrived on deck and directed his telescope towards the incoming ships.

"There are two ships Captain," called Darley, "both flying the flag of pirates, shall we break open the camouflaged cannons so that they can see we are a British warship? They will be sure to leave us alone if they see the extent of our cannon strength."

"Certainly not," said Captain Murphy, "prepare the ship for battle and do not strike the cannon camouflage until I give the order. Two more pirate ships at the bottom of the ocean will be a perfect end to my career."

"Are you sure Captain?" asked Darley.

"Don't question my authority Mr. Darley," came the response.

Darley turned to another man, a subordinate sailor standing nearby. "Relay the Captain's order to the men," said Darley.

On the pirate flag ship '*Ghost*' was the charismatic yet bad-tempered Captain Choler Joe. He called himself a Vice-Admiral of his fleet of two ships, *The Ghost* and another ship following behind known as the *Phantom:* though the real leader and Admiral of these two ships and many others was *Blackbeard* the infamous pirate. But Blackbeard and the rest of his fleet were elsewhere on that day.

Standing on the deck in his easily identifiable colourful orange and black striped trousers Choler Joe shouted, "Thirty minutes with this head-wind behind us and we shall soon be upon them. Admiral Blackbeard will be pleased with us on this day, once we have taken all possessions and sunk this target ship."

Looking through his telescope Choler Joe said, "They think they can fool me – flying the white ensign of a British Navy warship when they only have a scattering of cannon on the main decks and none below – they are not a King's Navy ship. They fool no-one. They are a merchant ship – probably full of treasures and bounty – which we will take for ourselves. Send a signal to *The Phantom.* Tell them to hold back. We will only need one ship to attack, there is no point wasting cannon shot. I and you men aboard our ship *the Ghost* shall take this vessel, alone.

"Shall I give the order to prepare for battle Captain Joe?" asked his first mate.

"Yes," replied Choler Joe, "we will take three sweeps at them. On the first run we will hit them broadside at a distance of one-hundred yards and unleash our cannon fire on them. On the second broad side sweep we will do the same and on the third run we will come alongside and fight hand to hand. Pass that information onto the men. Get the grappling hooks ready and the men to the cannons. We have a ship that is smaller and faster than theirs. We shall sail from the west to the east and catch her port side."

"We are coming under attack," shouted Captain Murphy of the King's ship. The pirates are positioning their ship to run at us broadside. All officers remove your hats and jackets. I don't want to give them any indication that this is a British Navy warship – until it's too late for them to retreat."

The Captain began to remove his tricorn hat and naval jacket; the rest of the officers followed his orders.

Tobias Watson shouted to the two soldiers guarding the Spanish prisoners. "Take them below and lock them up. Call on the other soldiers below; get them to come up on deck with their muskets. You two soldiers come back too. We have a fight on our hands. You shall all remove your jackets and hats and hide on deck so as not to alert the enemy to our numbers or identity. Hide your muskets until the Pirate ship is close by and the order is given to fire."

"All other men on deck who are not engaged in sailing this ship shall also hide, make sure your cutlass and knife are at the ready," shouted the Captain

Twenty-minutes later the pirate ship *Ghost* was closing in. Its bow near the stern end of the British ship. Shortly after that, *Ghost* was positioned less than one hundred yards broadside to the Royal Navy ship *HMS Grateful.*

"Can't see many sailors on her deck," shouted Choler Joe, "she is weaker than I first thought. I see a few cannons on her main deck but there is no one to man them. On my command, fire several shots into her sails. I think we can take her intact. We could use another ship for our fleet."

The pirate ship drifted a few more yards towards the East.

"Fire," roared Choler Joe as he climbed the rigging of his ship to get a better view.

Several cannon shots screamed through the air above *HMS Grateful* entering the mass of timbers, sails and rigging. Two cannon shots tore through sails and one hit the mizzen gaff which broke its fixture to the mizzen mast. It fell onto the poop deck missing the Captain and his officers by an inch.

"Send a signal asking for their surrender, I think we have made our point," shouted Choler Joe as he hung like a spider half way up the ship's rigging, looking at his conquest across the water, "I don't think that we need to fight a hand to hand battle, for I can see that there is not enough of the enemy to fight with. We should be done within the hour and on our way home."

But unknown to Choler Joe, his point had not been made to Captain Murphy of *HMS Grateful*.

Captain Murphy hollered – "fire cannons from the main deck. Kick out the camouflage on the lower decks and fire those cannons as well, shoot thereafter, at will."

Straight away, cannon fire emanated from the main deck of the vessel towards the pirate ship. The men below, on the middle and lower decks kicked out the timber camouflage and began firing their powerful cannons. There was an almighty barrage of fire power that hit the *Ghost* broadside. It took Choler Joe and his men by complete surprise. Shots took down the fore and aft masts and some penetrated the hull of the pirate ship. Within ten minutes of opening fire the pirate ship was in trouble. It was almost disabled, unmanageable and taking in water.

"Shall we board Sir?" called Darley.

"No," said the Captain, "we shall turn-about, go around three sixty degrees and hit her with more firepower. We don't know how many men they have aboard. It will also draw the second pirate ship towards us."

Within twenty-minutes the King's ship had circled the pirate ship and once more the *Ghost* was pounded into oblivion by the cannon fire of His Majesty's ship, *Grateful.*

The pirate ship was sinking.

"Pull away," shouted Captain Murphy, "we shall wait for their sister ship to come closer and attempt a rescue. When they do, we shall give them a good cannon pounding."

They watched for the next two hours as the pirate ship, *Ghost,* sank beneath the waves of the Atlantic Ocean. Some of the men aboard this doomed vessel, including Choler Joe, dropped four rowing boats into the water. As these boats became full to their capacity they allowed no more sailors to climb aboard. Any of the men in the sea – those who dared to put their hands onto the rim of the rowing boat – had their fingers battered by a wooden cosh. Soon, the pirates in the boats were rowing away from the scene. Many men had been left behind to drown – watched by the King's sailors of the ship *Grateful.* The second pirate ship, *Phantom,* remained on the horizon watching and waiting. It was clear that they were not going to rescue any of the men from the *Ghost;* not while Captain Murphy and his ship was nearby.

"It goes against my principles to let the second ship get away," called Captain Murphy to Lieutenant Darley.

"What is your intention Captain?" asked Darley.

"It saddens me to say that we have wasted enough time in this vicinity. It is also clear to me that the second pirate ship is not going to prompt a rescue. I think we must let matters rest and take their due course. We ourselves shall continue our journey to England. If we try to chase the second ship it will out-run us, for it is smaller and faster. Mr. Darley, set a heading of due-East, for England."

"Very well Captain," said Darley, as he issued the Captain's orders to the lower ranks.

"It's a pity. This is my last voyage in the King's Navy and I have sunk one pirate ship when I could have sunk two," said the Captain with a droll smile.

Eight days later, Choler Joe made it back to Blackbeard's flotilla of ships. At that time, Blackbeard and his fleet were moored off the coast of the Leeward Islands in the West Indies. And Blackbeard was none-too-happy to find out that Choler Joe had been so stupid as to attack a British Navy ship of war and lost one of his most prized pirate ships, *The Ghost,* and numerous ordinary sailors. Blackbeard made all manner of threats in front of his men about what he was going to do to the next British warship that passed his way; but history has proven that these threats were idle words.

Nothing more has been recorded in the annals of history about Choler Joe. Some said he was hung by the neck until dead aboard Blackbeard's ship of the fleet – the *Queen Anne's Revenge* – his body thrown overboard to the waiting sharks. Others said that Blackbeard's men keel-hauled him before chopping him up into little bits to feed to the seagulls. But whatever fate Choler Joe suffered – nothing was ever heard about him again and the exact detail of his final demise remains a mystery to this day.

Chapter 15

Defending the helm.

It was a mild pleasant evening aboard His Majesty's ship, *Grateful.* Three weeks and Christmas day had passed since the pirates had attacked. The new year of 1719 was to be upon them in a few days' time. Tobias Watson had been to see Captain Murphy about prisoner accommodation arrangements and the Princess had been given her own room. She was grateful to Tobias for his intervention in the matter. Tobias went further – he had the room cleaned out and washed down for the Princess. Then he positioned some furniture in the space. The Princess took this room, situated beside the cell of her fellow Spaniards Ronaldo Delaguila and Mr. Montez, and made it her own. Time went by and Tobias Watson met with the Spanish contingent every day. At night the prisoners were taken to their respective rooms and locked-in for the night. Two of the King's guards accompanied them where ever they went on the ship and stood guard outside their cells at night.

Most days the Princess and Tobias walked the main deck of the ship, talking and laughing. Sometimes they played a Spanish card game that she had taught him. It was clear to Tobias that the Princess had no Spanish diplomatic secrets worthy of imparting to the British – for she was a minor royal person – a young woman of about twenty-two years of age. She was just a small cog in the large hierarchy of Spanish Royalty. Tobias liked her and enjoyed her company.

The other two Spanish diplomats stayed close by, sometimes speaking to Tobias – but most of the time Tobias and the Princess only had eyes for each other. Tobias was indeed attracted to the Princess and she to him. She was his one vulnerability aboard this ship. His predisposition to her charm left him with a delicate weakness about him that would last every single moment that they were together. And whenever Tobias was alone in his bunk at night he would often think about the Princess. Tobias knew he was defenceless to her charms. He could do nothing about it; he found it difficult to resist her appeal. And yet, he could not ask the Captain to be relieved of this duty, because this would be a sign of weakness unbecoming to a junior officer of the King's Navy. The Princess knew this, but she wanted him. She wanted Tobias Watson more than anything. She yearned for this gallant, good looking, tall, British officer. She wanted him as her lover. It was an impossible situation.

One day on deck, as they walked beside each other towards the stern of the ship – with Delaguila and Mr. Montez following behind – something happened. It was a moment in time when an affair between the two of them could have begun. It happened when the ship rolled on the crest of a wave. The Princess appeared to lose her balance. She fell into the saving arms of Tobias Watson. That was the only time they held each other close. It was a moment when he smelt the fragrance in her hair and felt the softness of her cheek. It was a moment when their lips almost touched. Only the inner strength of Tobias Watson's character stopped him from embracing her. This was an instant moment of pure pleasure. The Princess melted into his arms and was ready to be seduced. It never happened of course. Afterwards, they never spoke about the incident. During the following weeks Tobias kept his distance from the Princess and concentrated his efforts on the diplomats, Delaguila and Mr. Montez. Some minor secrets of the Spanish diplomats were secured by Tobias Watson who diligently wrote them in his log – but it wasn't much. As for the secret of resistance that Delaguila had so proudly spoken of, Tobias managed to extract only part of the secret formula. Mr. Montez told him this section of the formula, *R1+R2 = the distance of potential travel*, in return for a ladle of rum. This secret Spanish formula, handed to Tobias Watson by Montez, much annoyed Ronald Delaguila.

"You have given my secret away to the enemy," exclaimed Delaguila as he took another drag on his cigarette.

Mr. Montez looked at Delaguila and growled a disapproving, "Who cares!" And for the first time aboard this ship, Montez smiled. In fact, after that, he beamed a broad smiled every time Tobias brought him a ladle of rum.

The formula of resistance meant nothing to Watson or to Captain Murphy. They were both men of considerable book reading ability and knowledge – yet neither could comprehend its detail. Tobias Watson pondered on this formula night after night, but he never understood it.

One late evening, around ten-o'clock, Tobias was undertaking his duties when he passed the prisoners' cabins. There were no guards outside the prisoners' quarters. That was unusual. Then, he heard a muffled noise.

He took a flickering oil lamp from a hook fixed on the hull of the ship and held it up to the cell door. He peered through the grill of the door and could see that Delaguila was asleep on the floor. Mr. Montez, however, was sitting upright with his back to the wall – growling, as was usual – though it was difficult to see if he was asleep or awake. Was he growling or snoring? thought Tobias Watson. The clasp to the door of the cell had a peg wedged into its metalwork, holding it locked shut. Everything was in order. But Tobias noticed that the peg in the door to the Princess's adjacent cabin was missing, leaving the door unlocked – though the door was closed.

Then he heard another muffled noise followed by a man's subdued voice, "Keep quiet, bitch."

Watson opened the door to the cell. In the corner of the darkened room he saw Darley holding the Princess from behind. Her blouse was torn revealing her ample bosom. He had one of his hands over her mouth and another around her torso.

"Leave her be," shouted Watson.

"Go back to your quarters Lieutenant Watson, that is an order," replied Darley.

"I will not," asserted Watson, "let go of her."

"The penalty of disobedience towards a senior officer is hanging by the neck," replied Darley as he struggled with his captive. "Watson, I will make sure you hang for your insubordination towards me."

Suddenly, the Princess bit Darley's hand.

"You bitch," he shouted as he let go of her and struck her across the face with the back of his hand.

This was Tobias Watson's moment. He lunged at Darley – fists clenched and battered him in the face several times. Darley fell to the ground. Moments later Darley regained his posture, stood to his feet and a fist fight between the two men began. It lasted a few minutes as they struck each other with bare fisted power until Darley got the better of Tobias Watson. Darley sat on top of an outstretched Watson – his hands spread around Watson's neck – squeezing… squeezing. Human life was draining out of Watson's body. His focus was almost gone, his face bleeding and his strength depleted. He could smell a repugnant whiff of whisky on Darley's breath. It was overpowering. The sweat from Darley's physical efforts to strangle Watson dripped from Darley's brow onto Watson's face. Tobias Watson was almost done for.

Then, as quickly as it had started, Darley's grip was released. He fell forward, the full weight of his body coming to rest on Watson. Darley's eyes were wide open. His face giving the expression of excruciating pain. He was not moving.

Tobias Watson struggled for breath for a moment while simultaneously pushing the weight of Darley's body away from his own. Then he saw that Darley was dead.

A few moments later a blood-soaked Watson had recovered enough to get onto his knees. He could hear the Princess sobbing. He looked around the room. Standing near to the wall of the cell in the semi-darkness was a man holding a bloodstained dagger. He did not speak – he just growled. It was Mr. Montez the diplomatic protection officer. Both men looked at each other before Mr. Montez glanced down at the knife in his hand. Then he flicked the knife around so that its handle was pointing towards Watson, before he dropped it to the deck.

Watson picked up the knife. He recognised it for it had a distinctive handle. He knew that it belonged to Lieutenant Darley.

Tobias once more heard the Princess sobbing. She was outside of the cell.

Tobias went to the weeping Princess and held her close in his arms to comfort her. Then he looked at her bruised face and arms.

"Thank you, Tobias, for saving me from that madman," she cried.

"What happened?" he asked.

The Princess began to sob once more as she began to recall the wicked event. Tobias looked around the area – trying to picture in his mind the sequence of events leading up to Darley's death. It was clear that the Princess must have opened the door of the adjoining cell to allow Mr. Montez to assist.

"Thank you, Mr. Montez," Watson exclaimed.

Montez merely smiled before growling in his usual manner, "Time for a sup of rum Mr. Watson, if you please."

Watson shouted at the top of his voice, "Guards… Guards."

Two guards of the King's Army came running towards him.

"Where have you been? You left your posts unattended," screamed Watson.

"No Sir," said one of the guards, "Lieutenant Darley ordered us to leave. He said that he had some questions to ask of the prisoners in private. We were following orders Lieutenant Watson, Sir."

Watson thought for a moment, "Thank you guards, I will take this matter to the Captain. Lieutenant Darley is dead in that cell. Put the prisoner, Mr. Montez, back into his own cell and secure the area. Do not move Darley's body until I get back."

"Very good Sir," replied one of the soldiers.

Tobias looked at the Princess. "You will come with me Princess Serafina. I shall give-up my cabin to you for this evening and you shall tend to yourself. I will also send the ship's doctor to you."

"Thank you," replied the Princess.

"It is not I that you should thank for saving you Princess Serafina," said Watson, "it is Mr. Montez."

At that moment the guards passed with Mr. Montez under restraint.

"Wait," ordered Tobias Watson, "release him,"

The guards let go of Mr. Montez's arms.

Tobias eye-balled Mr. Montez. "Thank you, once again Mr. Montez, for saving my life," said Tobias. "Guards, please put Mr. Montez in his cell and bring him a ladle of rum."

Montez said nothing – he smiled and just growled, as was usual.

Watson peered through the grill in the prisoner's cell door. Ronaldo Delaguila was asleep on the floor. He had slept through the whole ordeal.

Over the next few days Captain Murphy carried out a thorough investigation into the death of Lieutenant Darley – taking witness statement from the two guards – Watson, the Princess and Mr. Montez. He concluded that there was no case to answer regarding the death of Darley, for this man had committed a monstrous crime in attacking the Princess for his own sexual gratification. Further, Darley had almost killed Tobias Watson. It was only Mr. Montez's intervention – having been let out of his prison cell by the Princess – that had prevented Watson's death. The Captain also found one half-empty bottle of whisky hidden in the bunk-bed of Lieutenant Darley. It was the same labelled whisky that had been stolen from the King's stock – the remainder of which was traded with the Indians at *Little Water*.

Three weeks later the King's ship *Grateful,* reached its destination – The Tower of London, England, on the North banks of the river Thames. The following day the Spanish prisoners were delivered into the care of the warden of the Tower.

When it was time to say goodbye Ronaldo Delaguila smiled and bid his personal farewell. Mr. Montez growled in his usual manner while the Princess gently kissed Tobias Watson on the cheek, before taking the initiative and planting a kiss directly on his lips. Tobias Watson did not resist her charms. He threw his arms around her and held her close. It was a long lingering passionate kiss and for that moment in time nothing else mattered. "I will never forget you Tobias," whispered the Princess, "I shall miss you every day."

"Madam, I shall not forget you either," came Lieutenant Watson's curt reply as he stood to attention and saluted her;

though deep inside his body he felt it aching with the hurt and agony of this loss. This loss of a beautiful and wonderful woman who could have become his lover and lifelong friend. He would miss the Princess Serafina from Seville in the province of Andalusia, Spain.

"In better times, when our two countries are not in conflict, I would fall in love with you Tobias Watson," said the Princess.

Tobias Watson smiled. The Princess smiled too as she grasped his hand and held it for a moment.

"You are a wonderful lady," replied Tobias, "I shall never forget you. I will come back to visit you at the first opportunity."

"I will look forward to that," replied the Princess as the guard held her arm.

"Guard be gentle with her and look after her properly," said Tobias.

The guard did not reply.

Then the prisoners were led away. Tobias watched them as they were escorted across the courtyard to the White Tower. Three loud thuds on the mighty door were made with a wooden mallet and the door opened to allow the three prisoners and their guards to enter. Then the door was slammed shut. Tobias had a thought of regret – but he knew he could do nothing more.

Tobias left the Tower, bid farewell to Captain Murphy and the crew of the King's ship *Grateful*, before heading towards Greenwich naval training school.

Three months later, Tobias went back to the Tower and asked to see the Princess, but she had been transported elsewhere. The guards could not tell him where she had been sent. Tobias was bitterly disappointed.

Tobias Watson spent the next three years at the Naval training school. Throughout his time at Greenwich he continued to send money to his parents in Copperas Gap and wrote numerous letters to them to tell them of his achievements – though his parents could not read or write – so the Church Warden helped them out. After finishing training school, he was seconded to various ships serving under numerous captains before taking his final examinations at Greenwich. By the late spring of 1724, more than five years after he began his training, Tobias Watson emerged from this great institution on the day of his graduation as a first Lieutenant in the King's Navy.

But he was not the same man that had entered the training school five years before. His boyish southern Copperas Gap accent had been erased, and he spoke the words of a gentleman – slightly effeminate but effectual and with a decisive warm personality that would ignite his likeability in everyone that he met. Tobias Watson was now a refined well-spoken gentleman of knowledge. He did not know it, but he was to about to become the finest Captain in the King's Navy.

Chapter 16

A sparkle in her eyes.

On the 17th June 1724, twenty-seven-year-old Tobias Watson returned to Portsmouth Harbour. He found the street where Mr. and Mrs. Morse ran their lodging house and knocked on the front door. It had been some years since he was last at the premises. Mr. Morse opened the door. He looked a little older than the last time Tobias had seen him, but he recognised him instantly.

"Good afternoon Mr. Morse, my name is Tobias Watson and I sent you a message by postal service, booking a room for two nights."

"Come in Sir. What was your name again?" asked Morse as he looked in the guest house diary.

"It's Watson. I am first Lieutenant Tobias Watson of the King's Navy," came the reply.

"The King's Navy you say," replied Morse as he studied the facial features of Watson, "I never forget a face Lieutenant Watson, or a name. I believe that you have stayed at this establishment before, have you not?"

"Yes Mr. Morse I have stayed here before. You have a very good memory; it must be six or seven years since I was last here," said Watson.

"Yes, I remember. Did you not stay here with a young man by the name of William? Then the pair of you went off to the Americas on your adventures," replied Morse with a smile.

"That is correct Mr. Morse," said Tobias Watson as he thought about his deceased friend for a moment, "your memory is exceptional, but sadly…"

"Something is wrong Lieutenant?" asked Morse.

"My friend William was killed in the Americas," said Watson.

"Oh, that is sad," came the reply from Morse, "never mind, go through into the dining area Lieutenant and I will get Mrs. Morse to show you to your room. I must go outside now. It's time for me to do my job as a watchman at the docks."

"Still doing that job Mr. Morse?" inquired Watson.

"Yes, I am still doing that job. Every day I find one or two young men sitting on the dockside. They wonder which way they shall go or which ship to board," replied Morse, "and I bring them back here to tell them what best to do. We look after them for a few days, until they get on their feet, and then they go off and find adventure – just like you and William did all those years ago."

Watson smiled. "Mr. Morse, you and your wife provide a very useful service to these young men," replied Watson, "may that continue."

It had indeed been a long time since Watson was last at this establishment. He thought for a moment about his life – how he had arrived in Portsmouth all those years before and all those adventures and times of sadness during the intervening period. Then he thought about Molly, his first love and the sadness surrounding her death.

"Goodbye, Lieutenant Watson," said Mr. Morse, "I will see you again later today, probably at evening supper."

Mr. Morse went out of his front door into the streets of Portsmouth while Tobias stepped into the dining room.

Sitting at one of the dining tables was a familiar face.

"Don't I know you?" asked Tobias as he approached the table. It was the shopkeeper, wearing his sheepskin apron. The shopkeeper did not reply. He just stared at Tobias Watson.

"Yes, I know you," said Tobias once more.

The shopkeeper again, did not reply.

The shopkeeper's eyes moved from side to side, watching, piercing, and thrusting his persona into the personal space of Tobias Watson.

Sitting next to the shopkeeper was a fisherman. The fisherman just growled. This was the same pair of men who

Tobias Watson had spoken to the last time he stayed at the lodgings many years before.

Suddenly, the shopkeeper spoke. "I'll see you in the future."

"Yes, I remember you," said Watson, "you said those words the last time I spoke to you – what do you mean by that?"

"Good morning Sir," came the voice of Mrs. Morse as she came out of the kitchen into the dining area.

"Good Morning madam," said Tobias as he turned away from the fisherman and shopkeeper to look at her.

He continued, "Are these two gentlemen your regular guests?" as he pointed his hand towards them.

"What two gentlemen?" asked Mrs. Morse.

"These two..." Tobias looked back to where the men were seated at the dining table.

There was no one there. They had vanished.

Tobias stood in stunned silence for a moment as he tried to comprehend this mystery. They could only have vanished – for otherwise he would have seen them leave the room.

"You are the only guest in my house young man," said Mrs. Morse.

"Are you sure?" replied Watson.

"Yes," came the reply, "you must be tired Mr. Watson for your eyes are playing tricks upon you."

"Never mind Mrs. Morse," said Watson, "would you be kind enough to show me to my room and I shall arrange for my belongings to be delivered from the stagecoach station."

"Very well," came the reply, "please follow me."

Later that day Tobias Watson boarded the Admiral's flagship moored at Portsmouth docks and knocked on the door to his quarters.

"Enter," demanded a stern voice.

Tobias Watson opened the door into the Admiral's quarters.

"Come in Watson," said a smiling Admiral Carden.

"Thank you, Sir," replied Watson as he entered the room before standing to attention to salute the Admiral.

Admiral Carden returned the salute before shaking Watson's hand.

"Well my boy," said an excited Admiral, "it's been more than five years since we last met and now look at you. You are a fine upstanding Captain in the King's Navy. You passed the Navy's course with flying colours – didn't you. It is the highest result that any student at the naval college has ever achieved."

"Well thank you Sir," replied a slightly embarrassed Watson, "did you just call me a *Captain*?"

"Yes, I did, Captain Watson," said the Admiral. "The reasons you are here are two-fold. The first being, that I am promoting you to a Captain in his King's Navy with immediate effect."

"Well, I am lost for words," replied a delighted Watson.

"Then say nothing," replied the Admiral, "and I have some more news for you Captain."

"What is that Sir?" asked Watson.

Do you remember your friend Mr. French, who died in the Americas and left goods and monies to his brother?" said the Admiral.

"And that his brother had also died and that, as far as I knew, there were no other known relatives" said Watson.

"Yes," replied the Admiral, "and I advised you that you should see my legal friend because I was sure you would be the sole beneficiary of his estate."

"Yes, that was quite a few years ago Admiral," said Watson.

"Well the matter has been settled in a court of law," replied the Admiral, "and you are indeed the beneficiary of Mr. French's estate. It is more than a thousand guineas, quite a sizable sum. You are a very rich man Captain Watson."

"I am surprised," replied Watson as he took a moment to remember his former friend and mentor – for without Mr. French's tuition he might never have learnt to read or write, and for that Tobias Watson would be forever grateful.

“The funds have been transferred to a naval account in your name Captain Watson. Here are the papers for that account. Spend it wisely,” said Carden.

Watson took the papers and looked at them. He felt a tinge of sadness at the loss of his friend, Mr. French, who had died in tragic circumstances, killed by Red Indians in the Americas many years before.

“I shall deposit some of this money into a Trust-fund dedicated to helping poor young men achieve their sailing ambition,” said Watson, “I know just the man to administer this fund in Portsmouth harbour – his name is Mr. Morse –he can use the fund for short-term accommodation for those young men until they find a ship to sail on and your legal firm can audit the Trust-fund.”

“Very magnanimous Tobias,” replied the Admiral, “we are always looking for bright young men to join the King’s Navy.”

Watson’s mind returned to present matters. “I should say a special thank you to you, Admiral Carden, for all that you have done for me. I believe that you should also receive congratulations, Sir… on being elevated from the position of Captain to Admiral this past year. I read about your promotion in a military communication.”

“Thank you, Captain,” replied the Admiral, “my old friend Admiral Hurding retired and I was promoted, but it’s a bugger really – because I don’t get out to sea as much as I used to. But I do get to see my wife and children more often. Now, come and sit-down Tobias. Tell me all about your time at the college. I knew it, I just knew it, the very first time I clapped eyes on you, I knew you would make a successful sailor in the King’s navy. Now where did I first meet you? Was it at Bath town harbour in the *Americas*?”

“I believe that it was in Boston, Massachusetts, in the *Americas* Sir,” said Watson.

“Yes, that’s right,” said an animated Admiral, “it was then that I knew you would make a very fine officer. I could see something in your personality. And here we are, Captain Watson. Let us toast your success.”

The forty-five-year-old Admiral went to his oak drinks console, took two glasses, which he filled to the brim with Navy rum. He handed a glass to Watson.

"Thank you, Sir," said a relaxed Watson.

"Let us drink a toast to your future," called the Admiral.

"And your future too," exclaimed Watson.

"Hmm," said the Admiral, "what's left of it. Here we go Tobias – *bottoms up.*"

Both men drained their glass of this undiluted alcoholic beverage – fit for a seasoned Navy man. Tobias didn't much like the taste of rum, but he thought it impolite not to drink it on this special occasion. The two men sat down and spent the following twenty-minutes talking about old times before getting onto another matter. The second reason why Captain Tobias Watson was in the Admiral's quarters on that day was that he was to be given command of a Naval ship called *St. Aubyn*.

"She's an old ship but it will do you well, Captain Watson, as your first command," said Admiral Carden.

There was a knock on the Admiral's door.

"Enter," shouted the Admiral.

A well-dressed woman, about forty years old, holding the hand of a child aged about eight walked into the Admiral's quarters.

"Stephen," she said, before seeing that Tobias Watson was in the room. "Oh, I am sorry Stephen, I did not realise you were busy."

"Come in my dear," said the Admiral, "let me introduce you to one of the finest Captains in my fleet."

The Admiral and Tobias Watson got to their feet.

"Tobias, this is my wife Annabel and my daughter Alice," said the Admiral.

"I am very pleased to meet you," said Watson as he held out his hand to greet Annabel, "and I am very pleased to meet you too, young Alice."

The blue-eyed young girl looked up at Tobias Watson and smiled before hiding her face in her mother's dress.

"She is a little bit shy today," said the Admiral.

Tobias smiled, “I am very pleased to meet you both.”

“And where’s the other scally wag,” the Admiral continued.

“He’s at home with Nanny – playing with his tin soldiers,” replied Annabel.

“Pity, I would have liked him to meet Tobias,” came the reply, “I want him to meet the finest young naval officer in the world. One day Tobias, I want my own son to join the Navy.”

“Stephen, you know that he’s not interested in the Navy,” replied Annabel.

“Sadly not… he prefers the Army,” replied the Admiral, “but I am working on him.”

“Your son, Admiral?” inquired Watson.

“Yes, my son, he and young Alice are twins, born within one hour of each other,” said the Admiral, “and he prefers the bloody Army to the Navy.”

“Stop it Stephen,” scolded Annabel, “he’s only nine years old.”

The Admiral changed the subject, “What brings you here Annabel?”

“Stephen, you haven’t forgotten that you are home for supper tonight?” asked Annabel.

“Yes, I think I am at home this evening,” said the Admiral, as he thought for a moment while trying to remember.

Suddenly a spark of his memory ignited. “Yes, I am at home. We have a special occasion to celebrate.”

“Good,” replied Annabel, “then I shall see you this evening at the house no later than six-o’clock. Why don’t you bring this fine young man with you for supper? Tobias, I have heard so much about you from the Admiral. He’s been watching your progress in the Navy. Has he told you?”

Watson smiled – unsure of what response to make.

“Don’t embarrass the man Annabel,” said the Admiral, “and what a marvellous idea. Tobias won’t you come for supper this evening? You can meet my son Henry. Maybe you can get him to like the Navy… eh?” The Admiral broke into a hearty laugh.

"I would be very pleased to come to your house for supper," replied Watson.

"Then that's settled Captain Watson," said Annabel, "well, I shall leave you two to talk about ships and things or whatever you men talk about and I shall see you both later. Goodbye."

"Right... let's get back to business Captain Watson," said Admiral Carden.

"Yes Sir," came the reply.

"You are to take command of His Majesty's ship *St. Aubyn* tomorrow morning. She is moored in this harbour," said the Admiral.

"I have seen her," replied Watson.

"You have?" inquired the Admiral.

"Yes Sir, I make it my business to walk the docks and to see what ships are in harbour. It's something I often do when I visit a port," replied Watson, "and as I pass each ship, I check their rigging for irregularities."

The Admiral smiled. "Always on duty young Sir," he replied.

"Yes Sir," replied Watson.

"You shall take some three months to familiarise yourself with your new ship and its crew Captain Watson," said the Admiral, "then I have a mission for you, but I shall not discuss this until nearer the time."

"Very well, Sir," said Watson.

"So, take some time to undertake sea-trials aboard your ship Captain Watson," said the Admiral, "and I shall see you tonight for supper."

The Admiral went to his desk and scribbled something on a piece of parchment.

"Here's my address Tobias, supper will be at seven. Could you arrive at say, six-thirty?"

"Yes, of course Admiral Carden," replied Tobias Watson as he saluted.

Later that day Captain Tobias Watson, wearing his navy dress uniform, made his way to number 22 Anchor Way, a very large house near to the British Naval base. Tobias knocked on the door and the butler of the household let him into a large entrance hall where he took his sword and hat.

"I will show you to Lord Admiral Carden," said Barnes the butler.

"*Lord* Admiral, did you say," said Watson.

"Yes Sir, I did," came the unflinching reply. "His lordship's appointment was announced at six minutes past six o'clock this evening by the Admiralty.

"You mean… since I saw the Admiral this afternoon he has been elevated to the position of a Lord Admiral?" inquired Watson.

"I couldn't possibly comment," replied the butler, "follow me Sir and I will take you to the Lord Admiral and Lady Carden."

The butler led Captain Watson into an adjoining room. The décor was magnificent and certainly befitting a Lord and his lady. Lord Admiral and Lady Carden were standing by the fireplace admiring some miniature portraits on the mantelpiece.

"Come in Captain Watson," called the Lord Admiral.

"Welcome to our house," added Lady Carden.

Tobias strode the thirty feet distance to them and outstretched his hand to greet the Admiral.

"I see congratulations are in order *Lord* Carden," said a smiling Watson as he shook the Admiral's hand, "and you too Lady Carden," as he kissed her hand.

"Thank you, Captain Watson," came the simultaneous reply from them both.

"Of course, I have known about this honour for weeks. But I have not been allowed to say anything until the public posting at naval headquarters. That was done about half-an-hour ago," said the Admiral.

"Well it seems a shame that I will interfere with your celebrations tonight," said Tobias Watson.

"On the contrary my man," replied the Admiral, "you are here to celebrate with us and so are the other forty guests who have been invited. It is my Scottish Ancestry that has led to my appointment, not necessarily my naval background – but the

Navy are not complaining, they don't mind a Lord or two in their ranks. Some of my Scottish relatives are here tonight. I shall introduce you to them. They and my other guests are through that doorway, Captain Watson, in the ball room. Barnes, our butler will show you the way. We will be through soon… we are just waiting for another two guests."

"Oh, I see, you have a pre-planned celebration," replied Watson. "Well, thank you for my invitation, I really do appreciate your kindness Lord and Lady Carden."

"Follow me Sir," called Barnes the butler.

Tobias Watson was led into the ballroom to the sound of joviality and music, where he joined the other guests. Later, they moved into the dining room where they sat down to a roast supper of lamb, with starters of Custard Fish Yum, which was promptly served at seven o'clock. In the corner of the room a pianist played a tune accompanied by a violinist and bassist.

After the first course had been cleared away a child peered around the open doorway.

"Sass… sass," she called to the Admiral. Behind her was a boy of about the same age. They were both accompanied by their nanny.

Admiral Carden saw the child and laughed, "Oh yes, I haven't forgotten," he mouthed to the blonde girl. He had of course forgotten; that was until he had been reminded. The Admiral hit the table with his gavel to attract the attention of his guests.

"Ladies and gentlemen," boomed the Admiral, "our children are going to bed and would wish to say goodnight to you all."

The children entered the room with their nanny and said goodnight. The guests sitting around the dining table called 'goodnight' to the children.

"But before they go to bed, they want to sing you a song," said a cheerful Admiral.

A huge "Ahhhh" emanated from the female members of the group.

"Ladies and Gentlemen, may I present our twin children, our son Henry and daughter Alice… Maestro if you please," called the Admiral to the pianist.

The audience clapped hands to encourage the youngsters.

The nine-year olds stood side by side, Alice wore a red dress with a pink ribbon in her hair and Henry was wearing the child uniform of a British soldier with a wooden sword and leather scabbard affixed to his belt.

Girls and boys, come out to play,
The moon doth shine as bright as day;
Leave your supper, and leave your sleep,
And come with your friends, into the street.

(Artist Unknown)

At the end of the song the audience politely clapped their hands, and some of the men cheered.

The boy Henry pulled his sword from its scabbard and shouted, "Who wants to fight me?" with that kind of aggressive bravado that only nine-year-old boys have contained within their personality.

Tobias was seated nearest to young Henry.

"Well I would fight you, young Sir," called Tobias, "but I have no sword – for Barnes the butler has taken it from me."

"I have a spare sword," replied Henry before scurrying out of the door – to return moments later with an identical wooden sword.

Tobias looked towards the Admiral for approval – which was given by way of a nod and a smile.

Henry handed Tobias the sword and they spent the next five minutes engaged in a play fight on the dining room carpet. Tobias spent most of this time on his knees to compensate for their difference in height.

"Come on Henry," called Alice, "hurry up with your fight because nanny says it's time for bed."

Tobias paused for a moment to look at this young girl. He had seen mannerisms like hers before; the way in which she spoke – her individuality, her demeanour, her temperament. Traces of her young character radiated around the room as she scolded her brother. Then he saw a wonderful sparkle in her bright blue eyes during that fleeting moment. She reminded Tobias of someone he once knew in Copperas Gap, someone who died so very long ago. Someone he loved so very much.

"Come, come," shouted the Admiral, "sword fights do not last for an eternity. Someone has to win, and someone has to die."

It was time to end the fight. That was the Admiral's orders. Tobias allowed his defence to falter and young Henry gained the advantage and stabbed him in the heart. Tobias fell down dead on the spot. It was a soft landing for the carpet quality was, to say the least, luxurious.

"I win," shouted an elated Henry as he held his sword high above his head with his right foot resting on Tobias Watson's chest.

Tobias Watson lay dead for a few moments to allow Henry to bask in his military glory. Then he stood up, thanked him and handed back the wooden sword of a loser.

Young Henry returned the tribute and thanked Tobias.

"Time for bed now," called nanny, "go and say goodnight to your parents."

The children kissed their mother and father goodnight before leaving the room with nanny.

The rest of the evening was a very pleasant one for Tobias Watson. He had never been to such a function where so many dignitaries and important people were gathered. There were some very high-ranking naval officers at the party and Tobias soon got to know most of them. His training at the military academy had put him in good stead. For Tobias Watson, the illiterate boy from Copperas Gap who once spoke with a southern regional accent, was now a well-spoken fascinating compelling gentleman of considerable knowledge. At ten o'clock that evening Tobias Watson returned to his temporary accommodation in the town of Portsmouth – Mrs. Morse's house. He knew that tomorrow he would formally take command of his first ship as Captain of the King's ship, *St. Aubyn.*

Chapter 17

Hostage. A beautiful Princess.

Captain Tobias Watson took command of the King's ship *St. Aubyn* on the 18th June 1724. Three weeks later, after extensive sea trials aboard his new ship, he returned to port and made his way to see the Lord Admiral Stephen Carden, in his quarters aboard his flagship.

"Come in Captain Watson," called the Admiral, "how are you getting on with your new ship?"

"It's a very fine ship Admiral," replied Watson, "and I have purchased a dog for the ship. He is a fine-looking long-haired Jack Russell. I have named him Patch, he is just the sort of animal for catching rats."

"That's good news. I shall have to meet this dog of yours Captain Watson. Well, I haven't got much time today Watson, so I will get straight to the point," said the Admiral.

"I want you to sail to Massachusetts in the Americas. The British colonists are having problems with the French. The French have been encouraging the Abenaki tribe of native Indians to attack British frontier posts. Like all wars it has a name. It's a war called the 4th Anglo-Abenaki or better known as Dummers war. Here are your written orders from the Admiralty," said Carden.

Admiral Carden passed the document to Captain Watson.

"Thank you, Sir," said Watson, "when do I sail?"

"As soon as you can Captain Watson," came the reply, "your orders are to support the war at sea, to disrupt French shipping to their colony known as *New France.* You will be under the direction of the acting governor William Dummer and the British military generals. On this voyage you will take two-hundred soldiers aboard your ship and deliver them to General Hawk in the Americas. Other British ships are also on their way with more troops."

“How long will this mission last?” asked Watson.

“I don’t know the answer to that,” replied the Admiral, “but I guess that you shall stay there for as long as this war lasts. That is all I have to tell you Watson. God speed on your journey.”

It was October 1724 when Captain Watson sailed for the Americas. Patch the dog went too and spent his sleeping hours in the captain’s quarters – while during his waking hours he was often with the ship’s crew barking his doggy orders at them. That was in-between catching rats of course. The ship arrived in Boston harbour in early December and almost at once began the task of disrupting French shipping further north. The ship and crew of the *St. Aubyn* remained in the area for just over two years. During this time Tobias Watson was mentioned in dispatches to the Admiralty for his heroics, leadership and sheer determination in supporting the British flag and colonialists. Captain Tobias Watson was a hero of the British people. Indeed, stories began to be published in national newspapers detailing his many military conquests and adventures. By December 1725 Dummers war was over. For the next two years the ship and its crew remained in the Americas and towards the end of 1727 the Admiralty ordered Captain Tobias Watson to sail to Gibraltar, off the coast of mainland Spain. His orders: to receive a new ship by the name of the *Astound* and to scuttle his present ship – the battle-weary old lady of the sea, *St. Aubyn* which was, by now, considered too old for the Navy’s modern-day purposes. Watson took command of his new ship the *Astound* and spent the next two years taking part in the Spanish war of succession in Europe; before returning to the Americas for five years as a support ship for the Chicksaw war and other conflicts against the French. It was around this time that he learned of the death of his Father, George; but he could not get back to Copperas Gap due to Naval commitments.

In 1734, Tobias Watson’s ship was positioned off the rock of Gibraltar. And that is where this story should end.

But there is one more final piece of this tale to tell. The astute reader of this manuscript will remember that the latter part of Chapter one paused, as Watson and his depleted crew sailed aboard his stricken vessel.

The *Astound,* you may recall, was at peril. The ship's master Mr. Brown was dead and so was the boy John – both crushed by falling cannons. Mr. Brown's spirit was now steering the ship *Astound* towards Fishersgate harbour 1734 England, and the spirit of the boy John was in the crow's nest. Patch, the elderly dog, watched Mr. Brown and whimpered at this ghostly sight. The ship had no other crew of ordinary seamen. Only five men were alive aboard this ship: Captain Watson, Lieutenant Roach, soldiers Bartlett and Hodges as well as an injured Robert Hotham, the ship's surgeon and carpenter. And worse, they were about to come under attack by a Spanish galleon. The *Astound* had no crew to defend itself against such a Spanish military onslaught for they had all mysteriously disappeared.

"Please prepare Mr. Brown's body for a burial at sea Lieutenant Roach," shouted Captain Watson, "we shall bury him within the next fifteen minutes before the Spanish galleon is upon us."

The burial was hastily prepared and carried out soon after. When it was complete Captain Watson turned to Roach. "Well, we are in a predicament Mr. Roach. An attacking Spanish ship is about to fire on us and we have no crew to defend us; and even if we did have a ship's crew, we have no cannon or shot to fire with, for our defences are strewn about the ship."

"With respect Captain, the only thing we can do is try to outrun them," replied Roach, "if we can get that wheel turned-about we can head for the Rock of Gibraltar. They will not follow us once we get near to the Rock."

"I agree, Mr. Roach," said the Captain, "but first let us consider our predicament. The steersman wheel will not turn-about, and we have an image of the spirit of Mr. Brown who appears to be setting a course for this ship. However, the reality is that it is possible that the ropes to the tiller are jammed. We shall go down to the tiller in the gun room on the middle deck and cut the ropes. Then we can steer the ship directly from there."

A few minutes later both men were in the tiller room where they found two ropes, some two feet apart, extending down from the steersman wheel through cut-outs in the main deck.

"Cut that rope Mr. Roach," ordered the Captain.

Roach took out a knife and began to cut one of the ropes. The knife made no impression upon the rope at all – even though Roach exerted quite an effort.

"The rope will not cut, Captain," exclaimed Roach.

"Here, let me see that knife?" asked the Captain.

Roach handed the knife to Captain Watson, who brushed his thumb across the sharpness of the blade.

"It seems sharp enough," said the Captain.

"It is Sir, it was sharpened just a few days ago," came the reply.

The Captain tried to cut the rope, but the knife made no indent into its fibres. He pulled his sword from its scabbard to try to cut the rope. It made no impression. Finally, the Captain found an axe in the carpenter's workshop and attempted to cut the rope – the axe-handle broke. Nothing it seemed would cut into this rope.

"I already told you that your plan will not work," boomed a voice.

Both men looked around. Before them stood the same strange looking bedraggled man wearing a lamb-skin apron. They had seen him before. He was dressed as a shopkeeper; quite out of context on a sailing ship. His name was Wentworth and he was an ancient soothsayer who acted for the forces of good.

Wentworth continued, "I told you that your ship is set on a pre-defined course for Fishersgate harbour near Copperas Gap, England and there is nothing you can do to alter this course. The Lord of the universe has ordered that you must go to this land to change the course of history – for if you do not something terrible will happen."

"What?" asked Captain Watson.

"You will find out," said Wentworth.

"What will the future hold for myself and my ship's company?" asked Watson.

There was no response. Wentworth's image faded into the woodwork.

Patch the dog began barking at this fading image. The Captain ordered Patch to be quiet.

Suddenly a female voice interjected. "Tobias, follow your natural instincts."

Watson looked around. The voice was that of Molly Moffatt, but Tobias could not see her.

Roach also heard Molly's voice.

"What is happening?" asked Roach, as he too looked around the area for this mysterious female voice.

The Captain did not respond.

Roach continued, "Captain, the Spanish will be upon us in the next few minutes. I fear that we will all be dead soon."

Watson ignored Lieutenant Roach.

"Molly, where are you?" asked Tobias Watson.

"I am here my lover, but you cannot see me," replied Molly, "do what you must and remember that we will be together when you die a mortal death."

"Well that won't be long," said a worried Roach, "the Spanish are near to this ship – can you hear their cannon fire?"

Once again, Watson ignored Roach.

"Molly… I love you," cried Tobias.

"Sir," exclaimed Roach, "I appreciate your declaration of love to this woman that I cannot see, but the Spanish are here, and I feel we must fight – even though it will be a fight to our death. There are only five of us aboard our ship – and one is injured. We are up against a Spanish ship of five-hundred men, we will die fighting – unless we surrender."

"We will never surrender," exclaimed Watson.

"Have faith in your Captain, Mr. Roach," called Molly, "I will leave you now, but I will return."

"Molly…Molly," Tobias screamed. But there was no reply, for she had gone.

Then, mysteriously, the roar of cannon fire erupted from the British ship, *Astound*.

"Did you hear that Captain?" shouted Roach, "it's impossible! The cannon fire is coming from this ship."

Both men rushed to the upper gun deck. More barrages of cannon fire were heard as the vibrations were felt throughout the ship.

On the upper gun deck the two men were privileged to a magical sight. There were a hundred sailors manning the guns. Watson and Roach ran down to the lower deck to see another hundred sailors. The cannons and shot that had been strewn about during the recent upheaval were back in their proper places, positioned exactly as they should be. The sailors were loading the cannons with gunpowder and cannon balls. They were firing at the Spanish ship – and better still, they were winning. The Spanish ship had succumbed to some serious structural damage.

"It is a mystery Captain," said Lieutenant Roach, "I don't understand it – where did these men come from?"

The Captain observed for a moment while the battle continued.

"Lieutenant Roach, look at the crew members closer," said the Captain, "they have that glow about them as did Mr. Brown and the boy John. They are the spirits of dead men. They are dead men walking in dead men's shoes."

"Are you all right Captain?" shouted one of the glowing men, as he took a sup of rum from a ladle.

"Yes," replied Captain Watson as he looked at a familiar face – before recognising him and smiling broadly. "Yes Mr. French I am fine. Go easy on the rum my good man, I don't want you to get drunk. Go about your business and do your fighting with the Spanish."

"Yes Sir, yes Captain Watson," replied French as he put down the ladle, "and one last thing Captain before I go…"

"Yes Mr. French," called Watson, "what is it?"

"Thank you for returning my new shoes," said French as he pointed down to a pair of shiny shoes on his feet.

"You are most welcome Mr. French," replied Captain Watson.

Mr. French smiled before disappearing into the crowd of fighting men.

Roach looked at the men loading and firing the cannons and gasped in amazement.

"These dead men are winning a battle for us!" called Roach in almost disbelief.

"Come on Mr. Roach let us make haste onto the main deck," shouted Watson.

The two men watched as the barrage of fire from the *Astound* hit their Spanish target again and again. The *Astound* turned and weaved through the waves on a perfect trajectory suited to the battle to hand. A mysterious force was controlling its speed and direction. Soon, there was only a fifty-yard distance between the two ships. The men on the Spanish ship ceased firing. Their ship was a wreck – its masts, sails and rigging torn to destruction – its bow taking in water. A white flag was raised, as high as they could get it on the damaged timbers of the Spanish ship.

"Cease fire," shouted Captain Watson.

The cannon fire ceased. At that moment the two soldiers, Bartlett and Hodges, came onto the deck. They had left the injured Robert Hotham in the sick bay.

"They are surrendering Captain," said Roach, "I find it quite amusing that an entire Spanish company are surrendering to five Englishmen."

"And some two-hundred English spirits," interjected Watson, "but we cannot accept their surrender, for once they realise there are only five of us they will eject us from our own ship. We must continue to destroy them."

"Continue firing at will," ordered Captain Watson at the top of his voice. It was a bit of a longshot for he did not know if the English spirits aboard his ship would accept his command.

Hodges and Bartlett cheered at the Captain's decision.

There was silence for a moment. Then the barrage of cannon fire began once more. Watson was indeed in command of the ship's fire power.

Just then Roach spotted something on the main deck of the Spanish Galleon.

"Captain Watson," he exclaimed, "I see a woman on the deck of the Spanish ship."

"Lend me your telescope," asked the Captain.

Roach passed his telescope to Watson who proceeded to look through its lenses of magnification – towards the Spanish ship.

"My God," Watson exclaimed before shouting as loud as he could, "cease firing, cease firing."

The cannons fell silent.

"What is it Captain?" asked Roach.

"The Princess Serafina of Seville is aboard the Spanish ship," exclaimed Watson.

"With respect Sir," said Roach, "there is nothing we can do – we must continue to sink the Spanish ship, for if we give them leeway they will over run us."

Captain Watson thought for a moment before looking at Hodges and Bartlett. As he did so the residue of smoke from the aftermath of the *Astound's* cannon fire, faded away.

Wentworth the soothsayers voice was heard once more. "Captain Watson, the spiritual fighting force of your sailors has now been re-called. Your fighting force has been depleted. You must use your wit and skills to continue."

"We are done for now," called Roach, "you should not have ordered a cease fire Captain, for we have now lost our fighting prowess."

"I will not allow the death of this Princess. She is my friend," said Watson, "and less of your insolence Roach. I command this ship – not you. Now, I need one man to volunteer. I want you to put one of our quarter boats into the water, raise the white flag of peace and row to the Spanish ship with a message from me."

"Is that wise Sir?" inquired Roach. "What is a Spanish Princess to us?"

"Do not question my authority Roach," said Watson, "it is my duty to save the lives of the five men aboard this ship and where possible the lives of our enemies too; though I don't know why the Spanish attacked, for I do not believe we are at war with them at this present time."

"I will do it," said a determined Hodges.

"You risk your life Hodges," said the Captain.

"I know," replied Hodges.

"This is what you are to say to the Spanish Captain Mr. Hodges," said Watson, "that I will spare all of their lives aboard the Spanish ship in return for one hostage – that hostage will be the Princess Serafina. You will promise on my behalf that we will not harm her but take her back to England – tell them no more than that. Then, if they agree, bring her back to this ship in the quarter deck rowing boat. You will give them my word that once the Princess is aboard this ship we will sail away and leave them to drift until one of their own ships find them."

"Very well Sir," came the reply.

"Whatever you do Hodges," continued the Captain, "do not tell them that there are only five of us aboard this British ship. If anything, you must indicate we have a compliment of some six-hundred men at the ready to board their ship," said Watson. "Do you understand Hodges?"

"I understand you Captain. But what should I do if they refuse?" asked Hodges.

"You are to come back with that message and I will reconsider our options," replied the Captain.

"Why don't we just sail off and leave them," asked Roach, "the Spanish ship is disabled, and we certainly don't need a Spanish Princess."

"Ahhh, but we do," replied Watson, "for we are a lone British ship and we shall be sailing several hundred miles around the coast of Spain. If we encounter another Spanish ship of war, then we simply produce our hostage and they will back off. They will let us travel freely to our destination in England."

Roach thought for a moment.

"I have to say Captain," said Roach, "that your plan is a clever one considering our circumstances. But Captain, would you kill the Princess? That is, if the Spanish ignored your threat?"

Captain Watson did not reply to this question for he knew that he would never kill this beautiful Princess. Only Watson knew how special the Princess was to him.

"Thank you, Mr. Roach," replied the Captain, "now take heed man – the two of us must remove our officer's uniforms and dress as ordinary sailors. The Spanish will think something odd if they see officers launching a quarter deck rowing boat."

Within minutes they were dressed as ordinary sailors. With the help of Hodges and Bartlett they lowered the small vessel into the water and affixed a makeshift white flag to the stern of the boat. Hodges got into the rowing boat, picked up the oars and placed them into the rowlocks.

"Remember Hodges – be as cautious as you can," called Captain Watson as he stood on the deck looking down in the boat.

"Good luck mate," shouted Bartlett to his fellow soldier.

Hodges set-off, gently rowing the boat towards his objective. The others watched as he completed the short journey to the Spanish ship. The rowing boat was tethered to the Spanish Galleon and Hodges climbed aboard, assisted by a few Spanish sailors.

"This is the moment where we learn of our fate," warned Captain Watson.

They watched from the English ship and could see that there was some discussion between the Spanish Captain, the Princess and Hodges. This lasted for over half an hour. The Princess was actively engaged in the conversation. It was likely that because of her ability to speak excellent English she was translating the terms from Hodges to the Spanish Captain.

"Come on Hodges, do the business," said Bartlett under his breath.

Then, they saw in the distance that the Spanish sailors were escorting and assisting the Princess into the quarter deck boat. Hodges followed and the two of them cast off from the Spanish ship and were en-route back to the *Astound*."

"Make no noise whatsoever – not until they are aboard this ship," ordered Watson.

The small boat came alongside the Astound. Bartlett assisted Hodges and together they helped the Spanish Princess up the rope ladder to the main deck. Once on deck she adjusted her clothing to make herself comfortable and looked towards Captain Watson.

"Tobias," she purred as she fluttered her eyelashes, "how nice to see you again. Why are you dressed like an ordinary sailor?"

"Princess Serafina, it is so good to see you again. It's been fifteen years, two months and three days since I last saw you," replied Tobias, "I am Captain of this ship, though today for reasons too detailed to explain right now I have decided to dress as an able seaman."

"How can you be so certain that it is fifteen years, two months and three days since we last spoke?" she inquired.

"I am certain," came the reply, "I keep a diary."

"And you have the audacity to demand that I am to be your hostage," said the Princess as she smiled to display her natural beauty; a beauty which Tobias Watson had not forgotten.

"Yes, I did ask for you to be my hostage Princess and for that I apologise," replied Watson.

"There is no need to apologise Tobias. Come and kiss my hand. I have missed you so much," said the Princess.

Tobias walked towards her. He kissed her outstretched hand before taking her in his arms and kissing her cheek. "And I have missed you Princess," he replied. "How did you get out of the Tower of London?"

"They kept us prisoners for a few weeks before releasing us in exchange for English prisoners that my government were holding," she replied. "Are you to take me back to the Tower of London, Tobias?"

"No Madam," he replied, "I will make sure you get back to Spain in due course – you have my word on that."

"Why then did you take me as a hostage Tobias?" asked the Princess.

"We men must do what we think is right during times of conflict," replied Tobias.

"And it is lucky for you that I agreed to be your hostage," said the Princess with a smile. "I agreed to your demands as soon as Hodges told me that you were the Captain of this ship. Captain Rodriguez of the Spanish ship was prepared to fight to the death rather than release me as your hostage."

"You agreed to be my hostage and put yourself in danger?" said Watson.

"Yes, I did Tobias," she replied. "Tobias Watson, I really don't mind being your hostage. You are the most pleasant and trustworthy Englishman that I know – I feel safe with you. My affection for you has grown this past fifteen years, though I never thought I would see you again."

"You flatter me Princess," Tobias replied before staring at her exceptional beauty.

The Princess noted his stare. "Tobias are you feeling all right?" asked the Princess.

"Yes, I am fine," came his reply as he broke his gaze upon her.

"Sir," called Roach, "we have hauled the quarter boat back on deck – might I suggest that we make sail."

"Very well Mr. Roach, make sail," replied Watson.

Instantly, the spirits of the ship's crew returned on deck before getting straight to work. The sails sprung to life, the steersman turned the wheel and the ship began to pick up speed due to a favourable headwind.

"Destination England," shouted an elated Lieutenant Roach, "I was not expecting the ship's crew to return for I thought that Wentworth said they had gone."

"Had you listened to Wentworth's words in detail Mr. Roach you would have heard him say that the spiritual *fighting force* of sailors was depleted; but he did not mention the spiritual *sailing force* who are now manoeuvring this ship," called Tobias Watson.

"Thank you, Captain, for clarification," called a thrilled Roach, "destination England," he repeated at the top of his voice.

"That will do me," said Hodges, the hero of the day.

"Come Princess," said Watson, "I will show you to your cabin. You can sleep in my quarters on our journey to England, I will sleep in one of the officer's cabins for we have plenty of room aboard this ship."

"That is very kind of you Tobias," she replied, as he led her below deck.

The Captain looked down at Patch, his dog, who had been watching him and the Princess. "Come on Patch I have a job for you – you can look after the Princess." The dog scampered into action and followed his master.

"We shall have dinner together tonight. That is, if you are free?" asked Captain Watson.

"Oh, I shall be free Tobias. I shall be free to see you every day, every morning and every evening; I shall be free to see you for the rest of my life if you want me to. I look forward to having dinner with you tonight," replied a delighted Princess before she looked at the dog, "and you too Patch."

The dog barked with delight.

The journey to Fishersgate Harbour at Copperas Gap, England, was to take a further twenty days. Tobias Watson had indeed been proven right. They came across two more powerful Spanish warships en-route that attempted to attack them but with the presence of their hostage, the Spanish soon backed-off thus allowing the *Astound* to continue its journey to England. The Princess was a most willing hostage to Tobias Watson and they resumed their friendship during those few days. In fact, by the time they got to Fishersgate Harbour, the Princess Serafina had fallen in love with Englishman Tobias Watson.

Chapter 18

Fishersgate harbour.1734.

On the 31st March 1734 the ship arrived offshore at Copperas Gap. They waited for the high tide before entering Fishersgate harbour under a haze of morning mist. Captain Watson had told Princess Serafina the story of the missing ship's crew. She found this difficult to believe at first and thought that Tobias was making fun, but in time, she realised that the ship did not have a proper crew and that it appeared to be navigating itself. It was only when the ship's sails were set or taken-in or when other naval actions were undertaken, did Princess Serafina realise that there were no mortal crew members performing these many tasks. The sails, rigging and beams moved on their own. It was all done by something inexplicable – perhaps it was magic.

"Drop the anchor and make the ship secure," ordered Watson, "we are in a tidal port and the waters of Fishersgate harbour will soon drain away. All of us will disembark for Copperas Gap on two rowing boats, for when the tide runs away the ship *Astound* will list heavily to one side. Hodges and Bartlett, you will take the injured Mr. Hotham in one rowing boat and find him a doctor. The Princess and Mr. Roach will travel with me in a second rowing boat."

"Very good Sir," came the reply from Hodges.

"You Patch," as the Captain looked down at his trusty Jack Russell dog, "shall guard this ship with your life." The dog barked and ran towards his master who knelt and made a fuss of him.

"Good boy Patch, I will see you in a few days."

They rowed their small boats the short distance from their ship to the beach, where they tethered the boats to a stake.

"Hodges would you and Bartlett take Mr. Hotham to the doctor? You will find his house further up the hill," ordered Watson. "How are you feeling Mr. Hotham?"

"As best as can be expected Captain – I was lucky I wasn't killed when those cannons came thundering my way – but they got my leg," replied Hotham, "I fear it may be amputated."

"Keep your chin-up and your leg attached Hotham," replied the Captain, "that is an order – we will soon have you with the doctor."

The two soldiers lifted Hotham onto a makeshift stretcher that they had constructed aboard the *Astound* and carried him up the hill to find the doctor.

"It seems very quiet here Mr. Roach," said Watson, "that's unusual for Copperas Gap. I would have expected to see the bustling sight of fishermen and their wives in the harbour filleting fish, children playing games and the farmers in the fields further up the hill tending to the animals on the land."

"I have not been to Copperas Gap before Captain," replied Roach.

"Come," said the Captain, "I know this place well. It is my birthplace. Let us ascend the steps from the harbour to the high road. There is a tavern called the Halfway House, where we can get refreshment and rooms for the night."

They ascended the timber staircase that took them up a steep grassed bank some ten-yards above the harbour. The coastal road ran from west to east and on the other side of the road stood the Halfway House tavern. Captain Watson tried to open the front door of the tavern. It was locked shut.

"Unusual," he said, "I have never known this place to be closed."

The Captain knocked on the door.

The door opened a few inches. A chain prevented it from opening further and a man peered through the gap. Tobias recognised the man as the innkeeper, though he looked much older than when he last saw him – eighteen years before.

"Are you open for business Mr. Jenkins?" asked the Captain.

"Depends who wants business," said the innkeeper.

"I am Tobias Watson. Do you not remember me Mr. Jenkins?" asked the Captain.

"Tobias Watson… Tobias Watson?" repeated the innkeeper with a vacant look upon his face. "How do you know my name?"

"I know your name because I used to live in Copperas Gap," said Watson. "I have returned after eighteen years."

"Tobias Watson – should I know you?" asked the innkeeper, "we don't see many captains of the King's Navy around here, not in Copperas Gap. They all go three-miles eastwards to Brighthelmstone for a bit of fun."

"I am the son of the late shoemaker and cobbler in this village, George Watson," replied Tobias.

The innkeeper thought for a moment. Then, his facial features changed to abhorrence.

"Molly," exclaimed the innkeeper, "you killed Molly! We do not want you in this village Watson."

The innkeeper slammed the door shut.

"It seems that he does not like you Captain," remarked Lieutenant Roach.

"Who is Molly?" asked the Princess.

"Molly and I grew up here in Copperas Gap. We planned to marry but she died in sad circumstances," replied Watson.

"I see, I am so sorry," said the Princess – not wishing to pry any further.

Suddenly, the door opened again. It was not restricted by the security chain anymore. In the doorway stood an overweight woman about sixty years old. She wore the clothes of a kitchen maid and held a rolling-pin in her hand.

"Don't take no notice of him," she said, "he's only the innkeeper, he thinks he's in charge of this establishment, but he is not."

"I am in charge woman," boomed the voice of the innkeeper, who was out of sight.

The woman turned towards the voice, "No you bleeding ain't," she continued, "you're a fool for turning away the good business of a captain of his King's Navy, a Lieutenant and a very well-dressed lady. Why I ought to throttle you on the spot."

"She is a Princess actually," said Roach.

The woman looked at Roach before looking once again at the Princess.

"A bleeding Princess… that's what she is," called the woman as she turned towards the out of sight innkeeper and hit him several times with her rolling-pin. "You turned down a bloody Princess you fool and half the flaming Navy as well. Lucky, I caught you. And yesterday I caught you again when you nearly turned away an Admiral of the King's fleet."

"An Admiral?" inquired a surprised Captain Watson.

"Yes, a bloody Admiral," replied the woman, "he turned away a bloody Admiral."

"He wasn't an Admiral," bellowed the voice of the innkeeper, "he said he was an Admiral, but he was not dressed like one. Dressed just like an ordinary toff he was."

"He was a bloody Admiral I tell you," said the woman, "he spoke all prim and proper like a gentleman. He arrived by ship. I could tell he was a man of importance."

"Everyone arrives by ship in this place," shouted the innkeeper, "*anyways* – never mind about the bloody Admiral – this man who stands before you is none other than Tobias Watson who was banished by the villagers eighteen years ago."

"I don't care who he is. If he has the money to pay for a room – then he is good enough for me," replied the woman.

Tobias smiled, then he thought for a moment. "May I ask who you are madam?"

"I am Deloris Jenkins, the innkeeper's wife. But not for much bloody longer… I can tell you. Do you know what it's like living with HIM," came the angry reply, before changing the tone of her voice to a gentle welcoming one, "please come in young Sirs and Princess. I take it that you will require three rooms at three shillings a night. How long do you require the rooms for, may I ask?"

"Let us say a week," said Watson.

"That's seven days, times three shillings, equals twenty-four shillings. No, it's twenty-two shillings, I think," said the woman as she counted the amount on her three fingers. "I have never been sure of counting money properly; not since I lost one of my fingers in the meat slicer."

"Twenty-one shillings for cash in advance," said a smiling Captain Watson, who was aware of her mathematical error.

"You drive a hard bargain Captain," replied the woman as she held out her hand to take the money.

"Madam, you are an astute businesswoman. I will need another room for three of my men – they will sleep together. Here, take another seven shillings." Captain Watson handed her twenty-eight shillings. "I will require a receipt," he said. "Now tell me about this Admiral that is on your premises," inquired Watson.

"He's no Admiral," said the innkeeper from the shadows.

"Shuddup you," said the woman aggressively before sweetly smiling at Captain Watson, "he's staying here in room fourteen," she replied. "Please come in, I will show you to your rooms."

Once the Captain had settled in his room and taken morning tea in the dining area, he met with the Princess and explained to her why he had left Copperas Gap all those years before. He told her about his one true love Molly, his family, her family and the people of the village. He spoke about how he had been banished from Copperas Gap after being given a stigma and how he had joined the navy to become a Captain of the King's fleet. The Princess was saddened by this story and very sympathetic. Then, Tobias Watson decided to knock on the door of room fourteen to satisfy his curiosity about this supposed Admiral. It would be very unusual to find an Admiral at such a modest establishment.

The door to room fourteen opened.

"I knew you would come to me," exclaimed the occupant, "Tobias Watson I have a task for you."

"I am shocked to see you Lord Admiral Carden," exclaimed Tobias Watson, "what are you doing here in a place like Copperas Gap? Why are you not in uniform?"

"Come in," said the Admiral, "where have you been Tobias? I called for you some time ago."

"I got here as soon as I could," came the reply, "but I know nothing of why I am here. Admiral Carden, what are you doing here? Where are your aides and officers?"

"I cannot tell you everything," said the Admiral.

Watson insisted. "Admiral, tell me what has happened? I will do my best to help though I do not have many men with me and one, the ship's carpenter Robert Hotham, has a broken leg. I also have a Spanish princess in my custody."

The Admiral turned away to look out of the window onto the port of Fishersgate bay.

Watson continued, "There are mysterious forces at work here Admiral. And there is a reason why I am here. I was told to be here in Copperas Gap many years ago by my friend Molly. I do not know what that reason is right now, but I believe that it is no coincidence that you and I are here in this place together."

The Admiral turned around and looked Watson straight in the eyes.

"I know nothing of anyone called Molly. Who is Molly? I personally asked for you to be sent here through the chain of Naval command," replied the Admiral.

Tobias thought for a moment.

"Never mind who got me to come here," replied Tobias, "the fact of the matter is that I am here right now and at your service Lord Admiral. You must tell me everything."

"Tobias," said the Admiral, "only you can save the people of Copperas Gap. They have been sent away by mysterious forces into a parallel universe. But there is something else you must know."

"Tell me your story Admiral," asked Tobias Watson.

"It's a long story Tobias, but one month ago my beautiful daughter Alice and my son Henry were kidnapped. They are both nineteen years old. I have not seen them since and have been in negotiations with their captors," replied the Admiral. "I am here to pay a ransom on the 2nd April at 12:00 noon. I have two of my most trusted sailors keeping a watch on the harbour."

"Are these the same children that I first met at your house in Portsmouth about ten years ago?" asked Watson.

“They are,” replied the Admiral, “they are my only children.”

“I remember them both,” said Watson with a smile, “And, if I remember correctly, I had a playfight with young Henry using a wooden sword.”

“Yes, you did,” said the Admiral, “Henry is now a Lieutenant in the King’s Army.”

“You wanted him to join the navy?” inquired Watson.

“I did, but I lost him to the army,” said the Admiral.

“Alice and he are twins if I remember,” said Watson.

“That’s right,” came the Admiral’s reply.

Watson thought for a moment.

“The second of April at 12:00 noon you say,” replied Watson as he pondered on that date in time, “Yes, that is the date that Molly told me to be here in Copperas Gap.”

“It is?” asked a puzzled Admiral.

“Yes,” came the reply from Watson. “What is the ransom that you must pay?”

“£500 in gold.”

“Five hundred pounds is a tidy sum Admiral,” replied Watson, “who is your point of contact with the kidnappers?”

“The man I met is a church Rector,” replied the Admiral.

“I know of him,” said Watson.

“He is a wicked man,” replied the Admiral, “not a man that should be a part of the church.”

“He is an imposter; I am sure of it,” revealed Watson.

“Why are your trusted sailors watching the harbour?” asked Watson.

“That is where the ransom is to be paid, though I do not yet have the finer details,” said the Admiral, “we might just see something down at the harbour that will help our situation. That is why we are watching the area.”

Tobias Watson thought for a moment using his analytical mind.

“Look Admiral,” said Watson, “it is March 31st today and the exchange between you and the kidnappers is due to take place in two days’ time. I will help you. But first there is something I must do. It will form part of my plan to get your children back to you safely."

"Thank you, Tobias – you always were the helpful sort," replied the Admiral.

As Watson left the room he turned to the Admiral, "you have the gold ransom with you?"

"I do," said the Admiral.

"Keep it well hidden, Admiral. Wait until you hear from me."

The Admiral nodded in agreement.

Chapter 19

The Conclusion.

The following morning a stagecoach arrived at Copperas Gap. There was a letter among its postbags, duly addressed to Lord Admiral Stephen Carden. The letter was from the Board of the Admiralty in Greenwich, giving specific orders of a detailed plan and instructions on ship's co-ordinates.

The Admiral made his way to the dining room hoping to find Captain Watson, but instead he found Lieutenant Roach.

"Stand up Lieutenant Roach," ordered Admiral Carden.

"Yes Sir," came the reply from a surprised Roach as he stood to attention, "bit of a shock to see you here Sir, in the dining room of this establishment – Sir."

"Yes, well never mind about that Roach," replied the Admiral, "I have received orders from the Admiralty and I want you to take the ship *Astound* with the Princess, the two soldiers Hodges and Bartlett and ship's carpenter Hotham back to Gibraltar. You shall leave by the *Brambledean mist* on the next high tide which is three hours from now."

"What is the *Brambledean mist*?" asked Roach.

"All the information you require is contained in these written orders," replied the Admiral as he passed the papers to Roach.

"What about Captain Watson Sir?" asked Roach. "I have not yet seen him this morning."

"Watson has gone on a pre-planned special mission. I was hoping to catch him before he left. However, now that he has gone I can tell you that you will not see him for a while," said the Admiral, "and your orders are to leave him behind. He will make his own way to Gibraltar once his mission is completed."

"Might I be permitted to know what his mission is?" asked Roach.

"It's something to do with an undercover operation here in Fishersgate harbour. I cannot tell you more," said Carden, "but it is nothing that should concern you Roach. Your orders are clear. You must take the ship *Astound* and its passengers back to Gibraltar."

"Then I will do my duty Admiral," said Roach.

"By the way, I have heard that ship's carpenter, Robert Hotham, has broken his leg. How is he now?" asked the Admiral.

"He is all fixed up," replied Roach, "and staying in one of the rooms here in this tavern. Yesterday, the doctor did a good job on him. He has splints on his leg and can walk with the aid of crutches. He thought he would lose his leg, but the doctor saved it from amputation."

"Good," said the Admiral, "then you can get him back aboard the ship and take him with you. Now I must go to a place nearby known as Southwick and wait. Tell no-one that you have seen me Roach."

"Yes Sir," came the reply, "safe journey."

After breakfast, Lieutenant Roach called on the princess and together they found Hotham, Hodges and Bartlett in their room. Roach told them of the Admiralty orders.

"You are to gather your belongings, we leave for the ship *Astound* right now – for the tide is at its highest," ordered Lieutenant Roach.

Bartlett coughed, "Sir, among our group we have three abled bodied men, an injured ship's carpenter and a woman," asked Bartlett, "how are we going to handle a ship the size of the *Astound* with such a small crew? Are the spirits of the dead sailors who brought us here to Copperas Gap still aboard to sail it?"

"I don't know," replied Roach, "but I have my instructions from the Admiralty. You do not need to worry about the detail – just follow my orders and assist to break some of the sails aboard the ship. We do not need many sails. Just enough to pick up a breeze to pull the ship into the *Brambledean* mist co-ordinates – and don't ask what the *Brambledean mist* is, for I am not sure myself. My Admiralty orders refers to this wonderous blue mist which will magically transport the ship to Gibraltar."

"What about Captain Watson?" asked Bartlett.

"He is to remain here at Copperas Gap," came the reply.

"We cannot leave Captain Watson behind," called the Princess.

"I am afraid that we must," replied Roach, "for those are my orders from the Admiralty."

"Well I am not going – I don't need to take orders from your Admiralty," she replied.

"I am sorry Princess – but I really must insist that you come with us," said Roach. "Hodges, Bartlett, take her to the ship – by force if necessary."

"I am sorry madam, but our orders are to take you to the ship," said Bartlett, "Mr. Hodges will assist you to the ship while I help Robert Hotham."

Hodges held the arm of the struggling Princess who threw several insults, in Spanish, at Roach before she was escorted towards the shore of Fishersgate harbour.

They re-grouped at the shoreline so that they could row the two small boats to the *Astound.* Last to arrive was Hodges but the Princess was not with him.

"Where's the Princess?" shouted Roach.

"The woman bit my hand and escaped," Hodges replied.

"You fool Hodges," came the reply, "we have no time to find her for we have to enter the Brambledean mist at a specific time. Everyone get into the rowing boats, we must get back to the *Astound* straight away."

Hiding in the bushes, watching the little rowing boats make their way back to the *Astound* was Princess Serafina. She watched as two of the ship's sails were slowly raised before a slight breeze filled their fabric. She looked on as Hodges cut the rope to the anchor with an axe and she saw the ship slowly begin to drift Eastwards within the harbour basin.

Suddenly, there were shooting stars all around the ship's masts. It was daylight and yet these stars were so bright they caused a spectacle that could be seen for miles. Ten million shooting stars engulfed the ship – and then it was gone. The ship had disappeared into a magical chasm that nobody knew was there. It was a chasm so great, powerful and mysterious – known only as the *Brambledean mist*. The Princess gasped at the sight of the shooting stars and watched the giant ship disappear. Roach and the other three would soon be back, in a parallel time, in the seas near to the Rock of Gibraltar.

Captain Watson had left the Halfway House tavern earlier that morning and headed for Eastbrook. He saw no-one on the short walk to his mother's cottage. This was unusual for a small bustling village like Copperas Gap. It would be good to see his mother. He had not seen her for eighteen years, though he had often communicated with his mother by letter and sent money to her on a regular basis. Nothing was better than seeing her for real. He was looking forward to it.

Arriving at the row of cottages he knocked on the front door to his mother's home. There was no response. He tried the door – it was unlocked.

"Mother," he called as he walked into the cottage.

There was no response for she was not there. He tried the cottage next door and the one next to that. He entered all of them right to the end of the row – to the cottage where Molly's mother lived. They were all empty. He found no-one.

'Where is everyone?' he thought, before deciding to walk up the hill to the church and the manor house. He found the church doors locked and no-one in residence at the manor house.

'How bizarre,' thought Watson.

He walked down the hill and passed the old apple tree in the meadow. It was swaying in the breeze on this spring day, the buds on the twigs getting ready to burst into flower. Tobias Watson stopped to study the tree. It brought back so many wonderful memories of his time with his one true love, Molly Moffatt. He thought about those times when they used to sit under the Apple tree and talk about their future together and their love for each other. It was here where they kissed for the very first time and so many times after that. And it was here that they first held each other close and declared their love for each other.

Then it began to rain. Soon a raging wind took off Watson's tricorn hat. The wind blew the hat towards the old apple tree. Tobias chased after it but did not catch it until he was beside the rutted trunk of the old apple tree. He felt the ruggedness of the bark on the tree and saw the weatherworn letters TW and MM carved into its rutted trunk. The letters had been there for more than twenty years. Suddenly the bright sunlight that surrounded the area turned to darkness. Heavy rain and thunder broke the silence of this spring day. Forked lightning spread all over the skies, with many powerful million-volt strikes of electricity hitting the earth with tremendous velocity. Large crevasses appeared in the land as the ground shook beneath his feet. This scene was just like the terrible dream that Tobias Watson so often had. Then, a howling hundred mile an hour wind began to take hold. It became increasingly powerful and lifted a rain-drenched Tobias into the air. Tobias grabbed a branch on the tree as the force of nature exerted a wrenching energy on his body. This put a persistent strain upon his grip.

"Hold on Tobias," shouted a voice, "hold on." It was Molly's voice, but he could not see her.

Then, as suddenly as the wind had started – it stopped. Watson drifted to the ground, unharmed.

"Molly, Molly," called out Tobias, but there was no response.

A deep loud laugh of what can only be described as an eerie, spine-chilling, frightening man's voice, echoed throughout the area. Tobias looked around trying to see where the howling scary laughter had come from or, more importantly, if he could see Molly.

The menacing frightening laughter of this man echoed around the area once more.

"Who are you? What do you want?" Tobias screamed as he looked around – but he saw no one. The sound of a musical flute could be heard in the distance. It became louder and louder before gradually fading away – until it could be heard no more.

Suddenly the ground beneath him opened-up and a huge crevasse, some ten-yards-long and three feet wide, cracked open in the earth. Tobias fell down the gap, but not too far, for he grabbed the root of the old apple tree that was protruding into the crevasse from the side of the broken earth. He hung for a moment, dangling precariously inside the chasm as he tried to gain a foothold in the sodden soil. But he could hold on no longer. He fell into the depths of the earth. But his fall was slowed by a magical upward draft of air.

He suffered slight bruising as he hit the ground deep beneath the earth's surface.

"Get up Captain Watson," boomed a man's voice.

"Who are you?" asked Watson as he looked around. He could see no-one.

"I am Barlott, the King of all this land," said the man, "what are you doing here?"

"Looking for the people of Copperas Gap," replied Watson.

"It is none of your business where they are. I have them working for me," shouted Barlott.

"Where are they?" screamed Watson. "Show yourself to me."

Suddenly, a ring of flames rose from the ground and a man appeared. Tobias knew this man. It was the Rector he had met outside the church in Copperas Gap many years before. The same Rector who tried to persuade Tobias Watson to deny that the child Molly bore was his own. It was the same Rector that had been in the saloon bar of prostitution in the Americas. The flames surrounding the Rector became higher and higher. The image of the Rector began to change to that of the Devil himself. His skin became a crimson red and his eyes yellow. Small curved horns began to form on his forehead. And a trident – a type of a three-pronged spear – appeared in his left hand. He let out a huge roar of inner-power followed by a devilish laugh.

"I knew all along that you were evil in some way Rector," screamed Watson, "from the very first moment I spoke to you at Copperas Gap. I knew you were from hell itself and that you had the devil inside of you. Now tell me where the people of Copperas Gap are? What have you done with them?"

"The people of Copperas Gap are somewhere safe, for now," he boomed, "they are herded together like lambs to the slaughter and so is the Lord of the Manor and his soldiers. This village and all the surrounding lands now belong to me, for I am a friend of the devil himself. With his help I shall rule these lands for the rest of my natural and eternal life."

"You are mad," screamed Watson, "only a madman sells his soul to the devil for power, glory and greed."

"You shall join your people soon," replied Barlott in a firm manner, "and then you shall join me in Copperas Gap which I shall re-name Barlott's Heaven. It will be my very own heaven. I shall be the ruler of you all."

"Go to hell," Watson replied.

"I've already been there, it's not such a bad place," said Barlott with a smile, "but now I am back to claim my rightful lands, Copperas Gap… with the help of my business partner and accountant, Lucifer."

Barlott once again screamed the laugh of a madman.

"Fight me like a real man Barlott. Come out in mortal flesh where I can see you," shouted Watson.

"I don't fight men like you," came the reply, "I am too important to waste my energy on a minion."

"You're a coward Barlott," shouted Watson, "I will never allow you to become my King. You will never be the King of my home town of Copperas Gap. I will find a way to fight you to the death."

"I am already dead," came Barlott's sarcastic reply, "but I shall not be dead for long. Lucifer is to bring me back to mortal life in three-days-time. Then I can begin to rule my lands and my human lambs. I will once again taste the fruits of the female flesh. I will once again taste the meat of my favourite dish of goat and boiled eyeballs. When I am human once more the first thing I shall do is slay a goat, then cook it to perfection."

"Then I shall fight you in three-days-time when you become a human being," demanded Watson as he took of his glove and threw it at Barlott.

"Very well Watson, you are irritating me now. If you must persist in your wild demands then I shall fight you and slay you," replied Barlott. "It will delay my breakfast of goat-meat and boiled-eyeballs, but no matter – it will not take long to dispatch you," replied Barlott.

A flash of lightning hit the floor of the crevasse. Thick grey smoke bellowed upward from the Earth. Three men appeared out of the smoke. They looked like pirates of the West Indies, each with a cutlass retained by their leather belt. They were the sort of men that Blackbeard himself might employ. They were indeed ugly thugs.

"Take him away," ordered Barlott, letting out a huge roar of inner-power followed by a devilish laugh. The flames around his feet grew tall – at least six foot in height. Barlott disappeared into the flames. Then, the flames extinguished and there was no sign of his former presence.

The pirates grabbed Watson, disarmed him and dragged him through a labyrinth of tunnels before throwing him in a prison cell.

"We will be back," said one of his captors, "and you will agree to answer our questions once you receive some suitable body pain in the torture chamber." Then, he slammed to door to the cell shut and locked the door.

In the half-darkness Tobias Watson could hear a young girl sobbing. He moved towards a lit candle affixed to the wall. He could see that it was a girl about nineteen years old.

"Who are you?" asked Tobias.

"Alice is my name," she sobbed.

"Are you the daughter of Admiral Carden?" asked Tobias Watson.

"I am," she said, "how did you know that?"

"Never mind child, I shall get you out of here," replied Watson.

"They have captured my brother too," she exclaimed.

"I know," said Watson.

"He is in another cell along the corridor," Alice continued," I have heard his voice."

Suddenly, there was a strange noise. Watson looked to the corner of the room. A pair of eyes looked back. "Who is that?" whispered Watson.

"It's a monkey," replied Alice.

Tobias Watson went closer to the pair of eyes. It was indeed a monkey and quite a friendly one at that. It was about sixteen inches in height and it wore a collar encrusted with diamonds; but those diamonds must be fakes thought Watson. Extending from the collar was a chain about three feet long.

"What is this monkey doing here?" enquired Watson.

"He lives here," replied Alice, "he was here when I arrived. He scared me at first, but I have got to like him. He has been my only friend. The guards tell me that he is known as a snub-nosed monkey and was brought to this country from China two years ago. He seems to like it in here – he stays with me most of the time but goes off now and again through the grill in the door and comes back with bananas. I am sure he has another home somewhere. He is very protective of his bananas but sometimes lets me have one to eat. They are very nice."

"Wait a minute... I have seen this monkey before," said Watson, "It was many years ago that I last saw him. He was with my personal attendant. Is this monkey with anyone? Is he with a man of Moroccan descent, a former sailor, perhaps?"

"I have seen no-one – other than the prison guards," replied Alice.

Watson thought for a moment about their situation.

"Who are these guards – do you know them?" asked Watson.

"They are the men of Barlott, a smuggler and pirate of Copperas Gap," she replied, "and they have demanded money from my father for my release."

What were you doing in Copperas gap Alice?" asked Watson.

"Nothing much," came the reply.

"Please tell me why you came to Copperas Gap; it might help me to better assess the situation," asked Watson.

"My brother and I found our certificates of birth quite by accident at home in Portsmouth and though most of the detail on the document was blurred it showed our place of birth to be Copperas Gap. So, we thought we would come to this place to find out more."

"Did you not think to ask your parents?" inquired Watson.

"They didn't want to talk about it," replied Alice.

"And what have you discovered," asked Watson.

"Well, nothing. The first person we spoke to when we arrived at Copperas gap was this man called Barlott. He is a Rector of the Church and seemed a nice man. He wanted to know all about us. So, we told him. And then…"

"Please continue Alice. This man is not a real Rector of the church: did he harm you?"

"No, he did not harm me," said Alice. "Then, my brother escaped. It is fortuitous that he did escape for he alerted our father, Admiral Carden to this location. But later my brother was re-captured. Barlott's men killed the sailors who were with him. Then Barlott's men brought my brother back to this terrible place. Barlott said we would be released when our father paid a ransom, but I do not know any more than that."

"I know that your father is here in this village my child, for I have seen him in Copperas Gap," replied Watson.

The girl sighed and thanked Captain Watson for telling her that her father was near-by.

Tobias Watson sat back to think about the situation they were in. He looked at the girl once more. It was strange. In her face he could see a similar feature to Molly Moffatt. In fact, she looked very much like Molly, but he must be imagining this. 'Could this be some trickery of the dim lighting in the prison cell?' he thought.

Later, when Tobias was asleep a voice gently spoke to him in his dream.

"Tobias… Tobias… listen to me, it is Molly, I have someone who wants to speak to you."

"Molly," exclaimed Tobias, "where are you?"

"I am near, but you cannot see me. I want you to know something that I am now permitted to reveal to you. Be prepared my lover for a surprise," Molly said sweetly.

"Tobias," whispered the voice of a man.

"I know that voice," said an astonished Watson as he sat up.

"Yes, it is Sequoya your Indian guide," said the man, "I shall show you and the other prisoners the way out of this jail. I shall be your guide."

"I cannot see you; where are you Sequoya?" asked Watson.

"I passed over to the spiritual side about a year ago," replied Sequoya. "Listen to me carefully and I will tell you of my plan of escape. When you, Alice and Henry get out of this place you will find three Indian stallions outside of the Halfway House tavern. Take them and ride westwards towards a place known as Shoreham-by-sea. Ride your horse's as fast as you can and get away from Barlott's men. When you arrive at Shoreham-by-sea you will find a spiritual band of Indian braves – they will be waiting for you. They are the warriors of the Oconee tribe. Chief Attakullakulla will lead these warriors. The Chief's spirit is here in England."

"Why that's impossible!" exclaimed Watson. "The Americas are over three thousand miles from Copperas gap."

"Nothing is impossible in the spiritual world," replied Sequoya, "the spirit of the Native Indians of the America's will be with you. They will protect you and the children until you reach Portsmouth harbour. It is certain that Barlott and his men will follow you. They will not be very far behind you. If they catch you, they will kill you. Now you will listen to me. I plan this escape to take place in 48 hours' time on the 2nd April at 12:00 noon. Be ready."

"But what about my men – the two soldiers, Lieutenant Roach, Hotham and of course the Princess? I cannot ride off and leave them behind," asked Watson.

"I have sent word to Admiral Carden via the Admiralty. He has ordered them to sail the *Astound* into the mist of the *Brambledean* portal," came the reply.

"The mist of *Brambledean,* what is this?" inquired Watson.

"It is a parallel time-portal. They and the ship *Astound* will be sent back to Gibraltar – unharmed in the same time zone from where they came, 1734," said Sequoya.

"And what of me?" asked Watson, "where shall I go?"

"You will ride to Portsmouth and deliver Alice Rebecca and Henry Tobias to their mother in Anchor way – their private house," said Sequoya. "Lord Admiral Carden will meet you en-route at a place known as Southwick and ride with you. I cannot tell you more than that Tobias, for your personal destiny is in the hands of the Lord of the Universe."

"Did you say Alice Rebecca and Henry Tobias?" asked Watson.

"I did," came the reply.

"Henry, the boy, has my name. He has Tobias, as a middle name, how nice," mumbled Watson.

"Yes," said the gentle voice of Molly. "He is your son Tobias… he is our son."

"What!" exclaimed Tobias Watson as he jumped to his feet.

"And Alice, who is sleeping before you right now in your dream is our daughter," Molly continued, "the children were taken from me shortly after they were born. They were taken for adoption by the Lord of the Manor, sent to Portsmouth and given to Admiral Carden and his wife who could not have children of their own."

"My God," cried Tobias Watson, "as tears of sadness ran down his face, before he looked down at the sleeping girl. I thought that there was one child… not two. I was told that the second child had died at birth. What is this life that brings so much sadness and pain to me? What has happened to me? That I have missed out on my children's young lives and their upbringing through my own stupidity of pursuing my own career. And I also lost you Molly because I selfishly wanted adventure beyond Copperas Gap. I am not worthy of living. I should have realised these facts when I saw something in this girl and the boy ten years ago at the Admiral's house. I should have known that she was my own flesh and blood. How stupid of me."

"Be quiet Tobias, for you will wake her," called Molly, "isn't she beautiful?"

"Yes, she is," replied Tobias in a whisper, "she is really beautiful, and she looks just like you Molly."

"You must never tell Alice or Henry that you are their biological father Tobias," continued Molly, "for they are happy with their life as it is – or rather they will be, once they escape from Copperas Gap and are reunited with their adoptive parents in Portsmouth. Enjoy your moments with them on your journey to Portsmouth for you shall return them to their adoptive parents before the week is out and you will never see them again."

"Now listen to me Tobias," interrupted Sequoya, "I will appear before you and tell of the escape plan – you must follow my instruction."

Very slowly the image of Sequoya appeared before Tobias Watson. In the distance behind him Tobias could see the Indian campsite of Hog Creek, beside *Little Water* in the Americas. The Indian guide continued to tell Tobias Watson of his escape plan and that he should wait until 11:00 am on the 2nd April before beginning to put the plan into action.

"But what about this place Copperas Gap," asked Watson, "where are the people? Where is my mother?"

"They have been banished from these lands by Barlott himself. A spell has been put on them and they remain in a limbo land in a parallel world to this one. They are working the land for Barlott," said Sequoya.

"Are they dead?" asked Watson.

"No," came the reply, "they will remain in the parallel world until Barlott is destroyed and removed from this real-time world and his spirit sent to Hell – for all eternity."

"Why is he doing this?" asked Watson.

"It's simple, he wants to use Copperas Gap for his own wicked purposes. He has sold his soul to Lucifer the Devil to gain himself further human life, power and glory."

"I am not sure I understand," replied Watson.

"You do not need to understand my friend," said Sequoya. "The ancient spirits of the Native American Indian will be used to cast a curse on Barlott who is known as a living spirit of negativity. The Lord of the Universe has requested Native American assistance. My people will banish him to Hell, for he is a man who tortures living people on this Earth – afflicting them with a Ghost sickness of a parallel world. Only when Barlott is banished from this Earth can the people of Copperas Gap be released to return to their homes."

"Why do the Innkeeper and his wife of the Halfway House tavern remain in Copperas Gap," asked Watson.

"Because they work for Barlott, they have already sold their souls to the devil. They look after this barren place of Copperas Gap when he is not here," replied Sequoya. "Barlott operates across this whole local area in the county of Sussex."

"What must I do Sequoya?" asked Watson.

Sequoya told Watson the details and within half an hour Tobias knew the plan. At this moment, young Alice began to stir from her sleep. Sequoya said that he could not let her see his image as it would frighten her, so he had to go. Then, he vanished.

"Did you have a nice sleep my dear," whispered Tobias to Alice.

The girl looked anxious, having been brought back to the reality of these terrible surroundings of a prison cell.

"Don't worry," said Tobias, "I will get you out of this place sooner than you think my girl."

"And now you must wake yourself Tobias," whispered Molly.

Gradually the dim light from the candle protruded into the darkness of his mind as Watson opened his eyes. Alice was sitting before him wide-awake.

"It will soon be time for us to leave this place," whispered Watson to the girl, "I shall now explain to you how we are to escape."

Two days later the guard came to the cell. Alice engaged in a conversation with the guard – as she had been told to do by Tobias Watson.

Watson attacked the guard from behind using the chain attached to the snub-nosed monkey. He strangled the guard until he fell dead. It was quite a struggle and I can tell you that the monkey was not pleased at all in being pulled about from pillar to post during this physical struggle between the two men. In fact, the monkey looked very dishevelled; with his straggly hair standing on end and squashed banana embedded in his fur.

"Look the other way Alice, I need to put the guard's clothes on," called Watson.

Alice did as she was told.

A few minutes later Watson was dressed in the guard's clothes. "Come Alice," said Watson, "we must find your brother."

They made their way out of the cell taking the dead guard's keys with them. The monkey followed. There was no one about and they soon found the cell that contained Henry. Tobias released the door and Henry was free.

Tobias looked the young Henry up and down. 'What a fine young man he thought. He is my son, but I can never tell him that.'

"Come, we must make haste," called Watson, "there is no time for introductions."

"Thank you," said Henry as he followed his sister and Tobias Watson.

The three of them, and the monkey, made their way along the tunnel, opening doors with the guard's keys before coming to a final heavy timber doorway which they opened into the salty fresh air and to the sound of squawking seagulls. They were midway up a steep grassed bank. They could see Fishersgate harbour below.

"Wait here inside the tunnel," said Tobias.

Tobias Watson went outside and clambered up the grass bank. At the top of the bank he peered through the long grass to see the Halfway House tavern on the opposite side of the road. Outside the tavern, as promised by Sequoya, were three of the finest, fully saddled, Native American Indian bred horses. They were tethered to a rail.

Tobias went back to the tunnel. He explained to Henry and Alice what should be done. They must get on the horses quickly and ride westwards to meet up with Chief Attakullakulla and the Oconee tribe who were stationed just outside of the village. Before long, the three of them and the monkey were standing beside the horses. Henry mounted one horse and Tobias began to assist Alice onto another.

Suddenly there was a loud voice, "Stop or I shoot."

It was one of Barlott's men aiming a musket at them.

"Keep going," whispered Watson to Alice as he turned his back on the man to assist her onto her horse. Here, give me the chain of the monkey; I will put my foot on the chain while you get your balance on the horse then I will pass it to you. He clasped his hands together and she put her foot in them. He lifted her up and she sat on the horse with her feet in the stirrup, holding the reins.

BANG. The man fired a single shot from his musket.

It hit Tobias Watson square in the back, breaking his spine.

"Go," shouted Watson as he staggered in considerable pain, thumping the butt of Alice's horse with the palm of his hand, "ride as fast as you can, I will follow-on behind you,"

Henry and Alice squeezed the sides of their horses with their legs and yanked the reins. The horses sprang into action and galloped away while the lone shooter frantically reloaded his musket. The snub-nosed monkey observed – making no attempt to run away as he could have done.

Tobias Watson watched his two children ride into the distance, the third passenger-less horse following behind. They headed towards Southwick and Shoreham-by-Sea. Suddenly, Tobias Watson succumbed to his injuries and fell to the ground. The door to the tavern opened and several people came out including the innkeeper of the tavern and his wife. Then the Princess Serafina came rushing to Watson's aid and knelt beside him.

"Tobias my love, where are you hit?" she asked.

"The pain is in my back," came the reply, "I cannot feel my legs anymore."

“I love you Tobias. I will nurse you back to health. I will get help from the doctor,” replied the Princess.

In the near distance, about fifty yards away, they could hear the sound of a hundred men or more approaching.

“It’s Barlott’s men,” exclaimed the innkeeper, “everyone get inside.”

“Help me get Tobias inside,” asked the Princess.

“Not likely, Barlott is the most dangerous man around. I know that because I work for him,” said the innkeeper, “we won’t have time to get Watson inside for they will be here in a moment. It’s best to get out of the way when Barlott’s in a mood. Anyway, the Captain looks done-for.”

The innkeeper, his wife and several bystanders disappeared into the Halfway House tavern leaving the Princess and Tobias Watson alone on the street.

“Tobias, I love you,” said the Princess, “I want us to spend the rest of our life together.”

Tobias smiled, “Go quickly my beautiful Princess – those men of Barlott’s will be here in a moment.”

“I will not leave you Tobias,” she replied.

“You must leave,” came the reply from Tobias. He knew that he would not survive his injuries and would say anything to get the princess to leave the scene. “My Princess,” Watson continued in a faltering voice, “will you go and find the doctor. Barlott’s men will do me no further harm for I am not a threat to them. Will you come back to me my beautiful Princess with the doctor.”

“I cannot leave you Tobias,” she said.

He smiled once more. “You must, for it is my only chance of survival – now begone my young beautiful lady, my very own Princess,” said Watson, “I shall see you later.”

A tear ran down the cheek of the Princess as she kissed Tobias full on the lips.

“I love you Tobias Watson,” said the Princess.

“And I love… arrrgh,” Tobias Watson did not finish his sentence for the pain in his back had become excruciating.

Barlott's men were very near, so the Princess fled the terrible scene towards the doctor's house.

Soon, Barlott's men were upon Watson.

"What have we here?" exclaimed one of the men as he looked down on Watson. It was Barlott himself.

"Mr. Barlott," said the man who fired the shot that brought Watson down, "the prisoners were escaping I had no choice but to shoot. Two of them got away."

"You did right," came Barlott's reply, "which way did the Admiral's children go?"

"Westwards, towards Shoreham-by-sea – riding on the finest horses that I have ever seen in my life," said the man.

"I didn't ask for a detailed condition report on the horses," came Barlott's sarcastic reply.

The men nearby laughed while the snub-nosed monkey looked at his seriously injured new master with a knowing sadness in his intelligent primate eyes.

Barlott nodded to around ten men mounted on nearby horses. "Get after them," he ordered.

The men on the horses galloped towards Shoreham-by-sea. Barlott then turned his attention to Watson.

"It seems we shall not need to fight a duel; by the looks of your injuries Watson you will soon be dead. Now tell me, where are those children heading?" he demanded.

"Go to hell," whimpered a pain-stricken Watson.

Barlott kicked Watson in the side of his rib cage. Watson screamed out in pain before drifting into unconsciousness.

"Take him away," screamed Barlott, "take him into the smugglers' tunnels. Wait until he regains consciousness and torture him, oh so very nicely and slowly, until he tells us where the boy and girl are heading. The snub-nosed monkey followed his new master as Barlott's men dragged Watson away.

Tobias Watson was dragged into the smugglers' tunnels and taken to a place known as the Crab house. It was a place where Barlott's men often took prisoners to torture – none ever survived. Their bodies were disposed of in the harbour; chopped up into little bits and fed to the slimy eels that lived deep-down in the murky waters.

And that's exactly what they did to Captain Tobias Watson. They tortured him until he died of his gunshot wound and those terrible torturous injuries they inflicted upon him on that afternoon of April 2nd, 1734. The monkey was sitting on Tobias Watson's chest at the exact moment of his death, pining for his new friend who was screaming in pain. One of Barlott's men saw the diamond encrusted collar on the monkey and decided to have it for himself. He took a swipe with his cutlass. It was a good shot for it chopped the monkeys head clean off. This despicable thug lunged for the diamond collar but as soon as he touched the diamonds the collar vanished into thin air.

Throughout the torture our hero, Tobias Watson, never revealed to his captors where his children were heading.

Henry and Alice were soon re-united with their adoptive father, Lord Admiral Carden, on the banks of the river Adur at Southwick. They rode westwards to the Marlipin Inn at Shoreham-by-sea where they embraced each other. The Landlord, a Mr. Jackson, offered refreshments and looked on with a smile. But there was no time to waste. A few minutes later they made their way towards Portsmouth Harbour some forty miles further west, under the spiritual escort of the Oconee American Indian tribe led by Chief Attakullakulla. Every person in every town and village en-route came out to cheer this glittering tribe, who were riding the finest Native American stallions. The warriors were dressed in traditional Indian clothes, beads and bones, each wearing a headdress made from the feathers of a golden eagle. They wore striking coloured war paint on their faces, whooping it up and chanting ancient songs as they rode past the English villagers. It was a wonderful sight for an ordinary English family to see. It has never been done since. The Indians, the Admiral and his children arrived at the gates of Anchor way in Portsmouth the following morning where their adoptive mother was waiting for them. The Admiral and his wife thanked Chief Attakullakulla and his warriors and as they did so the tribe of Indians vanished into thin air. They were never seen in England again.

A few days after Watson's terrible demise, evidence of his death began to filter out to the people staying at the Halfway House tavern. A distraught Princess Serafina was inconsolable.

Yet, unknown to the Princess, at that moment in time the spirit of Tobias Watson was in transit to that place called purgatory where he met with his Indian friend Sequoya. They talked about old times before getting on with the business of saving the people of Copperas Gap. Together, and with the help of the Lord of the Universe, they defeated the wicked Barlott who was summarily banished from having a mortal or spiritual presence on Earth for all eternity. Barlott was banished permanently to that prison known as Hell with no parole prospects whatsoever.

After that, Watson and Sequoya did what they had to do and once it was done the spell on the people of Copperas Gap was broken. The people returned to the village to carry-on with their simple lives – much as they had done before. Tobias Watson's mother returned to her little cottage at Copperas Gap and spent the rest of her life there.

In the following weeks the Princess Serafina visited Tobias Watson's distraught mother. Together they helped each other ease the pain of Tobias Watson's sad departure from this mortal world. In fact, the Princess moved into the little cottage and took Tobias Watson's old room for a few months. She felt closer to him when she slept in his bed.

The Lord of the Manor and all the people of Copperas Gap proclaimed Captain Tobias Watson and the Indian Sequoya to be village heroes. His mother was given the substantial sum of monies from Tobias Watson's naval bank account and that allowed her to live for the rest of her natural life in luxury. The Lord of the Manor allowed her to live in the little cottage, rent free, for the rest of her days.

One afternoon, after attending Copperas Gap church, the Princess Serafina was walking past the village monument of the unknown sailor when she heard the strange sound of multiple bells. Then, the gentle sound of a flute began to play. Suddenly, a shape appeared on the ground. It was a shape that grew right next to the statue of the unknown sailor. It was about four feet square and made of marble. It propagated upwards from the ground until it reached six feet in height. It was a plinth – much like the one next to it supporting the statue of the unknown sailor. Then, a pair of marble feet appeared on its top surface. The feet were not wearing shoes. Gradually the feet grew into legs and a torso, then a man's shoulders and a head. It was the statue of a Native American Indian dressed in the finery of his Indian clothing. It was one of the most excellent statues of its kind and, at the time, the only one of its type in England – depicting a Native American Indian warrior.

On the plinth a brass plaque appeared. Its inscription read '*Sequoya, The Native American Indian – a friend of Captain Tobias Watson and the people of the village of Copperas Gap, a hero to them all, England 1734.'*

She gasped in amazement at the beauty of this sculptured masterpiece and the power of its stature.

Then, while admiring the Indian sculpture, the Princess noticed out of the corner of her eye that the blurred facial features of the statue of the unknown sailor had moved ever so slightly. She stared upwards to study the indistinct face. Out of the blur, a man's face was magically being formed. It grew into the face of Tobias Watson. Below, on the blank brass plaque, an inscription was magically being engraved. It stated. *'Captain Tobias Henry Watson born, 1696 – died 1734, a hero of this village, friend to Sequoya the Native American Indian and to the American nation.'*

'If Sequoya was a friend of Tobias, then he is a friend of mine,' thought the Princess as she took some comfort from this amazing spectacle that had been created before her very eyes.

This statue of Captain Tobias Watson was, and still is, a tribute to the British Navy's finest eighteenth-century military hero who was born in the little-known village of Copperas Gap. It is a tribute to that special relationship between the United Kingdom of Great Britain and the Northern states of the Americas.

A tear ran down the cheek of the Princess as she studied the features of the man she loved more than anyone else in the world; before she stepped forward to kiss the plinth supporting the statue of Captain Tobias Watson.

A few weeks later it was time for the Princess Serafina to leave England. The King of Spain had called for her through diplomatic circles. She had stayed in the village of Copperas Gap for more than six months, much more than she ought. She said her goodbyes to the people of the village before she spoke in private to Tobias Watson's mother. The Princess Serafina of Seville in the Province of Andalusia returned to Spain on a British naval ship via Gibraltar and nothing else was heard of her after that, except that in time it was acknowledged in the history books that the Princess Serafina was instrumental in negotiating a lasting peace between Spain and England.

As for the two statues, Tobias Watson and Sequoya. Well, they remain at Copperas Gap to this day; but unless you know where they are located, you will never find them.

After Captain Tobias Watson was murdered by Barlott's men, his spirit travelled to that place beyond mortal life. He, at last, met Molly as his equal, in a spiritual form. She was and still is his one and only true love and he considers her to be the most beautiful spiritual girl in the Universe. He greeted Molly somewhere in the clouds over Copperas Gap, on the golden steps leading up to paradise. They kissed passionately, before Tobias nibbled her earlobe – which always made her giggle.

Together, they began to walk up those golden steps towards the gates of heaven, hand in hand, as happy as they ever were, with a special love and lust for each other. It was to be a love that would last… for all eternity.

But it didn't quite happen like that – for on that day Molly was ordered to enter heaven, alone. Tobias was told to wait outside. Tobias watched Molly enter the Kingdom of Heaven and through the threshold of the entrance doorway he could see two of his friends… young William and Mr. French. He also saw his father, George. Then he saw his former Moroccan attendant and heard him playing a wonderful tune on his musical flute, but he could not see the snub-nose monkey.

They waved to him and smiled. But Tobias could do no more than wave back, for on this day he was not permitted to enter the after world. Suddenly the snub-nosed monkey appeared beside Tobias Watson outside the gates of paradise. He wore a diamond encrusted collar around his neck that had a short piece of silver chain attached. The monkey looked-up at Tobias and smiled before he grasped Watson's hand.

The Lord of the Universe had one last task for Tobias Watson. He was ordered to return to Earth to fulfil that mission. Only then would the Lord of the Universe allow him access into the pleasures of Heaven, and of course to be re-united with Molly Moffatt.

It would be a while before Tobias Watson would see her again.

The End.

Read the next book in the series.

The Ghost of the Fishersgate Mariner.

ISBN 978-0-9955382-5-2

Available at all good bookshops, Waterstones online and at Amazon

Printed in Great Britain
by Amazon